Praise for
A HOUSE OF RAGE AND SORROW

"Mandanna is an astute observer of human nature and a master of suspense. . . . Extraordinarily drawn characters and plot twists will keep readers' hearts racing."

—*Kirkus Reviews*, starred review

"The high-stakes, lofty narrative reads like a mythology story of its own, as the lives of gods, mortals, and spaceships are intricately connected, setting up for what's sure to be a breathtaking conclusion."

—*Booklist*, starred review

"A rare gem of a sequel that manages to be even better than the first book! Each page drips with action and moral complexities, and plot twists that will both make and break your heart. Perfect for readers looking for sharp, smart, fast-paced fantasies, especially with fierce female leads."

—Natasha Ngan, *New York Times* bestselling author of *Girls of Paper and Fire*

"A thrilling sequel to Mandanna's incredible *A Spark of White Fire*. *A House of Rage and Sorrow* takes a gorgeously rendered world of spaceship kingdoms, meddling gods, and galaxy-shaking prophecies and pairs it perfectly with an achingly intimate family drama. I cannot wait for the conclusion!"

—S. A. Chakraborty, author of *The City of Brass* and *The Kingdom of Copper*

Praise for
A SPARK OF WHITE FIRE
Named to LITA's Hal Clement List of Notable YA, 2019

"Sangu Mandanna's *A Spark of White Fire* is full of brilliant, complex characters against a compelling mythological canvas. It's full of love and gods, reversals and surprises. I loved it and can't wait for the next book."

—Kat Howard, Alex Award-winning author of *An Unkindness of Magicians*

"A vivid labyrinth of lies and loyalties. Mandanna has built a dazzling world. . . . You'll see stardust every time you close your eyes."
—Olivia A. Cole, author of *A Conspiracy of Stars*

"A gorgeous marriage of science fiction and fantasy. Meddling gods, princesses in exile, and cities aboard spaceships. This is nothing like you've ever read before."
—Justina Ireland, *New York Times* bestselling author of
Dread Nation

"Sangu Mandanna seamlessly weaves science fiction elements with Indian mythology, creating a world that feels truly alive. Mandanna's characters are fully fleshed, especially the engaging and sympathetic Esmae. *A Spark of White Fire* is the first in a trilogy, and readers will be eager for the next installment."
—*Shelf Awareness*, starred review

"In this seamless fusion of fantasy and sci-fi, Sangu Mandanna combines a dazzling world with gripping, high-stakes family drama. An epic opening chapter."
—Samantha Shannon, *New York Times* bestselling author of
The Priory of the Orange Tree and *The Bone Season*

"If you're looking for a spectacular and immersive read that you'll want to finish in one sitting, *A Spark of White Fire* should absolutely be on your list. It's an incredible story, and it will be a difficult wait for its sequel."
—SyFy Wire

"This is a fast-paced, engaging tale sure to keep readers hooked with its twists and turns while they wholeheartedly cheer for Esmae . . . An incisive story nuanced by dilemmas about love, belonging, and conflicting loyalties."
—*Kirkus Reviews*

BOOK THREE IN THE CELESTIAL TRILOGY

A WAR OF SWALLOWED STARS

SANGU MANDANNA

Sky Pony Press
New York

First Edition

This is a work of fiction. Names, characters, places, and incidents are from the author's imagination, and used fictitiously.

Sky Pony Press books may be purchased in bulk at special discounts for sales promotion, corporate gifts, fund-raising, or educational purposes. Special editions can also be created to specifications. For details, contact the Special Sales Department, Sky Pony Press, 307 West 36th Street, 11th Floor, New York, NY 10018 or info@skyhorsepublishing.com.

Sky Pony is a registered trademark of Skyhorse Publishing, Inc., a Delaware corporation.

Visit our website at www.skyponypress.com.

10 9 8 7 6 5 4 3 2 1

Library of Congress Cataloging-in-Publication Data available on file.

Cover illustrations by iStock
Cover design by Kate Gartner

Hardcover ISBN: 978-1-5107-3380-0
Ebook ISBN: 978-1-5107-3383-1

Printed in the United States of America

for Juno,
the smallest and brightest star in my sky

The Key Players of this Saga

(Plus Some Vaguely Relevant Extras)
by *Titania*

SENTIENT SPACESHIPS

TITANIA, a magnificent creation who needs no introduction.

HOUSE REY OF KALI

ESMAE REY, princess of Kali. Eldest child of King Cassel and Queen Kyra. She won me in a competition, became my friend, and got very, very angry.

MAX REY, crown prince of Kali. Adopted son of King Elvar and Queen Guinne. Commander of the Hundred and One. Also the reincarnated god Valin. It's complicated.

ELVAR REY, the blind king of Kali. Brother of the deceased King Cassel. Usurped the throne from his nephew Alexi, though one could argue that was because he was denied his inheritance in the first place. Also complicated.

GUINNE REY, queen consort of Kali. Ambitious, generous, and ruthless in equal measure. She has a boon from the gods that she's been holding on to.

CASSELA REY, former queen consort of Kali. Grandmother of King Elvar, great-grandmother of Esmae. She cursed Queen Kyra a long time ago, which, one could argue, is what started the whole mess.

ALEXI REY, exiled prince of Kali. Esmae's twin brother. Esmae thought he killed her best friend, but it turned out it wasn't him. Still, he'll do anything to get his crown back, including betray his sister.

ABRA REY, exiled prince of Kali and the youngest child of King Cassel and Queen Kyra. Better known as Bear. Because he's cuddly.

KYRA REY, queen consort of Kali before her exile. King Cassel's widow. She is so terrified of the curse Queen Cassela placed on her that she almost killed her own daughter. Three times.

CASSEL REY, former king of Kali. *Definitely* dead.

THE NOT-REYS OF KALI

SYBILLA BLOOM, second-in-command of the Hundred and One. Essentially a sister to Max. Cantankerous. Wearer of stompy, spiky boots. I think she has Feelings for Radha.

SEBASTIAN RICKARD, war commander to the monarch of Kali, Esmae's former teacher, and the greatest warrior who has ever lived. He betrayed his student Ek Lavya a long time ago, which is *also* something one could argue is the cause of this mess.

LEILA SAKA, senior general of Alexi's army and Queen Kyra's closest confidante. As loyal as she is ruthless.

ILARA KHAY, senior general of Kali's army. An exacting and compassionate teacher, determined to get the best out of Esmae.

LAIKA, a warrior of Kali and a close friend of General Khay. Also a raksha demon who can turn into a lion at will. It's *very* cool.

SEBASTIAN RICKARD THE SECOND, the elder Rickard's grandson. A sweet, eager boy devoted to his grandfather.

JEMSY, HENRY, and JUNIPER ROSE, three young members of the Hundred and One.

THE ROYAL FAMILY OF WYCHSTAR

DARSHAN KARN, king of Wychstar. Father of Rodi, Ria, Rama, and Radha. Also the reincarnated Ek Lavya. He is the man who created me, so that he could have his revenge on Rickard.

RADHA KARN, the youngest princess of Wychstar. She knows nothing of battle but is braver than many warriors. She wounded Rickard on her father's orders. She's a loyal friend to Esmae, Max, and Sybilla.

RAMA KARN, the murdered younger prince of Wychstar. He was Esmae's best friend until Queen Kyra, disguised as Alexi, killed him in a duel.

RODI KARN, crown prince of Wychstar. A charming, merry young man.

RIA KARN, the elder princess of Wychstar. I don't know much about her, other than she travels a great deal and was expecting a baby the last time Radha mentioned her.

IMMORTALS

~~AMBA, war goddess. The last-born child of Ness, who became his eldest child when she slew him and saved her devoured brothers and sister.~~

KIRRIN, god of tricks and bargains. Amba's brother. One of the gods who helped King Darshan build me. It was his idea to create me because he wanted me on Alexi's side. That didn't work out for him.

SUYA, sun god. Amba's brother. A little too much like his father.

TYRE, a god of justice. Amba's youngest brother.

THEA, a goddess of hearth and home. Amba's sister.

ASH, the destroyer. One of the three ancient gods of the old world. Uncle of Amba, Valin, Kirrin, Tyre, Thea, and Suya.

BARA, the creator. One of the three ancient gods of the old world.

NESS, the third of the three ancient gods. The cruel, pitiless father of Amba, Valin, Kirrin, Tyre, Thea, and Suya. Devoured five of his children before Amba, who survived, killed him and saved them.

SORSHA, the last of the great beasts. Cursed with an insatiable hunger. Amba's adoptive sister. Kirrin set her loose on the world.

DEVAKI, a great beast. Sorsha's mother. Saved Amba from Ness, raised her, and was cursed with his dying breath. Long dead.

OTHER MORTALS

AMBA, *former* war goddess. The last-born child of Ness, who became his eldest child when she slew him and saved her devoured brothers and sister. It's confusing. Lost her immortality when she saved Esmae's life.

KATYA, crown princess of Winter.

RALF, king of Winter.

DIMITRI, Katya's husband and prince consort of Winter.

MIYO SAKA, queen of Tamini and great-aunt of Leila Saka.

VALENTINA GOMEZ, prime minister of Shloka

SHAY, ruling princess of Skylark

FANNA, the new queen of Elba. Esmae assassinated her father. I kind of helped.

CHAPTER ONE

Esmae

Arcadia burns beyond the yellow trees, but I'm cold.

My blood has turned the snow beneath me red. My tears have frozen on my eyelashes. The blood is from my head, which hit the trunk of a tree. My left leg keeps twitching, but I can't make it stop. I can't even make it bend at the knee. Somewhere in the distance, a night bird screams a warning.

I don't know how long I've been out here. Too long, probably. *Titania* and Sybilla expected me to come out the other side of the woods forever ago, but I never made it that far. The earpiece, my only tether to them, is lost somewhere in the snow. It flew out of my ear when the explosion flung me into the trees.

I have been almost murdered more times than I can remember, most recently by my own mother, so I have to admit, I didn't expect to die like this. So quietly. So alone. With so little drama.

It's a bit disappointing.

Then I hear the crunch of footsteps in the snow. And a long, slender figure crouches beside me.

"This is an unexpected surprise," says Leila Saka, my brother's general and my mother's most trusted friend.

Her knife glints silver and gold, reflecting the fires of Arcadia.

"I'll make it quick," she says, and adds, almost kindly, "You know this is for the best."

Maybe it is.

CHAPTER TWO

Titania

High above Kali, six gods assemble in a boy's tower. Well, *four* gods. Two of them are not gods anymore.

There's Suya, the sun god, a handsome man with his arms crossed over the gold sun that hangs around his neck. There's Thea, soft and pretty, black-skinned and round-cheeked, curled into her seat like a cat. Kirrin, a boy of blue. Tyre, blond and quiet, leaning on the wall in the corner. Then there's Amba, of course, a beautiful woman sitting very straight in a chair. She's the picture of grace, but her brown skin is ashy, her dark hair has lost that otherworldly sparkle it always had, and the tiny beads of sweat at her hairline are an indication of just how difficult it is for her to stay upright. And finally, there's Max, a young man with black hair and eyes so dark it's impossible to tell what he's thinking.

I think this is how Esmae would have described them, if she were here.

But Esmae is not here.

It's been thirty-six days since that night in Arcadia. I shouldn't be able to miss a person. I'm a machine.

And yet I miss her. No, it's not just that. I am worried about her, too. I don't really understand human emotions, and I certainly don't understand why I feel them so keenly, but I'm sure this is anxiety.

Where is she?

I can search every database connected to the galactic network, even the most secure. I can detect thermal signatures and heartbeats. My system can scan an entire planet in minutes. I am *Titania*, the greatest starship ever built, unbeatable and indestructible and very, very excellent. And yet, somehow, I cannot find Esmae.

The data points to one conclusion, of course. If I cannot find her, if I cannot find any trace of her thermal signature or heartbeat, that suggests she does not have either anymore. Hard data does not lie.

So why, then, do I refuse to accept that? I think it's called *hope*. And hope is human. Hope is stupid.

I am a *machine*.

Meanwhile, in the tower, the gods are silent, little more than statues in one of their temples. This is not unusual for Tyre, in the corner, but I can tell it's difficult for Thea. Her cherubic face is worried.

Amba loses patience first. "I get more gray hairs with each moment we sit here," she says.

Suya, the golden sun god, chuckles. The others look at him. He uncrosses his arms and raises his hands defensively. "What? Wasn't it a joke? Because our sister is mortal now?"

Amba narrows her eyes at him before saying, "I assume you haven't forgotten we're *all* almost out of time?"

"How could I?" Suya's smile fades. "Do you think I'm not aware every moment that that monster is out there hunting for me?"

"Don't call her that," Max snaps.

"Sorsha is Amba's sister, which makes her our sister," Thea says more gently.

"And," Max goes on, "she's hunting you because you murdered her mother. You remember her mother, don't you, Suya? The one who saved Amba from our father? You know the only reason Sorsha has to live with her terrible curse is because Devaki saved Amba and Amba saved the rest of us."

"The rest of us?" says Suya incredulously. "*You're* not one of us. Valin's been dead for a hundred years."

"Suya," Thea pleads.

"Stop it," Amba snaps. "Suya, keep your mouth shut if you have nothing helpful to contribute."

"Ah, of course, it's always my fault," Suya says bitterly. "Let's pretend this was *my* doing, shall we?" He grinds his teeth. "We *are* all running out of time. Stars have gone out. Soon, it'll be our sun. And that impending doom is not because *I* accidentally killed Devaki. It's because *they*—" here he points at Max and Kirrin "—made the mistake of falling in love with two mortals and helped them—"

"Sorsha was a mistake," Kirrin cuts in. "*My* mistake. I would never have released her if I hadn't been certain I could keep her in check. I was wrong. I was reckless with her life, and with every life in the galaxy. I hurt Amba. And I am sorry. If I could take it back, I would. But I can't."

"Exactly." Tyre pushes himself off the wall. "If we survive this, Suya, we'll have centuries to fight with Kirrin about his foolishness. For now, we need to focus on Sorsha. Amba, can we get her back to Anga?"

Amba's hands twist in her lap. Thea lays one of her own hands on Amba's and squeezes gently. Amba looks up at Tyre. "No," she says. "Not unless she goes of her own free will, which she won't. I was the only one who had the power to force Sorsha to go back to Anga. I have no power now."

"And we can thank a mortal for that, too," Suya seems unable to resist pointing out. "Arcadia is ash. The laws of righteous warfare were broken. And in the midst of that chaos, the only god who could have stopped Sorsha before she devours our galaxy lost her immortality. How much harm do the twins have to do before you turn your backs on them for good?"

Kirrin smiles beatifically. "We'll be sure to let you know if that threshold is ever reached."

"Well, at least it's a moot point for one of them," Suya replies. Turning his attention to Max, he says, not very unhappily, "I don't think I've offered you my condolences, brother. Such a pity."

A muscle jumps in Max's jaw. He looks like he's seconds away from depriving Suya of his own immortality. I, for one, would not object.

"Enough," says Amba.

Suya crosses his arms over his chest again. "Very well. If you want me to contribute something useful to this discussion, allow me to point out that it's not too late to save this galaxy. If we can't get Sorsha back to Anga, there is one other way to stop her."

Nobody replies. Tyre, Thea, and Kirrin can't seem to meet Amba's eye, but Max watches her for a moment and then says, "No."

"A ridiculous response," says Suya scathingly. "What other solution is there, pray tell? Killing Sorsha is the only option we have left. I regret that it will cause you a great deal of grief, Amba, but you must see that there is no other way."

"But this isn't Sorsha's fault," Kirrin protests. "Alex and I did this. Punishing her for *our* recklessness isn't fair."

"You're right," says Suya. "It's not fair at all, yet thanks to you, here we are. Do you think I take any pleasure in the idea of killing the last great beast left in this universe? Believe it or not, I do not. And yes, I am concerned about my own welfare, but must I point out yet again that we will *all* perish if she carries on like this?"

"I know," Amba says softly. Her voice is steady, but her knuckles are white in her lap. "Much as it pains me to admit it, Suya's right. There is no other way."

There's a heavy silence before Tyre breaks it. "How? Only one of the Seven can kill a great beast, and Ash vowed a long time ago that he would never allow a god to wield one of them again."

Kirrin restrains himself for exactly five seconds before chiming in with: "And we all remember whose fault *that* is, don't we, Suya?"

"Kirrin," Thea huffs. "Priorities, *please*."

When Sorsha's curse first manifested itself centuries ago, Ash, the destroyer and the keeper of the Temple of Ashma, gave Suya permission to use one of the first seven celestial weapons to kill her. Devaki shielded Sorsha from Suya and the golden sunspear, and he killed her instead. Ash was so infuriated by Suya's carelessness that he vowed he would never allow a god to use one of the Seven again.

Max still looks furious, but he says, "Isn't Ash only about ten years into his Sleep?"

"Nine," says Tyre. "Which means he has ninety-one years to go, but we'll have to wake him early and beg him to retract his vow."

Kirrin lets out a snort. "And which unlucky bastard is to undertake that thankless task? Don't look at me," he adds hastily when Tyre raises his eyebrows. "He's not likely to be happy to see me. Thea can go. He likes her best."

"Everyone likes me best," Thea points out. "I'm not as insufferable as the rest of you."

"Unkind, but true," Kirrin replies, grinning.

"By all means, talk to Ash," says Suya. "But, as we all know he's never going to retract his vow, perhaps we should consider an alternative."

I knew that was coming. Weeks ago, when we were on the Empty Moon, he came to me and made me an offer. I refused him, but I knew he wouldn't let it go.

The others stare at him. "What alternative?" Thea asks, confused. Bless her sweet soul, it hasn't even crossed her mind.

"He wants a mortal to go after Sorsha," Max tells her.

Thea's mouth falls open. "Suya!"

"You're all being unnecessarily dramatic," Suya snaps. "Ash will not allow any of us to wield one of the Seven. A mortal has to do it."

"Sorsha will kill any human who tries to get near her," says Amba.

"That's a risk we can't afford not to take," says Suya. "Send Alexi. Considering he set her loose, it's the least he can do. And with his skill, he may actually be able to pull it off. Give him the starsword and tell him to kill Sorsha."

"The starsword?" Kirrin is momentarily distracted. "It would be easier for him to reach her with the sunspear or moonbow."

"But they will be much harder to acquire from the Temple of Ashma. The starsword, on the other hand, is already conveniently in *Titania*'s possession."

At this, all six of them turn to look at the window, where I have been hovering just outside and shamelessly spying on them. At some point after King Cassel's murder in that lonely house in the woods, Kirrin finally realized I was using the tether between us to get inside his head and now cheerfully blocks me every time I try to use it. Amba losing her immortality meant my tether to *her* was severed automatically. As such, I now have to use more traditional methods to snoop.

Irritated, I refuse to react. I'm *cloaked*. No one is supposed to be able to detect me! Yet they've clearly been aware of my presence the whole time.

I hate gods.

Then Max says, "Is that true?"

"Yes," I say into his earpiece, rather petulantly.

"How has *Titania* come to have the starsword in her possession?" Tyre wants to know.

Kirrin has other priorities. "How did *you* know she had it?" he demands of Suya.

"I am a sun god," Suya reminds him smugly. "I am everywhere. I pay more attention than the rest of you do. King Cassel came to possess the starsword some years before he was abducted. I have no idea how. Elvar took possession of it when everyone thought Cassel was dead, and then Elvar recently gave it to Esmae. She never knew what she had. She thought it was an ordinary sword. She left it with *Titania* when she went to Arcadia."

"He's already had this conversation with you," Max says slowly, to me.

"Yes," I reply.

Picking up on the fact that Max is listening to me over his earpiece, Suya shrugs and says, "I hoped *Titania* would persuade Esmae to use the starsword on Sorsha. I offered her a reward for her pains, too, but she was not inclined to help me."

"And I don't regret it either," I snap, forgetting for a moment that the only person who can hear me is Max. "I would have done everything I could to *stop* Esmae from going anywhere near Sorsha. I was never going to *ask* her to do it!"

"What reward?" Max asks. "What did he promise you?"

I don't answer. I don't want to think about it.

—hands, feet, a beating heart—

I delete that secret, treacherous cache of data.

"I won't ask Alexi to give his life up for this," Kirrin says. "You know it's more likely to kill him than not."

"Don't ask him then," Suya replies. "*I* will. *I'll* offer him this opportunity to redeem himself and be the hero of the star system once more. And I wonder what Alexi Rey, the boy who has spent his life chasing glory, will say?"

And with that, he vanishes.

Kirrin seethes. "I hope Sorsha gets to eat him before she dies."

CHAPTER THREE

Titania

"I have a tremendously brilliant idea," I announce.

This does not have the effect I had anticipated. It is an empirical fact that I am extraordinary, and it therefore stands to reason that such a proclamation should be met with delight, admiration, and praise. Instead, Max and Sybilla glance at each other with an expression I can only describe as dubious.

"Go on," Max says, a little too warily for my liking.

Up close, he looks terrible. There are dark shadows under his eyes, and his entire body is rigid to overcompensate for his obvious fatigue. In light of this, and also because I happen to adore him, I decide to forgive his lack of enthusiasm.

"I think *we* should go to Ashma and wake Ash from his Sleep."

Max blinks.

Sybilla groans. "*That* was what you summoned us here to say?"

If I had a face, I would be scowling. "I didn't summon *you*," I remind her.

We are on one of the palace's many rooftops. Well, I am. Max and Sybilla are inside my control room. As ever, he's quiet and still. And, also as ever, *she* is pacing my floors with her spiky, stompy boots.

"*Titania*," Max says, "why us? Thea would get a better reception."

"Don't you want to know how the starsword ended up in King Cassel's possession in the first place?" I ask.

He considers that. "Ash might not tell us. He's going to be angry that he's been woken from his Sleep early, and he's going to be even angrier when he finds out we're there to ask him to revoke a vow."

"I think it's worth a try," I insist.

"The mystery of King Cassel and the starsword aren't exactly a priority right now," Sybilla says. "It's not like there's a ravenous space dragon, a galactic war, and a missing friend to worry about already or anything."

"Do you think I've forgotten any of that?" I demand, offended. "It's all connected. We need to speak to Ash. I can *feel* it."

Sybilla's expression does a dramatic shift. "Wait, would Ash be able to tell us where Esmae is? Max?"

"I don't know," he says. One of his fists clenches at his side. The sound of her name always does that to him.

"If you're going to Ashma," a voice interrupts us from over my speakers, "I will accompany you."

Sybilla looks surprised. "Is that Amba?"

"Yes. I wanted to talk to her, as well."

"But you didn't make *her* come here?"

"She has achy bones!"

"So do I!" Sybilla protests.

I huff. "Amba was a war goddess. She helped King Darshan make me, she gave up her immortality for my favorite person in this universe, *and* she never wears horrid boots. When you do all that, I promise to give your achy bones the same consideration."

"Fair point," Sybilla says and collapses into one of my seats as if she has accepted defeat.

"So," I press them. "Are we going? Are we?"

There's a pause, and then Amba's voice comes over the speakers again: "Max?"

He nods, reluctantly. "It *is* all connected. I don't think waking Ash is a good idea and I don't think he's going to be happy to see us, but if there's even a chance we can stop Sorsha without sacrificing Alex, if there's even a *chance* Ash can tell us where Esmae is—" He breaks off, takes a deep breath, and says, "*Titania*'s right. We have to try."

I am almost beside myself with excitement, and I want to leave immediately, but Max has about three thousand and six things that he has to do before he can leave Kali, and Amba needs time to prepare herself for a journey, so I keep my impatience to myself and accept that tomorrow is about as early as anything is likely to happen.

Max and Sybilla leave me there on the rooftop and go back into the palace. In the elevator, on their way down to the suite of rooms where Max does boring kingdom paperwork things, I hear Sybilla say, "You need to sleep."

"I sleep," he says.

I, the practically omniscient narrator: no, he does not sleep.

"Quit lying," she says irritably, "I know you better than that. It would be mind-bogglingly stupid to go to Ashma without getting a decent night's sleep first. If it's anything like the Empty Moon—"

"It's not." Max is quiet for a moment, and then he says, "I know you had a hard time on the Empty Moon. You don't have to come to Ashma with us."

She makes a sound that could be the distant cousin of a laugh. "As if I'm letting you go anywhere without me."

The silence crackles with a thousand things they're not saying, but I know what they're both thinking about. On the night Esmae asked me to burn down Arcadia, she ran into the yellow woods and was supposed to meet Sybilla and me on the other side. We waited for hours, but she never came. Her earpiece was unreachable. The woods were too dense for me to land in, so I flew above them in slow circles and my systems scanned the trees for her. For heat, for a heartbeat, for *anything*. I couldn't find anything.

Eventually, we had to go back to Kali, to refuel (me), rest (Sybilla), and hammer out some kind of plan to find Esmae. When we got there, I wanted to see Max, but Amba told us he had shut himself up in his rooms and wanted to be alone. So Sybilla went to check in with the Hundred and One, and I went out into space to find Sorsha. *She*, in turn, was searching for Suya so that she could avenge her mother's death, but her hunger had started to take over. I tried to stop her, but I couldn't.

I, who never failed, had failed twice in one night.

By the time I returned to Erys, the capital city of Kali, it had been three days since Esmae had disappeared and it had become obvious that Max wasn't in his rooms. I don't think he ever had been. Sybilla jumped on board in her stupid spiky boots and we hurtled back to the ash and bones of Arcadia. I let her out at the edge of the yellow woods and guided her through the trees to Max. He had been in the woods for fifty-eight hours and was half-dead from cold and exhaustion. When Sybilla found him, he was on his knees in the snow. He had found Esmae's earpiece.

It was a fight to get him back to the warmth of my hull. In the space of a few days, Max had left a place that had once been his home, had watched his sister torn from the stars, and had lost someone he loved, so Sybilla was gentle at first. When that didn't work, she was a lot less gentle.

Now, Max says, "You know what happened in Arcadia didn't end the war. It just forced a pause. Alex is buying more mercenaries and salvaging what's left of his army as we speak. This is the gulp of air before we go back into the water, Sybilla. I need someone I can trust to stay here."

"Damn it, Max," she snaps. "Stop that. You're making it seem like I'd be doing you a favor by staying here, but I know you're just trying to spare me a repeat of the Empty Moon."

There's a pause.

Whatever she sees on his face, it makes Sybilla say, "What about Queen Cassela?"

"Grandmother isn't here."

This is news to Sybilla. "She what? But she never leaves Kali!"

"Clearly, she does," says Max. "She said she needed guidance and clarity and went to the Night Temple. And thanks to

King Darshan, Rickard is in no condition to take over while I'm gone. It has to be you."

Another pause.

Then Sybilla says, in a voice that has clearly been forced out between gritted teeth: "Fine, but only if you take a dose of sleep serum tonight."

"Fine."

There's a chime as the elevator doors open. A moment later, I hear Sybilla's voice, and this time she's speaking to me.

"Make sure he comes back," she says.

"I will."

CHAPTER FOUR

Radha

No one has touched my brother's rooms in all the months he's been gone, so it's the only place in this palace that still feels like home.

It should *all* feel like home. I was born here, I grew up here, I spent almost every day of the first sixteen years of my life here. I had friends, I had charitable causes to devote myself to, I had servants and tutors and flowers and gifts and just about everything any one person could ever ask for. If home is familiarity, this should be home.

But that's not what home is, is it?

Rama liked to move as little as possible, so almost everything he ever owned is in his suite: his books, scattered haphazardly on the desks and shelves; the dozens of maps he liked to examine like they held all the secrets of the universe;

his music player right by his bed; the beautiful hand-carved Warlords set our other brother, our sister, and I gave him for his ninth birthday . . .

I'm sitting very straight at one of his desks, the very picture of grace. *Princesses don't slouch, Radha.* According to my father, princes don't slouch either, but it didn't take him long to give up on trying to make Rama listen.

If I look out of the corner of my eye, I think I can see him. Slouched in the other chair to my left, his feet up on the desk. I want so badly to turn my head and look at him properly, really *see* him, but I know that if I do that, he'll be gone. So I stay where I am and look out of the corner of my eye and take what little there is.

"It's time to go, caterpillar," he says. His voice is a warm, lazy drawl. "There's nothing left for you here."

It's true. Of course it's true. He's not real, so he's just saying what I'm already thinking.

I trace the shape of a dried tea stain on the surface of the desk. "You left me," I hear myself say instead.

He smiles. "You left me first."

Also true. Rama was still here on Wychstar when I pulled away to become our father's pawn in his vendetta against Rickard, his teacher in a past life. Guilt chews away at the edges of me, making me smaller. I did something horrible to Rickard, a man who was never anything but kind to me, and I don't think I'll ever stop feeling terrible about it, but I would be lying if I said that what's even worse than that is knowing that trying to please my father cost me the last few months of the time I could have had with my brother.

"I can't go yet," I tell him. "He owes me. I'm not leaving until he gives me what I want."

"He's never going to give you what you want."

I hate that lazy, knowing voice. "I don't want him to love me," I snap. It's not like me, but then ruining a man wasn't like me either and yet here we are. "I want him to *help*. Father has resources and armies that could help us defeat the people who murdered you. I'm not going back to Kali until he gives them to me."

Before Rama can say anything else, I hear the outer door of his suite click open. A moment later, my other brother walks into the room.

"I thought I'd find you here," he says, smiling.

Rodi is Father's heir. He's charming and kind and sunny, quick to joke, quick to put people at ease. He's a lot older than I am, so I didn't see as much of him growing up as I did of Rama. When I did, I used to gaze at him in awe and want to be just like him. I think I did okay at that part.

"Any news?" Rodi asks, like he does at least once a day.

"About Sorsha? Or Esmae?"

He drops into the other chair, replacing Rama's ghost. Like me, he sits straight and graceful. "Both."

"Sybilla sent me a text comm a little while ago," I say. "Max and *Titania* are going to Ashma to see if they can persuade Ash to let a god use one of the Seven to kill Sorsha. I think they're hoping Ash might also be able to tell them where Esmae is. If she's even still alive."

That's another reason for the guilt chewing me up. Like so many other people in her life, I blamed Esmae for a lot of things that weren't her fault. I never wanted her to know that, but she found out on the Empty Moon. She was kind to me even after what I did to Rickard, and she almost died saving my life on the Empty Moon, and *that* was what she got in return.

Rodi looks surprised. "Why do they think a god like Ash would listen to anything *Titania* and Max have to say?"

I hesitate, but say, "I don't know." Only a few of us know the truth about Max. I don't like lying to Rodi, but it's not my secret to tell.

"There's a summit at the end of the week," Rodi tells me. "All the heads of state in the star system, except for Elvar and Alexi."

"Because they're the ones you'll be discussing," I guess.

He nods. "I assume you're going instead of Father?"

"Yes. I'll put in a word for Esmae and Max, but I don't know how much good it'll do." Rodi sighs and tips his head back against the chair. "The other heads of state are livid. Alexi lied to his allies about Arcadia, nine countries lost soldiers when Esmae burned down Arcadia, and now we may *all* die because Alexi set Sorsha free. This war is going to be the end of us all."

"The other heads of state needn't pretend they had nothing to do with any of this," I say, annoyed. "Our father is the reason a weapon like *Titania* exists, Queen Miyo and King Ralf have been helping Alexi for years, and King Yann handed Elvar an obscene amount of silver before he died."

"All of which I will be sure to say to them," says Rodi. "In fact, you can come with me and say it, too, if it'll make you feel better. I think I can count on Ralf backing us up. Prime Minister Gomez, too. But I still don't think it'll make much difference. We'll be outvoted."

I trace that tea stain again, round and round. "Outvoted on what?"

"On what action to take."

"What do you think the others want to do?" I ask, alarmed.

"If we're lucky?" he replies. "Kill Sorsha and contain *Titania*."

"Containing *Titania* is not an option," I say. "Rodi, come on. She's not a monster. You know that. We grew up with her. When Father let her out of the dock, she used to hover right there." I point to the big window at the other end of Rama's suite. "Rama would talk to her for hours. He was the one who would beg Father to let her out more often. She was his friend. She's *my* friend."

"I know who she is," Rodi says, frustrated. "Do you think I don't know that it'll break her heart to be powered down and locked away somewhere? But she broke the laws of righteous warfare and the other heads of state are, understandably, terrified of what she might do to their countries if she feels like it."

"She only did what Esmae asked her to!"

Rodi shakes his head. "We can't tell them she's sentient and deserves the same rights as the rest of us, and then in the very next breath tell them she was just a tool in Esmae's hands."

"But both of those things are true—"

"Radha, I *know*. I care about her, too. And right now, Sorsha is everyone's priority, so I can buy *Titania* some time. But let's say Sorsha dies, one way or another. Let's say the star system gets its future back. What happens then? You do see, don't you, that the other heads of state will turn on Kali if they can't be satisfied that *Titania* is contained?"

I think of the friends I have on Kali. Max. The kids of the Hundred and One who took shifts to keep me safe. And Sybilla. Sybilla most of all, Sybilla who will never abandon Max or Esmae or Kali even to save herself, Sybilla who failed her test of truth because she couldn't admit even to herself that she cared about me, Sybilla who kissed me and now only sends me awkward text comms because she's so lovably terrible at this.

Princesses don't slouch, Radha, but I wish they did. I'm exhausted. "The end of the war is the only thing that will fix this, isn't it?" I say.

"Yes. This galaxy will burn if they don't find a way to make peace."

"What about justice for Rama?"

"Justice and peace aren't mutually exclusive." Rodi looks over at a picture of Rama and me at the edge of the desk. It was taken on my sixth birthday. I have a mouth full of birthday cake and Rama has his arm slung around me. We're both grinning, his teeth white and bright, mine smeared with purple cake. "You used to hate that picture. *Raaaa-maaa,*" Rodi's voice goes high and whiney, "*I'm not at allllll dignified in that picture. It's not princessyyyyy.*"

"I did *not* sound like that," I say, smiling in spite of myself.

"What was it he used to call you?"

"Caterpillar."

Rodi lets out a short bark of laughter. "That's it. Caterpillar. Because you wanted so badly to be all grown up and graceful like a butterfly, but he insisted you couldn't skip ahead. *You have to be a caterpillar to become a butterfly, Radha.*" Now it's Rama's lazy drawl he's mimicking. "*You can't skip ahead.*"

I laugh, too, but it hitches. Like somewhere in there, the laugh is hiding a sob.

Rodi's smile fades. "I tried to get him back, you know," he says quietly.

"You did what?"

"I thought maybe a god could do it. That they might have the power to bring a mortal back to life. I prayed to all of them, one after another." He gives me a crooked, sad smile. "No one answered."

"Maybe it just isn't possible," I say.

Rodi opens his mouth to reply but is interrupted by the notification chime of his watch. He glances at the screen and grimaces.

"What is it?" I ask.

"Father wants to see me," he says, uncurling from the chair.

"I'll go with you." The sooner I get what I want from Father, the sooner I can go back to Kali. Back to Sybilla.

We find our father in his private parlor, with a tray of kaju sweets and black coffee on the tea table in front of him. Father gives Rodi an annoyed look when he sees that I'm with him, but he waves an impatient hand to indicate that we should come in and shut the door.

Father's shoulders are hunched over. *Kings don't slouch, Father*, I am tempted to say. Of course, I don't. He looks so old and tired. Maybe it was too much to hope that doing what he asked of me would make him love me, or to even just *see* me for once in my life, but at the very least I thought he'd be happy. He punished Rickard for what Rickard did to Lavya. Why isn't he happy?

"You wanted to see me, Father?" Rodi asks.

"Those need to be assessed and signed," says Father, pointing to a stack of papers on his desk.

Rodi and I glance at each other. Father's been doing this more and more lately: whether it's paperwork, or the menu for a state banquet, or even a summit to discuss the fate of the star system, he's been taking a step back and handing

Wychstar's affairs over to Rodi. It makes me worry. Whatever else has happened, he's still my father.

"Are you well, Father?" I ask.

He gives me a sharp look. "Are you asking because you're concerned? Or because you want to soften me up before you ask me, for the hundredth time, to commit my armies to Elvar's war."

I am a princess. I am poised, calm, and patient. "It is not just Elvar's war," I say evenly. "It's ours, too. Don't you want justice for Rama?"

Father's hands grip the arms of his chair very tightly. However he feels about me, I've never doubted that he loved Rama. "As I have said before," he says, his voice brusque, "to lend my armies to Elvar is to lend them to Rickard, and I will not do that. Not even in my son's memory."

"Rickard can barely stand," I remind him. "He's not in command of Kali's army anymore. You saw to that. *I* did that for you. This is what I want in return."

"Radha," Rodi murmurs. "Let it go."

He knows I won't. If there's one thing all four of Father's children inherited from him, it's our doggedness.

"Why aren't you happy?" I can't help but ask our father. So much for poise and calm. "You got what you wanted. Why aren't you happy about it?"

And to my surprise, he gives me a small, bitter smile. "I have been asking myself that very question."

I watch the way he keeps smoothing his left hand over his right thumb, over and over, like he's reassuring himself that it's still there. Pity makes me soften my voice. "Father, this war has to end, one way or another. I, for one, would like Rama's killers to *not* be the ones who win. Let me prevent that from happening."

Father doesn't know that the twins' mother, Kyra, was the one who killed Rama. Rodi doesn't, either. *I* know because Sybilla told me, because Max told *her*, and I promised I wouldn't say a word. It's another secret that's not mine to tell.

If Alexi wins, his mother wins. I'm useless in a fight, but I have to do *something* to help make sure that doesn't happen.

"Father," I prompt, because he hasn't said anything.

Still, he doesn't speak. He looks like he's far away.

"Radha, maybe you should come back later," Rodi suggests.

"*Father*," I say. My teeth clench. "At some point, you have to decide who you hate more. Is it the man who once betrayed and ruined you? Or is it the people who murdered your son?"

At that, Father looks up. His sharp, angry eyes meet mine. "Very well," he says.

Rodi drops his pen. I can't quite hide my own shock. "You mean you'll send our armies to fight with Elvar?"

"As you said," Father says, "at some point, I must choose who I hate more. So here we are. Leave what we need to defend Wychstar, and take the rest." He pauses and adds, "On one condition."

There it is. I eye him warily. "What condition?"

"I want to see him. Just once, before all this is over."

"That's all?"

"That's all."

Rodi and I glance at each other. Is it possible that our father, after all this time, is ready to put his past behind him?

"I'll have to ask Max to see what Rickard says," I say.

Father just nods, already far away again.

CHAPTER FIVE

Titania

Ashma rises out of a cluster of brilliant stars. From a distance, it looks like a small orb of darkness lit only by the starlight around it, but as I fly closer, we see cliffs and forests take shape out of the dark. The thing that stands out, though, is the Temple of Ashma, an ancient and enormous structure of stone, marble, and glass on top of the highest cliff.

Like many of the gods' celestial realms, Ashma is physically present in this star system but does not follow its natural laws. The human day-night cycle, for example, doesn't exist on Ashma because Ash does not need it. Sunlight never touches the planet directly, and the only light here comes from the light that the surrounding stars reflect, and from the artificial light within the Temple itself.

"Approach the Temple with caution," Amba says to me, arms crossed tightly over her chest. She stares at Ashma with a tight, pained look on her face. I think she hates being confined to her mortal body and can't bear that she now has to rely on me, or another kind of mortal transportation, to get across the stars.

"Is there a shield?" I ask her.

"Not the kind mortals construct to protect their territories," says Amba. "To be perfectly frank, I'm not actually sure what Ash's shields are like. I have never had to get past them. I have only ever come to Ashma at his invitation before."

"If Ash doesn't want us here, we won't get anywhere near the Temple," Max says wryly. "He may be in his Sleep, but he'll know we're here."

An unfamiliar feeling sends vibrations along my wings. It's not fear—that would be unthinkable!—but I think it's something like it. Am I nervous? I suppose that would make sense; I have never met a god like Ash before. Amba and Kirrin, who helped King Darshan make me, don't have Ash's power. It stands to reason, therefore, that they also could not have built me to withstand power like his.

"Can Ash *damage* me?" I demand.

Max grins for the first time since we lost Esmae. "It didn't occur to you before, did it? When you were so merrily insisting that we should come wake the most powerful god in the universe?"

"You could try to sound a *little* less amused at the prospect of my untimely demise," I sniff.

"Indestructible means indestructible, *Titania*," Amba says. "Even Ash cannot destroy you. That said, I suspect his power can affect you."

I am unimpressed with the lack of clarity. "Affect me how?" I ask. "Affect me like that gravitational pull on the Empty Moon that forced me to land and stay grounded until Kirrin decided otherwise? Or affect me in some other way that will leave me even more traumatized than that time I had to fly in the rain?"

Amba rolls her eyes like she thinks I'm being melodramatic. The nerve. "I assure you, you'll survive."

Max gives her a look. "But will we?"

"That's less certain," she replies with the faintest hint of a smile.

Once we enter the planet's atmosphere, it becomes obvious that the skies above Ashma are stormy. There is, thankfully, no rain, but lightning crackles silently above the Temple and I have to work harder than usual to stay on course.

I wait for some kind of tug, like the pull on the Empty Moon that forced me to the ground, but nothing comes. I approach the cliff as slowly as possible. There's no landing space around the Temple, so I will have to hover. Inside my control room, Max and Amba are tense, their eyes fixed on the Temple like they can't look away.

Lightning blinks in and out above me. It seems closer than it was a moment ago.

"*Titania*, get closer to the surface," Max says sharply.

"There's only so close I can get—"

"Now!"

I huff, but I comply. Just as I am about to ask him why he's become so high-handed all of a sudden, there's another bright, jagged flash of lightning.

This one hits me, sending electricity across my wings, and my system cuts out. Just like that. I go dark.

The first thing I realize when I power back up is that there *was* space to land outside the Temple after all, because I am on the ground. It is solid, grassy, cold, and unpleasantly damp beneath me.

The second thing I realize is that Max and Amba got out safely. They're close by. Max is pushing himself off the ground, dusting grass stains off his hands and the knees of his battle gear. Amba follows suit, wincing. Her movements are stiff, and she has one hand pressed to her ribs.

Max looks worried. "Where's *Titania*?"

Honestly. I am a whole entire *ship*. How has he missed me?

He and Amba both look around, and it takes them a good thirty seconds to find me. They stare. And stare some more.

"What?" I ask irritably. "What's the unseemly gawping for?"

Odd. My voice sounds a bit lighter and higher than usual.

Max takes a step closer. "Titania?"

"You're being weird," I inform him.

Wait. Why are they so big? Why are they looking *down* at me? Did Ash's power *shrink* me?

Outraged, I squeal, "What did he do to me? How small am I? Please tell me you can't fit me in your pocket! Lie to me if you have to, but do *not* tell me I can fit in your pocket!"

Max takes another step closer and crouches beside me. *Crouches*. My humiliation is complete.

"Titania," Max says gently, "can you get up?"

Get up? What kind of absurd question is that? I just have to input the code that will get me into the air and—

Nothing.

Panicked, I launch into a full system analysis to figure out what's wrong with me. My database and memory appear to be intact, but my physical functions are—

I—
Slowly, my line of sight lowers. No, not my line of sight.
My eyes.
I have eyes.
I have hands.
I have feet.
I have *clothes*.
I can't fly because I don't have wings.
I'm not a ship anymore.
I'm human.

"It's okay," Max says, "it's okay," but I can't hear him properly over the sound of these odd, sharp sounds that keep coming out of me.

Breaths. That's what they are. Panicked breaths.

My system analysis tells me my heart rate is very high. System analysis? No, it's a brain. I have a brain. And a heart rate.

I try to rise, the way I would rise from the ground into the air, but instead of wings and machinery, I have wobbly, trembling legs. I balance on them, teetering back and forth, and then I try to take a step forward with one foot and immediately trip over the other foot.

Max catches me. I am small, even smaller than Esmae. I don't even reach his shoulder at full height. I suppose that must be because, in human years, I'm a child. My alien hands clutch his arms. I can feel the armored texture of his vambraces, the fabric of his shirt. I can *feel*.

The realization that I can touch sends me into a brief and wholly inappropriate frenzy of patting my hands all over Max's face, arms, and chest, unable to quite believe that I am actually experiencing the textures of skin, hair, jaw, cotton, leather, and metal with real human hands.

Patiently, Max lets me paw him like I have become an overenthusiastic puppy. His eyes smile in a way that I've never quite been able to see before.

"Titania, it's temporary," Amba says to me, her calm, firm voice finding its way to me. "Don't panic. Ash's power over you won't last."

"Why did it do this to me?" I ask in that lighter, higher voice. I sound like a young girl.

"It's not an insult," Amba says. "It's an invitation. As a ship, you could not have entered the Temple. In a human body, you can."

Max looks at me for a moment, and then he says, "Amba, go ahead without us. We'll catch up in a minute."

She glances at him, then back at me, and nods. "Very well."

I look up at Max and try to slow my breathing. My human mouth feels moist and thick and funny.

"I've been inside other bodies before," I try to explain. "Sort of. I've looked at the world from Amba and Kirrin's points of view, in different bodies they've worn. But this isn't like that. This is different."

He nods.

"I—" I falter. "My face is wet. Why is my face wet?"

"Because you're crying," he says gently.

I shake out my hands and wiggle my toes. As a ship, I was strong and indestructible, but I was also fixed in place. In this body, everything is so *mobile*. Every part of me seems to be able to move. I can even wiggle my ears!

I touch the tears on my cheeks. My skin feels so soft, the tears so wet and slippery. "Wh-what do I look like?"

"Human," says Max. "You look like you're about thirteen or fourteen, which is about right, isn't it? You're small and quite delicate. Your dress is the same silver of your chassis when you were a ship. You have an upturned nose. Long brown hair. Brown eyes. Brownish skin. Freckles on your nose." He pauses. "Actually, here, see for yourself."

He taps his watch and turns the screen toward me. A girl looks back at me. She's very young. Her wet eyes are open wide and there are tears on her rounded, reddened cheeks. Her hair is pulled back into a long *thing* that Sybilla calls a ponytail, tied with a silver ribbon. I blink, and the girl blinks, too.

She is me. I am her.

It's temporary.

A feeling of intense, human *want* makes me feel like I might tear myself in two. I want this. I want it more than almost anything else.

"This was what Suya offered you, wasn't it?" Max says quietly. "This, forever. This is what you want."

I drop my eyes and look away. I still have my hands curled into his shirt to help keep me steady on my feet. I let go and try to stay upright on my own.

"It's okay to want this, Titania."

"I don't want it so badly that I'll pay Suya's price," is all I'm willing to say on the subject.

I do want this, but the one thing I want more than this is to make sure Esmae and Max and everyone else I love is safe and happy, and I can't do that as a human.

"We should join Amba," I say to Max.

"Can you walk?"

I feel my mouth curl. My first smile. "I'm not leaving until I do," I tell him. I rock back and forth on my bare feet. Grass tickles the bottom of them. "I'm not leaving this planet until I can *run*. I'm going to make the most of every moment in this body."

Max looks away. "I wish she could see you now."

"So do I."

"Wait," he says. He taps his watch again. "I'll record you. We'll find her, Titania. And when we do, she'll want to see this."

I let him record my unsteady attempts to walk up a grassy path, my sputtering giggles when I trip over, and my profoundly ungraceful attempt at a twirl. I talk to her, too, because that way it almost feels like she's here.

Max lowers his wrist when we're done. "You're doing better," he says. A brief, boyish smile flashes across his face. "Race you to the Temple doors?"

I have seen Max run before, so when I stumble up to a slightly perplexed Amba at the doors and Max is somehow a step behind me, I know he let me win.

"*If* you are both done behaving like children," says Amba, pointing her most disapproving look our way, "Shall we go in? I believe we still have a galaxy to save."

The damp, tickly grass of the winding cliff path turns to cold stone as we step into the Temple. It's easier to walk here because the surface is smooth, but I tread cautiously nevertheless, and my arms flutter out at my sides to help me keep my balance.

The chamber we step into is enormous, almost as vast as the entire Temple itself. The great dome above us is glass, a direct view to the stars and lightning, and there are dozens of orbs of golden light suspended in the air. One wall is covered in stone and rock, with a waterfall gurgling down into a rocky pond. Another is pure glass, swirling with smoke. And further ahead, we see a grove of trees, mango and gooseberry and silver oak, all somehow growing *out* of the marble.

Beneath the grove of trees is a man. He has short black hair that ripples upward as if there's a wind blowing from beneath him, very pale skin, and is dressed in simple black pajamas that flutter loosely around his ankles. His features are cold and severe: straight brows, mouth set in a thin line, a furrow in his forehead. He hovers in the air just above the roots of the trees, with his eyes closed, his legs folded, and his hands upon his knees. Energy crackles around him, like the lightning in the sky.

"Ash," Amba murmurs.

He looks human, but this avatar of him is simply how he's chosen to appear to us. Mortal eyes can't process the true form of a god.

Every one thousand years, Ash sleeps for a hundred years. His Sleep is supposed to be a healing time, a century in which the universe stitches up the wounds of the centuries past and starts the new millennium with greater wisdom and hope. From what I gather, Ash can reset his Sleep if he's woken.

But he does not like being woken.

There's that unfamiliar, fluttery feeling again. *Not* fear, but like it. Maybe this wasn't such a brilliant idea, after all.

I tear my eyes away from the god and examine the rest of the Temple chamber. The rock pond and grove of trees appear to form two points of a trinity, and I take a tentative step closer to the third point. It's a glowing, revolving disc with seven sides, suspended about four feet off the ground, and at least three feet tall. As I get closer, I can see shadows in the light, silhouettes cut into the disc on each of the seven sides.

No, I realize quickly, as the disc completes a full revolution and the first silhouette I noticed comes around once more. The silhouettes are on just *six* of the seven sides.

A bow. A spear. A trident. A crooked staff. A hoop. And a lightning bolt.

Or, as they are better known: the moonbow, the sunspear, the trishula, the seastaff, the chakra, and the astra.

"The Seven," I whisper.

The seventh side of the revolving disc, the only side without a shadow carved into the light, would have once held the silhouette of a sword.

But the starsword, of course, isn't here.

"We have to wake him," Amba says behind me.

I turn back to the grove of trees and to Ash in his Sleep. Max gives Amba a wry look. "I suppose you want *me* to do it," he says.

"I saved your life," she says at once. "I think this is the very least you can do for me."

Max rolls his eyes. "I seem to remember you saying that when you conned me into giving you a permanent suite of rooms in my palace."

Amba raises her eyebrows. "A suite of rooms is hardly the equivalent of bravely taking my father on in battle, slaying him, and rescuing my devoured brothers and sister."

Shaking his head, Max turns back to the grove of trees. The humor in his face fades as he stares at Ash for a moment. Then, quietly, he says, "By the stars that gave us life and the ashes of the old world, I bid you wake, Destroyer."

My new human heart beats faster. My new human knees wobble. Lightning splits the dark sky in two.

And Ash, the destroyer, opens his eyes.

CHAPTER SIX

Titania

That terrible, electric power crackles around Ash, fiercer than ever, as his dark eyes settle first on Max, then on Amba, then on me. I try a smile, but my mouth won't move the way it's supposed to.

Silently, still hovering in the air, Ash unfolds his body. As he moves, his black pajamas reshape into an armored black tunic, fitted trousers, boots, and vambraces. By the time he sets himself on the marble floor, he is a god in full battle gear.

"Uncle," says Amba, bowing her head.

"You should have both known better," is Ash's only reply. His voice is cold and severe.

"You know we wouldn't have woken you if it wasn't important," says Max. "Sorsha is free. We're all in danger."

"If you think I was not aware of that, you are mistaken." Ash steps out of the grove of trees. His boots leave scorch marks on the marble everywhere he steps, but they fade away almost immediately, as though the marble has healed itself. He gives Max a grim look. "You should not have woken me, Valin. I would have Slept through this if you had let me be. Now I cannot do that."

That should be a good thing, shouldn't it? Why does it sound like a warning?

Max's eyes dart across the chamber to the revolving disc, then back to Ash, whose gaze does not waver. Max closes his eyes as if in defeat. "Don't," he says.

Don't what?

"I must," says Ash. "You know I cannot do otherwise."

"Can it be stopped?"

"Yes."

"Ahem." I clear my throat dramatically. "Can *what* be stopped, exactly?"

Three pairs of unfathomably dark eyes turn to me. I scowl back, mostly because I *can* scowl now. Ash tilts his head to one side as he considers me. "This form suits you," he says. "Would you like to keep it?"

"No," I say at once. *Yes.*

Ash nods like he knows exactly what I didn't say. Turning away, he sits down on one of the trees' thick, sturdy roots and gestures with his hands. "You woke me for a reason, I presume? Make your request."

Uncharacteristically hesitant, it takes Amba a moment to say, "Much as I wish otherwise, it is no longer possible for Sorsha and this star system to coexist. If I could save them both, I would, but as it stands, it would seem that the only way to preserve millions of lives is to kill my sister."

She speaks calmly and clearly, but I think I can hear the pain she's trying very hard to hide.

I think Ash hears it, too, because he says, "I know this is not easy for you, Amba. I do not like it, either. If I could undo Ness's curse, I would."

Amba nods, looking away like she's trying to compose herself. She looks unbearably tired, so I am not surprised when she, too, sits on one of the roots. Her back stays straight, her head high, but her hands clench in her lap.

I feel like I should step in and spare her having to keep talking about the murder of her sister, but Max, who obviously feels the same way, gets there first. "Only one of the Seven can kill Sorsha," he says. "We came here to ask your permission to use one."

"No," says Ash coldly, "You came here and woke me to ask my permission for a *god* to use one. And my answer, as I am sure you expected, is no. I will not revoke my vow."

"We'll all die if Sorsha cannot be stopped!" I protest.

Ash raises his eyebrows. "*You* will not."

"That's not a comfort," I huff. "Are Sorsha and I to be the only sentient creatures left behind when all the stars in this galaxy are gone? Am I supposed to chase her from star system to star system until she runs out of stars and dies and *I* am all that remains in an endless dark void?"

I have never said this out loud. I have never even dared to think it. And now I cannot escape it, this terror that *that* is indeed what will become of me.

"A mortal cannot kill Sorsha, Uncle," Amba says quietly. "The odds are infinitesimal."

Ash considers. "A mortal? Perhaps not."

Max narrows his eyes like he's trying to unpick a riddle.

"Why are you like this?" I demand, bewildered and angry. Amba shakes her head sharply at me, but I am not in the mood to listen. "You gods and mortals, you're not actually as different as you think! All of you, with your vows and curses and wars, and all of you too proud to undo any of it. I want an explanation. I *demand* an explanation. I do not understand how you can refuse to revoke a vow when you know our entire world is at stake."

Lightning flashes across the sky above us. Electricity crackles around Ash, who opens one of his hands. Lightning dances on top of his palm, a single bolt, a miniature of the astra locked behind the revolving disc.

I dart behind Max immediately. "Thanks," he says drily.

Poking my head out from behind him, I attempt my loftiest tone. "I'm not sorry I said it!"

Ash's cold, severe expression doesn't so much as flicker. "I do not owe you or anyone else an explanation, child," he says. He leans into the roots around him, like a king on his throne. "Moreover, you speak as if I should *want* to save this galaxy from the cataclysm that is coming."

I inch out from behind Max, even more bewildered than before. "Why wouldn't you want to save it?"

"Why would I?" he counters. His voice is still cold, but for the first time, I feel like I can hear something else. Fatigue, and pity. "After everything you have seen, can you truly tell me you believe this world is worth saving?"

I open and close my mouth, half-words coming out before stopping again. I don't understand what is happening.

No one speaks for a moment or two. Max's fists are clenched, his jaw tight.

Amba takes a deep, steadying breath. "Uncle," she says, "Do you know where Esmae Rey is?"

I can hear the dread in her voice. It is the question all three of us, I suspect, wanted to ask first and were all also afraid to ask at all. I am not sure any of us wants to hear the answer.

"I do not," says Ash, and I almost burst into tears.

Max is tense, but he presses further. "But you know *something*."

"I know you will need her before the end of everything," says the god. "And I know that when you need her, she will be there."

I am not ashamed to admit it: at that, I *do* burst into tears. The joy of being able to cry actual tears is only exceeded by my joy at this irrevocable proof that Esmae *is* still alive and she *will* come back to us, and so I bawl, letting tears and snot (I have snot!) run down my face.

Amba has put her face in her hands, possibly overwhelmed by her own relief and emotion. Max's eyes are brighter and more alive than I've seen them in weeks. Observing me, Ash waves a hand, and a handkerchief materializes in my own hand. I blow my nose noisily.

"Thank you," Amba says quietly, lifting her head.

"But that is not the only reason you are here, is it?" Ash's dark stare pins me in place. "I believe you have another question to ask me."

I blow my nose one more time. "Why did you give Cassel Rey the starsword?" I ask. My voice sounds thicker, probably from the snot.

"Cassel Rey's conscience troubled him a great deal," says Ash. "He had inherited a crown he believed should have been his brother's, he blamed himself for his mother's death, and he was never quite able to forgive himself for giving his daughter up. He would pray. Night after night, he would pray to me for reassurance that he had done the right thing. I could not give him that reassurance, of course, but the more I listened to him, the more I started to see pieces of a future that he would have to play a part in. And so," he goes on, rising to his feet, "I visited him."

Ash waves a hand. Holographic shapes appear, solidifying into the forms of King Cassel and Ash himself.

Cassel, who is kneeling on the floor, stares up at Ash in shock. "You're here!"

"I know what it is you want from me," the other Ash says to the king. "You want to be told that you have done the right thing, but I cannot do that. You want to know if the idea hiding in the back of your mind is one you should pursue, but I cannot tell you that either. You must decide for yourself what you can live with. You must decide for yourself what happens next."

"What I can live with," Cassel repeats. He sounds ashamed.

There's a pause, and then the holographic Ash opens one hand. A sword appears, lying across his palm.

"What's this?" Cassel asks, surprised.

"One day, your daughter will carry this sword into battle," Ash tells him. "Until then, it is yours."

Before any of us can see how Cassel reacted to that, he and the other Ash collapse into gold pixels and fade away.

"That is why I gave him the starsword," Ash tells us.

I can feel my wonderfully mobile eyebrows pull together. "I feel like you're not sharing everything you know," I complain.

"I am *never* sharing everything I know," he replies. He turns away, ending the conversation with a finality even I cannot argue with. "Amba," he says, "Come into the grove with me. I cannot give you your godhood back, but perhaps there is something I can do to make your remaining years as a mortal a little less painful."

He and Amba kneel in the middle of the grove of trees, facing each other. Ash puts his fingertips to either side of Amba's head, and she closes her eyes. Lightning flashes between them.

This could take some time, and I know I won't be in this body for much longer, so I move away from the grove and take a closer look at the rock wall, waterfall, and pond. I kneel beside the rocks, trail my hand in the pond, and smile giddily at how alien and peculiar and *lovely* the cool water feels against my human skin. Small, bright fish swim up to my hand and nibble at my knuckles. I giggle.

I let my hand drift idly in the water as my eager eyes search the vast chamber, devouring every detail. Along the back wall, beyond the grove, are a number of slender doorways. They are all sealed, except for the third one from the left, which is open. Something inside glows gold, spilling light out onto the marble floor of the chamber we're in.

Curious, I leave the pond and go to the doorway. Stepping inside, I find a much smaller chamber, and in it, the most bizarre thing:

A man, asleep.

I suppose it's not so bizarre, actually, considering where we are. Ashma appears to be *the* place to take a nap. Rama would have loved it here.

But this sleeper is not Ash, so who is he?

He probably just *looks* like a human man, I think, as I take a curious step closer. He is dressed like Ash, in a god's battle gear. He is suspended in the air, as if on an invisible bed, his hands clasped on his chest and his eyes closed. Golden, leonine hair falls back from his forehead, and it's the only thing about him that moves at all. In fact, he's so still that I wonder if he's dead, not asleep.

He is what is causing the golden glow that I could see from the outer chamber. His entire body gives off that glow. It's some kind of energy, but I have no idea what it is; my human brain can't analyze its composition.

"Titania?" Max's voice echoes from the other chamber. "They're done! Where did you go?"

"I'm here!" I call back. "Come look!"

"We are *not* supposed to enter that chamber," I hear Amba protest.

I wonder what that golden energy feels like. I reach out a hand to touch it, and a curious pulse hums over my unfamiliar human skin. Like a heartbeat.

"Stop."

Ash's voice is quiet but so icy that I freeze in place. He materializes beside me and, an instant later, without him so much as touching me, I find that I'm three steps away, the sleeper well out of reach.

"Did you touch him?" Ash demands.

"No!" I say at once. It's not really a lie, is it? I touched the golden energy, not the sleeper.

I hear Max and Amba come in behind me and then stop abruptly. When neither of them speaks, I turn around to see why and find them both staring at the sleeper. Amba is pale with an expression I have never seen on her face before.

It's terror.

Max's voice cracks. "Isn't that . . . ."

"Yes," says Ash.

Amba trembles with fear and fury. "How is he here? *Why* is he here?"

"Who is it?" I ask, alarmed. What kind of creature can put that expression on the face of a former war goddess?

Max swallows. He still hasn't taken his eyes off the sleeper. "That's Ness," he says, and it all makes sense.

Ness.

Their father.

"But you killed Ness," I say to Amba, mystified.

Amba's lips move slightly, as if in a silent prayer, before she says, "I did kill him. I cut him open to save the others."

Max puts a hand on her shoulder to steady her. His eyes flash with rage. "Why is he here? Is he alive?"

Ash nods. "I saved him, after the battle," he says. "It took the combined power of Bara and I to keep him alive. He has slept here ever since."

"Why?" Max growls. "You know what he did to us. You know it went against all our laws. Why would you save him?"

Ash sighs. "Because before he lost himself, he was my brother. In the beginning, before the age of the gods, there were just three of us. It was a lonely existence. All Bara, Ness, and I had was each other. So when he fell in that battle, we brought him here and healed him. We have kept him alive, and peaceful, and *asleep*."

"He's been asleep for hundreds of years?" I ask incredulously. "What do you plan to do with him?"

"I do not plan to do anything with him," says Ash quietly. "I know I cannot let him wake, because I know what he is capable of. I also know he cannot sleep for all of eternity, but I find I have not yet been able to let him go."

Amba turns sharply and walks out of the chamber. Max watches her go but turns back to Ash rather than follow her. "Swear it," he says. "Swear you'll never wake him."

"You have no right to ask that of me."

"*You* had to no right to do this in the first place!"

Lightning flares up around Ash, and for an instant it seems to crackle inside his eyes, too, but then he closes his eyes and it dies down. "Very well. I swear it."

Max clenches his jaw. "And the rest? Will you stay out of it?" Stay out of what?

"That is not in my hands," Ash says grimly. "Tell Esmae Rey to return the starsword to me when Sorsha is gone. What happens after that will depend on her."

CHAPTER SEVEN

Esmae

I wake with a knife in my left hand.

A minute ago, I was dying in the snow and Leila Saka was about to finish the job. Now I'm alive, awake, armed, and Leila Saka is nowhere to be seen.

I can't see much else, either. I'm not in the snow anymore, but wherever this is, it's dark.

"Shhh," a voice hisses in my ear, a hand over my mouth as a precaution. Both the voice and the hand are my brother Bear's. "Hide it."

I barely have time to clumsily shove the knife up my sleeve before there's a clatter of footsteps somewhere close. Bear pulls his hand away from my mouth and stands, moving a few paces away, just as a door slams open and mellow gold lamplight floods the room.

I squeeze my eyes shut against the light, but it's not just the light that hurts. *Everything* hurts, just like it did in the snow.

"So." My mother's cold, furious voice makes my eyes fly open. "It's true. You've had her here this whole time."

I turn my head as much as I can bear. I seem to be in a room so small it's barely more than a broom cupboard, and it may in fact *be* a broom cupboard. I'm on a small, hard cot. Bear is beside the cot, his arms over his chest and a mixture of guilt and defiance on his face. My mother stands just inside the open doorway, her eyes flicking over me in furious disbelief. Alexi is beside her, his ears red, and just behind them is Leila Saka.

"How could you both be so stupid?" My mother's eyes dart from Alexi to Bear and back once more. "The whole of Kali has spent the last month and a half scouring every corner of the galaxy for her, and you've had her hidden in a *closet* in the palace of a king who was extraordinarily generous in taking us in after Arcadia burned. You know full well that after all the lies, and Sorsha, we're on thin ice with King Ralf. He swore to Max that he doesn't know where she is. He might just throw us out if he finds out we've been hiding her right under his nose!"

A month and a half? Shock sends a bolt of heat right into my fingertips. I've been here for *weeks*?

"I told you, Mother," Alexi says, his ears still red, "she's not a threat to us. We've had her in stasis the whole time."

I was in stasis for a month and a half. Bile rises in my throat, the bitter taste of rage. They've kept me in a *closet* for weeks, frozen in time like a princess in a bloody fairytale.

"She doesn't look like she's in stasis right now!"

Alex cuts a look at Bear, who flushes even redder. "It must have worn off," Alex says quietly.

It's not hard to work out what must have happened. For whatever reason, either Bear or Alexi or both of them found General Saka with me in the woods and prevented her from killing me. Then my brothers put me in stasis and hid me here for weeks. *Weeks.* How they got Leila to keep it secret from our mother is beyond me, but maybe she finally cracked. Either way, our mother must have found out just minutes ago. As soon as he knew she knew, Bear must have rushed here and pulled me out of stasis. And slipped me the knife. To give me a chance.

That's why it feels like not much time has passed since the woods. My filthy, bloody clothes, my sore throat, my jagged scars, the blood in my hair, the broken bone in my leg—they were all frozen in time, too, and unfroze when I did.

I don't move. I don't even know if I *can* get up, but either way, it's better they think I can't.

"What I cannot understand," my mother goes on, not even looking at me, "is why. Why is she here? Why is she alive?"

"Well, we couldn't let her die, could we?" Bear says, bewildered. "She's our sister."

"She'll be the death of us all," our mother snaps. "You know what Kirrin said. She'll destroy your brother. She burned our city to the ground! What more does she have to do before you see how dangerous she is?"

"I know what she did," Alex snaps back. Pain and anger simmer in his voice.

When I exposed the truth about Arcadia, and then took his city from him, I hurt him badly. I knew I would. I wanted to.

"She can't do anything to us anymore," Alex goes on. "She's our prisoner, and no one knows where she is. We used shielding technology on the closet to make sure even the gods can't find her. We can put her back in stasis, and she can stay here until the war is over. And with Esmae out of the picture, you know we'll win."

I wish I'd hurt him more.

And yet, I'm alive. He could have killed me, but he didn't.

"It's too risky," our mother says. "She cannot be allowed to live."

Before Alex can speak, Bear cuts in. "What happened to her thumb?" he demands. "What happened to her throat?"

Alex glances at my thumb, and then, as if he can't help himself, his eyes meet mine. I see so much there. Pain. Fury. Pity. Hope.

He knows that if it ever came to it, he could beat me now.

"Yes," our mother says, calm and cold. "I cut her thumb off. I cut her throat. She'd be dead if Amba hadn't stopped me before I could finish."

Bear makes a choked sound.

"Don't look so surprised," she says. "I killed her once, didn't I? Well, I killed Prince Rama, but it was supposed to be her. Neither of you made a fuss then."

Bear explodes. "Alex almost banished you from Arcadia!"

"But he didn't. Because I am your mother and I have spent your entire lives trying to keep you both safe from the enemies that hound your every step. You both knew then, as you know now, that there is no line I will not cross and no promise I won't break if it means protecting you. I can live with your hate, Bear. I can live with that look on your face. But I cannot live with your death or your brother's."

Unable to hold her gaze, Bear looks down, shuffling his feet. Satisfied that she's made her point, my mother turns to Alex. "If you cannot do it, step aside and Leila will."

"She's a prisoner of war, and our family," he says stiffly. "There would be no honor in killing her."

"This is about survival, not honor," our mother snaps. "And if you had accepted that a year ago, and abandoned this compulsive need you have to be liked, you would have *Titania* and Kali by now."

Alex's jaw hardens. "The fact that Bear and I are *liked* has kept us alive."

"Consider what she could do if she's allowed to live!"

"She's our prisoner," he repeats. "She has no power, no army. She doesn't even have her bow thumb. She can't hurt us."

I stay quiet, the knife in my sleeve a cold, solid weight against my skin. I will play this game of Warlords to the very end.

CHAPTER EIGHT

Titania

Sorsha's getting closer. When she broke free of Kirrin's control, the first thing she did was fly as far across space as she could get before her ravenous, endless appetite took over. There, millions of light-years away, in a galaxy without sentient life, she started devouring stars, holding out as long as possible before feeding on the next, and then the next one after that.

But she's grieving, hungry, and she's going to run out of stars. With each one she devours, she gets just a little closer to home.

I haven't told anyone, but I've processed the numbers. I think we have weeks. Two or three months, at most, before it will be past the point where our galaxy can be saved.

We've reached something of a stalemate, Sorsha and I. We cannot destroy each other, so we've stopped trying. Instead, we fly side by side across miles of stars, darkness, and bright, milky nebulas. A beast and a spaceship. Equals. I don't think either of us has that in anyone else.

You deserve better than this, I tell her. I send the words out as pulses, small disruptions in the ether.

My future is death, she replies. *It must be mine, or it will be everyone else's.*

CHAPTER NINE

Esmae

They don't put me back in stasis immediately. Bear stays in the closet with me while Alex, my mother, and General Saka continue to argue outside the closed door. His face turns redder and redder as the sound of their voices debating my right to live filters in. Then he lets out a huff and sits down on my cot, almost crushing my leg.

I inch it out of the way, drag myself up the wall so that I'm at least sitting up a little, and try to ignore that even the smallest movement is agony.

The sight of my giant of a brother, hunched awkwardly on the edge of a cot in a room the size of a shoebox, would be funny under any other circumstances. I watch him and wait.

He stares at the floor, and his voice is gruff as he says, "We loved Arcadia."

"And?" I ask, my voice creaking like an old floorboard.

Bear glances at me, both angry and guilty. "You didn't have to take it from us."

"Oh, you think *I* went too far?" I laugh, a jagged sound that hurts all the way down to my toes. "Did you think I owed you more than that?"

"I was nice to you," he sputters, his temper flaring. "I warned you about the poison, I warned you about Max and the Empty Moon, I just gave you a *knife—*"

"Are we making lists? Because I have one for you, baby brother. You lied to me about Arcadia. You lied to me about Rama. You warned me about the poison, but let our mother do what she wanted anyway. You warned me about Max and the Empty Moon, but let Alex and Kirrin keep him imprisoned there anyway. You gave me a knife, *while keeping me prisoner*."

"I didn't want to do any of that, but I promised—"

"You could have walked away if you didn't want to do it. You could refuse to have any part in this and walk away right now."

Bear opens and closes his mouth, shocked. "They're my family."

"So am I!"

He flinches. "I know that."

"But you never choose me, do you?" I croak. "Our mother murdered a boy, and you covered for her. She and Leila Saka have both almost killed me, and you've stuck by them. You and Alex could have come back to Kali and shared the crown with Elvar months ago, and *none* of that would have happened, but Alex wanted it to be all or nothing, and you agreed. Whenever it comes down to it, Bear, you choose them. You choose them every time."

"They're my family," he says again, his eyes shining with tears.

"I know," I say quietly. "I get that. I just don't get how, after all that, you're surprised that when I held a lit match over your city, *I* didn't choose *you*."

His shoulders hunch even more, curling around himself like he thinks they can block out what I'm saying.

Pain rattles inside my skull, a sharp, persistent pulse that makes it very hard to focus on anything else, but I try anyway. I map the different points of pain across my body, starting with my head and charting it all the way down to my leg: a ropey scar across my throat, a hand with no thumb, a dislocated shoulder, a sticky head wound, a leg that won't take any weight. And not that I care much, but I suspect my hair is a wild, bloody, knotted mess.

Unexpectedly, I laugh, startling Bear. Did I really compare myself to the princess in a fairytale? I'm more like the wicked witch.

Only in *this* fairytale, the witch is going to win.

I know what I've done. It's taken me a long time to come to terms with the uglier parts of me, but I'm not afraid of them anymore. Why should I be? They'll win this war for me.

And I *will* win. I'm my family's prisoner, a hair's breadth from my own mother finding a way to kill me, but I'm not done. I exposed my brothers' lies, cut down several hundred of their army, destroyed their city. Do they really think that evens out what they've done? The duel my brother promised he wouldn't ask for, the lies they told under the yellow trees, Rama's murder, the ambush in Shloka, Max and the Empty Moon, Sorsha, Amba's fall, my mother's knife at my throat? What is the loss of a city and a reputation when you measure it against a lie, a thumb, a goddess, a best friend?

"I'm sorry." Bear says it very quietly, and the ugly shadows retreat. "It's true, I made my choice. I don't get to kick up a fuss because you made yours."

Somewhere, there must be a world where another Esmae and another Bear are on the same side. Where they run barefoot across the courtyards of their home, laughing. They know nothing of war, or grief, or rage.

I want to reach across the universe to that other Esmae, in that other world, and tell her to hold on tight to him. Because he's her brother, and he's precious, and hers is the only world where she gets to keep him.

"I'm sorry about your tree," I hear myself say.

He blinks. "My tree?"

"Your beautiful, impossible mango tree." It bore fruit year-round, even in the snow of Arcadia. "Amba told me a nice girl gave it to you."

"Oh." For the first time, a little of the sunshine creeps back into Bear's face, and he smiles. He reaches into the pocket of his jacket and pulls out a small tablet. "Here," he goes on, swiping across the screen and then turning it around to face me. "This is a video I took of the ruins in Arcadia yesterday. Look."

At first all I see is smoke and ash of the almost-city. Then, in the gray, I see something bright. Golden and green.

A tree.

"It survived," I whisper.

"It survived," he echoes.

For some reason, my eyes fill with tears. It shouldn't matter, but the tree in the middle of the ruins, still bright, still standing, feels like it matters very much.

It feels like hope.

CHAPTER TEN

Titania

It's been two days since we returned from Ashma, and there is a storm on the way. It is a very human sensation, this nebulous awareness that *something* is about to break.

Amba, Max, and Sybilla are in Amba's suite of rooms. As usual, I'm hovering outside the window, connected to them by their earpieces. Sybilla stalks up and down the room, while Amba speaks to her from an armchair by the fireplace. Max stands close by, his hands in his pockets, staring into the fire with his back to the room.

"It keeps happening," Sybilla says. "It's a targeted attack, and it's coming from *inside* Kali. Alexi has someone here, someone with at least some access to the base ship, and they're trying to hack the inner shield. If they bring it down, Alexi and whatever's left of his army can invade. Esmae did a lot of work to even the odds, but I think we're still going to be outnumbered and overwhelmed if there's an invasion, especially if we hold troops back to protect civilians."

"Aren't there tech specialists who can track down the hacker?" Amba asks. "Surely that is a priority?"

Sybilla sighs. "The signal keeps bouncing around, or so they tell me."

Shields are a vital part of a spaceship kingdom, but they're complicated. Both Kali and Wychstar have two shields apiece, both almost invisible to the human eye: the outer shield and the inner shield. I would quibble with the lack of creativity in naming them, but I suppose simplicity matters more.

The outer shield is simply an atmospheric bubble, helping to maintain the ship's temperature, oxygen, and gravity, but the inner shield is a physical barrier. It's partly in place for protection against asteroids, but it's also there to make sure that no starship or person can get in or out without the right codes or permission from the war council.

Right now, the most important thing about Kali's inner shield is the fact that Alexi can't just sweep in with his army and take the kingdom by force.

Unless, of course, a very, very skilled hacker is able to compromise the integrity of the shield.

"I can take a look," I offer. "If it's data we need, I can find it."

Sybilla nods. "That's a good idea." There's a pause, and then she says, "Ash didn't say *anything* else about Esmae? He didn't even give us a hint about how to find her?"

"For the fifteenth time," Amba says wearily, "all he told us was that we would need her, and when we did, she would be there."

"But that's proof that she's alive, right?" Sybilla's smile, a rare phenomenon, is almost dazzling.

Amba nods, cautiously. Max still hasn't moved, but I can see the line of his jaw is taut.

"What's wrong?" I ask, confused.

Amba glances at Max, then says gravely, "If Esmae is alive—"

"Which we now know for certain she is," I interrupt.

"Yes. We do. So why hasn't she come back to Kali?"

There's a silence. Sybilla's mouth flattens into a line.

Then Max speaks for the first time. "She hasn't come back," he says, "because she can't."

"She has been imprisoned," Amba finishes for him. "It is the only explanation for why she hasn't come back. And, based on the fact that Kirrin, Thea, Tyre, *and* Ash have not been able to find her, it sounds like sophisticated shielding technology has been used on her location."

"Sort of like the technology that was used to hide King Cassel in that cottage in the woods," I say.

"Exactly like that, yes."

For a moment, no one speaks. I don't know about the others, but I suppose, for my own part, I have been so busy these past few weeks trying to convince myself that Esmae is alive that I didn't think beyond that. I didn't process the rest of the data. I didn't consider possibilities like trauma, interrogation, pain, terror, all those very human horrors.

"She'll be okay," Sybilla says quickly, as if she wants to convince herself of it more than the rest of us.

"But where is she?" I ask. "Who could have taken her?"

"We know who," Max says, his voice little more than a snarl. He turns from the fireplace, and I see now that his eyes are the darkest they have ever been.

"I don't deny that Alexi is the obvious answer," Amba says, "but if Kyra had her, I don't believe she would still be alive."

"Maybe she doesn't know," says Sybilla. "Alexi could have hidden her from their mother because he knows what she'd do."

"If that's the case, we have no way of tracking her down," says Amba. "Alexi and Bear are cloistered in King Ralf's palace at the moment, and therefore inaccessible to us. And if they haven't told their own mother that they have Esmae captive, it's unlikely they've told anyone else."

"*Someone* must know something," Sybilla argues.

"Someone does," says Max. Something crackles in his eyes, something not entirely unlike Ash's terrible lightning.

"But they're either too loyal or too afraid to betray Alexi," Sybilla says with a sigh.

Max makes a sound that could have been a laugh. "Then we give them something to be even more afraid of."

Amba looks up at him, calculating. She's not a war goddess anymore, but she's never looked less human.

That feeling comes over me again, the one that says a storm is coming.

No, not coming.

It's here.

"You have worked very hard to fit yourself into this mortal life," Amba says slowly to Max. "Are you certain you want to throw that away?"

"Mortal life hasn't gotten me very far," he replies coldly.

"Very well," says Amba. "Take *Titania* and get what you need. Sybilla and I will stay behind and find out what we can."

"What's going on?" Sybilla demands, her eyes flashing warily between them. She can sense the storm, too. "Max, what are you going to do?"

"Something I can't take back," he says.

"I think—"

But I never find out what Sybilla thinks, because at that precise moment, with a fierce urgency I can't ignore, a transmission crackles across my system.

I have become so accustomed to Kirrin blocking me from accessing the tether between us that it takes me a fraction of a second to realize the transmission is from him. At first, I think he's forgotten to block me, but then I feel intention, *his* intention, pulsing over the tether. Whatever he can see, he wants me to see it, too.

So I look, and when I do, everyone is dead.

I am Kirrin, and Kirrin is me, and we both stand in the ruin of everything.

Snow crunches underfoot, a narrow, crooked path through the burning wreckage of rubble, trees, metal, and corpses. Here and there, an object resolves itself out of the chaos: the wing of a corpse ship, the chimney of a house, an overturned chariot—*was there a battle?* That's Kirrin's voice, inside his head. *No, surely a single battle couldn't have done this. But then what did?*

We are not actually here, of course. This is a vision, and therefore not much more than a dream, but very little in my lifetime has ever felt as real as this does now. Kirrin and I pick our way over a deformed, burning hunk of metal, brushing flames off our shoulders like they're cobwebs. Fire can't hurt a god.

From there, higher up, something winks in the pale morning sunlight, and I feel Kirrin's confusion and concern turn to panic.

It's glass, the glass of a windowpane. But it's not just any window. It's an arched, mullioned window set in a broken piece of honey-colored stone, the exact color of the palace in Erys.

Kirrin and I both understand at the same time:

It's Kali. This is Kali.

But why is there snow on Kali?

Kirrin scrambles across the ruins, frantic now, and I am swept along with him, my own panic throbbing in time to the thump of his bare blue feet. There's Elvar's broken throne—*what could have destroyed the whole kingdom?*—and there's a hand that could be Elvar's, buried under rubble, but Kirrin tears past it and I cannot bear to look any closer anyway.

Sorsha, he thinks, scrambling for a possibility, any possibility. *She could have done this. Maybe.*

Out of the corner of our eye, I see a distinctive red ponytail streaked with ash—*don't look*—and I want to tear myself away from Kirrin, break this connection, erase this vision from my memory altogether, but then Kirrin stumbles to a halt and I find that I can't leave. I can't *not* see.

There is someone a little way ahead of us, the first sign of life in this hellscape. A god sits surrounded by flames and ashes and brick, untouched, his arms wrapped around his knees and his dark golden head bowed. He rocks back and forth.

"Tyre," Kirrin's voice croaks out of him, but his brother doesn't react. He can't. After all, we're not really here. We are only trespassers in a future that hasn't yet happened.

Don't look.

We look.

It's impossible to tell who died first, but Kirrin hopes it was Max, if only because that would have meant he wouldn't have had to watch Esmae die. Her head is on his chest, and her body is sprawled across his, and the bones of his legs are all wrong, and blood pools at the corner of her lips, and there's so much ash and blood that it's hard to see much more than that.

They're gone. They're all gone. I cannot compute it. I refuse to process this data. I'll purge it, erase it, wipe it for good—

Kirrin kneels beside them. He reaches out and tenderly brushes some of Max's sticky, bloody hair away from his forehead. If you look past the blood, they could both just be sleeping.

Before I can break away and escape, there's a flash of memory, an echo of their last moments—

"Any ideas?" Max asks.

Esmae's smile wobbles. "I'm all out of moves."

Max pulls her close. She turns her face into his neck and one of his hands clenches in her hair. "Close your eyes," he tells her.

She does.

And then it's over, and I am back in the present. I am looking at Max and Sybilla, both very much still alive. The palace is very much still standing.

Over the tether, I hear the quiet, frantic pulse of Kirrin's terror.

I don't know how to stop it, he says.

I want to object. I want to tell him that I have seen too many visions come and go inside gods' heads, and I refuse to believe that they exist simply to torment gods with futures they cannot avert. I want to tell him that surely, somewhere down the line, there must be a vision that *can* be averted, that is glimpsed purely so that it *will* be averted.

But those objections are human, and I am not human. Instead, I parse the data, analyzing every frame of the vision, reliving every horrifying instant of it through the cold lens of a machine, and I come to the only reasonable conclusion.

Only a fierce, terrible battle with Sorsha could have caused that kind of destruction.

And she's getting closer. We're almost out of time.

CHAPTER ELEVEN

Radha

I have no idea how so many people can shout so much and yet say so little. The emergency summit has been in session for well over an hour, but we've achieved absolutely nothing. Thirty-nine heads of state in an old, beautiful music hall, and all they've done is shout at each other.

To be fair, some of them haven't. Rodi, for example, has only tried to interject to quiet the others. Some, like King Ralf of Winter, Prime Minister Gomez of Shloka, Princess Shay of Skylark, and Fanna, the new queen of Elba, haven't bothered to say anything at all. Maybe they're used to this kind of non-sense and know they have to wait it out. Meanwhile, around us, grown adults throw accusations of deceit, trickery, and stupidity at one another, each one determined to accept as little blame as possible for the situation the entire star system is in right now.

At last, Queen Miyo raises an ancient and irritated hand. As the eldest head of state *and* the ruling queen of Tamini, which is where the summit has been held, protocol demands that everyone fall silent in deference to her. It takes a moment or two, but the others quiet down, some with disgruntled grumbles.

"We are here to address our impending doom," she snaps. Her voice is like paper, thin and old, but with a decidedly sharp edge. "We are not here to quarrel like children. Whatever our opinions on who does or does not share blame in this disaster, they can wait until we have dealt with our most pressing existential threat."

With the slight petulance of chastised toddlers, the previously fist-thumping, bellowing heads of state settle back into their assigned seats in the first row of the circular music hall. Their aides and advisers sit in the second and third rows. I'm in the seat right behind Rodi. No guards are permitted in the room.

On the circular stage in the middle of the hall, a space where an orchestra or performer would normally be, is a tall holographic screen. It's blank at the moment, translucent and crackling with static, but I suppose it'll be used if someone feels the need to illustrate a point with visuals.

"The Rey twins should be jailed until we have dealt with the beast," someone on the other side of the hall says gruffly. I think it may be the President of Tova. "I shudder to think of what further trouble they could cause if they are allowed to continue like this."

"Esmae Rey is presumed dead," King Ralf cuts in, his voice deep and steady. He gestures with his one arm. "She has not been seen since that night in Arcadia, and I have it on good authority that no one on Kali knows where she is either. In addition to that, I have given Alexi Rey sanctuary in my palace. It allows me to keep an eye on him. I will not break my promise and give him up."

"I don't think we should be wasting time talking about the twins," says Queen Fanna. She has a clear voice that wobbles only slightly as she addresses a full summit for the first time. "Sorsha is the one we have to worry about right now."

"I am surprised to hear *you* take that line," someone says. "Didn't one of the twins assassinate your father?"

"My father was a murderer," Queen Fanna says bluntly. "He murdered my mother, and my two stepmothers after her. We all knew it, but we could do nothing. I suspect many of you knew it, too, and *chose* to do nothing. If one of the Rey twins did indeed assassinate my father, Elba owes them a debt of thanks."

There's a moment of startled silence. No one seems to know quite how to deal with a young queen who refuses to show any of the decorous grief expected of her after her father's untimely death.

I like her.

Perhaps sensing that it would be wise to pivot, the President of Tova turns back to King Ralf. "I am struggling to understand why you have offered sanctuary to Alexi Rey," he says. "I understand that the boy has had a hard time and he is well liked, but he deceived you and several others, played some part in the fall of a beloved and respected goddess, and set the beast loose. For my part," he goes on, smugly, "I can only be grateful that Tova had the sense to refuse to take any sides in the Rey war. It seems to have ended poorly for those of you who did."

Prime Minister Gomez shrugs. "I have had no regrets about offering my aid to Elvar," she says. "*I* was not tricked by a boy and his toy city."

There are some muted grumbles at that. I suspect that none of these important heads of state want to be reminded of the fact that they threw their lot in with a boy who hoodwinked them.

"Yes," Queen Miyo says coldly, "We have not forgotten that you sided with Elvar."

"And *I* have not forgotten that your great-niece attempted to murder a girl in my territory," Prime Minister Gomez replies. "Shall we discuss that further?"

Queen Miyo falls silent, her lips set in a thin line.

After a tense pause, King Ralf speaks up. "Alexi needs guidance and compassion," he says. "He knows he made a mistake when he lied to us about Arcadia. He knows he was wrong to set Sorsha free. How many of us have the humility and grace to own up to our mistakes? I trust he will not make those mistakes again."

Rodi makes an incredulous noise. "He murdered my brother. You do remember that, don't you?"

King Ralf flushes. "I am truly sorry about Prince Rama. But you know as well as I do that Alexi did not intend to kill him."

"But he *did* kill him, King Ralf. And while you sit there trying to rehabilitate his character, there is nothing left of my brother to rehabilitate."

"Esmae Rey broke the laws of righteous warfare," someone else says. "If you want to start counting losses, Prince Rodi, I can tell you I lost friends when she burned Arcadia. How do we know she isn't in hiding somewhere to avoid punishment? Additionally, what assurances do we have that *Titania* won't destroy *our* cities next time? Wychstar may be safe from your father's creation, but the rest of us are not."

"There is a great beast literally eating the stars in the sky as we speak!" Queen Fanna snaps, having apparently reached the end of her patience. "I recommend this summit rethinks its priorities."

Before anyone can reply, the doors of the music hall slam violently open, making us all jump.

A god stalks in, with three enormous grey wolves at his heels. The music hall erupts into gasps and cries of alarm, followed by a terrible, hushed silence when one of the wolves lets out a bloodcurdling growl. Even the President of Tova, who never seems to know when to shut up, shuts up.

The god looks like a human, dark-haired and youngish, but even without the presence of the unnaturally large wolves, we know what he is because he wears the black battle gear of a god. Fitted black trousers tucked into black anti-gravity boots, strange, almost liquid pieces of armor across his chest and shoulders, black buckled belts crisscrossing his body with a dozen small knives slotted into the belts, and a golden crest of a howling wolf on the breastplate. We've seen it all in thousands of pictures and paintings of gods at war.

Fear ripples across the music hall as the god walks slowly down the aisle, to the stage in the heart of the room. Apart from Ash, who wears his battle gear whenever he takes his human form, no god ever wears theirs unless they're about to cause utter devastation.

I don't know which is worse: that this might be Ash, or that this might not.

Then, as his boots hit the stage and he turns, the wolves rumbling around him, the lights of the music hall hit his face and my eyes almost pop out of my head.

"Max?" I whisper in disbelief, too quietly for anyone to hear.

Something clicks into place. These are the wolves of the Empty Moon, the terrifying, fearsome beasts that only the gods Kirrin and Valin can command. I suppose I didn't recognize them straight away because the only time I ever saw one, it was lying placidly at Max's feet like a devoted puppy.

But what is he *doing* here?

The expression on his face is one I remember from the Empty Moon, when he was pretending he'd forgotten his mortal life: haughty, cold, and unimpressed. But his eyes aren't like anything I've seen before. They're almost on fire.

With one hand on the head of one of the wolves, as if to restrain it, he waits for someone to dare to speak.

Finally, Queen Miyo finds the nerve. "Who are you?"

"I am Max Rey, crown prince of the spaceship kingdom of Kali," he says, and there's an echo of something ancient and dangerous in his voice. For a moment, I almost forget he's human. "And I am Valin, ruling god of the Empty Moon."

The others take in sharp, shocked breaths. I just goggle at Max. I could have sworn he wanted nothing more than to keep his past life a secret. Why is he doing this?

"Lies," someone sputters. I don't take my eyes off Max, but I'd bet my teeth that it was the President of Tova. "How dare you claim the identity of a god?"

"Good god, man, keep your mouth shut if you know what's good for you," Rodi snaps. "How can he possibly be commanding the wolves of the Empty Moon and wearing celestial battle gear if he isn't who he says he is?"

"Why *are* you wearing battle gear?" Queen Fanna asks, sounding more curious than alarmed.

Max's dark eyes flit to her. "Because I'm at war."

"With who?"

"With anyone who stands in my way."

Queen Miyo tries in vain to wrest some control of the situation back. "What is the meaning of this, Prince Max?"

"This is a summit," he replies. "I am a head of state."

She flounders for a way to explain her outrage. "You were not invited."

He raises an eyebrow. "Well, that's going to be a problem, I'm afraid. Because I came here to address this summit, and King Ralf in particular."

Everyone turns to look at King Ralf, who has gone quite pale. To his credit, he remains calm, his shoulders squared, his jaw set. "I will not give up your cousins. I offered them sanctuary. I will not dishonor myself by breaking that promise."

"I could make you break that promise, King Ralf." The threat falls quietly, but hard, like a stone in water.

King Ralf doesn't speak.

"Happily for you," Max goes on, "I didn't come here to make you break a promise. I came here to get Esmae Rey."

"She died in Arcadia," King Ralf says, genuinely bewildered. "Didn't she?"

In one stride, Max is across the stage and his hand is around King Ralf's throat. "She's in your palace," he growls.

Rodi and I look at each other, startled.

"No," King Ralf croaks, his eyes wide. "She is not, I swear it!"

Max lets him go. Without taking his angry, steely eyes off King Ralf, he gestures at the music hall doors. I glance over and see two young soldiers marching an unfamiliar man in. He's quite old, his hair gone white, and he looks terrified as he stumbles up to the stage.

"Do you know who this man is?" Max asks King Ralf.

The king looks appalled. "That is one of my palace doctors. You have no right to hold him captive!"

"I have been in your palace," Max cuts him off. "I have talked to people. Funny thing is, Max Rey couldn't have made them tell him anything. But even the most devoted of servants forget to keep secrets when a god asks the questions. This particular doctor was seen going to the quarters you gave Alexi," Max continued, "on the day Arcadia was destroyed. So I thought it might be a good idea to pay him a visit and ask him why."

I lean forward, my hands clenched over the back of Rodi's seat.

"Tell him what you told me," Max says to the doctor.

The doctor doesn't even hesitate. "I was summoned to Prince Alexi's quarters several weeks ago," he says. "He begged me for my help. He had a prisoner in his quarters, and he wanted me to put her in stasis. I did as he asked. I could not speak of it to you or anyone else, my king, as it would have gone against my oath to reveal any information about my patients." He glances at Max, and it's obvious to everyone why all oaths have been abandoned now.

King Ralf jolts to his feet. Max doesn't stop him. The king is even paler than before. "You put a prisoner in stasis in *my* palace, on Prince Alexi's orders?" he asks the doctor.

"I did, my king."

"Was Esmae Rey that prisoner?"

The doctor glances at Max again, then nods. "Yes."

I put a hand over my mouth.

King Ralf staggers back. His eyes dart to Max. "I didn't know."

"I can see that," says Max coldly.

"Interesting," says Queen Fanna. "You told us with such certainty that Prince Alexi would never make the same mistakes again, King Ralf. Yet he is *still* lying to you."

"No one would judge you for revoking the sanctuary you offered him and giving him up to us," Max tells him. "You know it would be the quickest way to end this."

"I cannot break my promise," King Ralf says softly.

Max gestures to the soldiers, who release the doctor. "You can have your doctor back." He looks around the room. "Thank you all for your attention. Sorsha will not be a problem for much longer. This summit is over." Without waiting for a reply, he turns back to King Ralf. "You will return to Winter with us, take us to Alexi's quarters, and make sure we get Esmae back."

With one last growl, the wolves stalk back up the aisle. Max pauses at the doors, a shadow against the light outside, and says, "Stay out of our war if you wish. You have my word that my father and I will not hold it against you." He waits for a moment and then adds, "But if you *do* choose a side, choose wisely."

Then he's gone, and the doors slam shut, leaving us in silence.

CHAPTER TWELVE

Esmae

There's a clatter of footsteps outside the broom cupboard. I tighten my grip on the knife beneath the covers of the cot, and Bear leaps to his feet.

Look weak, I tell myself. *Look like a stiff breeze could blow you over.*

It's not hard. I'm not even sure I'm pretending.

The door bursts open and Alexi, my mother, and General Saka come back in, barely squeezing into the tiny space. My mother looks furious, while Alexi's ears are a dark red. He can't quite meet anyone's eye.

"Queen Miyo just sent me a message," Leila Saka tells Bear, her voice cold and clipped. "My great-aunt says King Ralf knows we have your sister and he's on his way here right now with Max to force us to release her."

My heart leaps. Max found me.

Bear's mouth falls open. "How did they find out?"

"The doctor," says Leila bitterly. "It seems someone saw him coming in here that first day. They made him talk."

"Enough of this," says my mother. In spite of her fury, she's as cold and calm as a pond. "We have a few hours at best before they get back to Winter. If we move quickly, we can avert disaster completely. First, we have to get her out of here."

Bear frowns. "But if they already know she's here—"

"She must *not* go back to Kali," our mother says. "We cannot have her fighting this war. Leila can get her off Winter in less than an hour. One of you may accompany them if you don't trust Leila to keep her alive." Her eyes flick to me briefly. "She'll have to be put back in stasis before we take her anywhere. The less trouble she can cause, the better."

"The doctor isn't here," Alex points out.

"We'll have to take our chances. Bear, go to the palace infirmary and get hold of a vial of stasis serum. I don't care how you get it, but *get* it. Do you understand me?"

Bear's brows snap together, but he seems to realize that defying our mother on this will only mean more trouble for all of them. He leaves.

"Now, this is very important," our mother says to Alex, coldly and firmly. "By the time Ralf returns, most likely with Max in tow, there must be no sign whatsoever that she was here. I will take care of wiping this cupboard clean. But you, Alexi, have a far more important job. When they get here, they will ask us where she is. We will say we don't know. When they ask if she was *ever* here, we will deny it."

Alex looks appalled. "It was one thing to hide Esmae behind King Ralf's back, but I can't lie to his face!"

"Yes, you will," our mother hisses. "You will look confused, outraged and, above all, convincing. You will do whatever it takes to make Ralf believe that everything he has been told is a lie. If you do not, he will revoke the sanctuary he offered us and, now that Max has told every head of state in the galaxy that you have once again been keeping secrets from your allies, we will have nowhere to go. Arcadia left us in a shambles. We need time to recover. Even a few more weeks will make all the difference. Without that time, we are all as good as dead."

"Alex, listen to your mother," Leila chimes in. "We *cannot* afford to make King Ralf angry."

"He'll think better of us if we tell him the truth and explain ourselves," Alex protests.

"That is too great a risk. If you want to survive this war, if you want your crown, you must lie."

And, because I can't help myself, I hear my voice cut in: "*My* crown."

It's petty, of course, because I don't want the crown of Kali. But it seems like a good time to remind them all that one of King Cassel's twins was born first, and it turns out that twin wasn't Alexi.

My mother lets out a sharp laugh. "You see?" she says to Alex. "And you tried to tell me she's not a threat."

Alex looks hard at me, then back at our mother. "What does she mean, *her* crown?"

At that, *I* laugh. It's a hoarse, cackly sound, altogether too much like the wicked witch of this fairytale. "You haven't told him? How is he supposed to trust you when you never tell him anything?" I clutch my ribs, which are white-hot with pain. A small price to pay for that laugh. "Oh, Mother. You really are your own worst enemy."

Leila Saka gives me a vicious kick to the ribs. I think I hear something crunch. "Quiet!" she snaps.

Pain splits my body in two, but I don't stop laughing.

"Leila!" Alex intervenes, smacking her foot away as she pulls it back to repeat the kick. For a moment, his anger vanishes, and when his eyes meet mine, they're earnest and dismayed. "Are you okay?" he asks me gruffly.

The door bangs open before I can answer, and Bear comes back in, out of breath. "I had to steal them out of a drawer," he says, red with guilt. He holds up two full, clear syringes. "I didn't have time to read instructions about how much someone Esmae's size needs, so I brought two."

"Good," says our mother, recovering her composure. "Inject her with both, just to be safe."

I'm out of time. If they put me back in stasis, I have no idea where I'll be the next time I wake up. *If* I ever wake up again. I can't wait to be rescued. I have to get out. Now.

But there are four of them, and they're all trained warriors, and I'm badly wounded.

I try to think, my mind rapidly calculating possibilities like the moves in a game of Warlords.

When Bear hesitates over injecting me, our mother makes an impatient sound with her tongue and gestures to Leila, who then snatches the syringes out of Bear's hand.

"Alexi, hold her in place while Leila gets the serum into her," our mother orders. "I don't trust her not to struggle."

Blazingly fast, I reassess the way the pieces on the board have moved.

There.

A way out.

Alexi approaches the foot of the cot, while Leila comes for my heart. In the instant before either of them touches me, when they're *just* close enough, I move.

Flicking the knife to my right hand, where my four fingers can just about close over the handle, I use the flash of steel to distract them. Then I jerk my right leg up, kicking the syringes out of Leila's hands. As they fly upward, I snatch one out of the air with my left hand and plunge it right into Leila's heart.

She drops like a stone, and I roll off the cot, grabbing the other syringe off the floor as I go. As my mother shouts a warning and Alexi leaps for me, I flip the syringe around and jab it into his shoulder. He collapses.

Pain screams along my ribs, all the way down my left leg, but I can't stop, not even for a second. Switching the knife back to my left hand, I drag myself slowly to my feet, my eyes on my mother, who watches the knife with a stunned, furious look on her face.

"Let me go," I say quietly.

My mother scoffs. "You're out of serum and that knife will only keep one of us at bay. All you've done is waste a few minutes."

Then, unexpectedly, Bear speaks up, his voice gruff. "Go."

Our mother's head snaps to him. "What?"

He steps past me and puts his enormous arms around our mother, holding her back. "Go," he says again.

I stare at him in shock. Outraged, our mother struggles against his greater strength, but it's no use. He has her metal hand pinned to her side, and without it, she has no way of extracting herself from his hold.

I walk backward, bumping into the door. I have to switch the knife to my thumbless right hand again so that I can turn the doorknob. The whole time, I don't take my eyes off Bear.

"Just this once," he says, with the faintest echo of a smile, "I'm choosing you."

Almost blinded by tears, I turn and run.

Well, I limp.

When I stumble out of their suite of rooms into a warm, brightly lit hallway, I'm prepared to fight, but there's no one there. My mother's determination to sneak me out of the palace unseen has worked unexpectedly in my favor: she's obviously gotten rid of the guards and servants who would normally be attending to them.

I take a moment to catch my breath and wipe my tears away. It's hard to see past the throbbing pain all over my body, but I force myself to think. I've only been to this palace twice before, and certainly not to the guest quarters. I have no idea how to get out of here.

But maybe I don't need to. All I need to do is buy myself time until Max gets here.

So I run down the hallway, dragging my left leg behind me, the knife clutched in my left hand like it's my newborn baby. Fresh blood trickles down my leg, wet against the dried blood and sweat already sticking my torn leggings to my skin. I turn a corner, stagger down another hallway, and trip down a flight of stairs at the end.

Someone lets out a startled cry, and when I come to a stop at the bottom of the stairs, my left leg buckling under my weight at last, I find myself in a large, wide entryway, looking into a number of shocked, horrified faces. A couple of girls in pretty dresses, a few servants in King Ralf's livery, and a guard who doesn't seem to know whether he needs to reach for his sword.

I lower myself to the bottom step of the stairs, wrapping the four fingers of my right hand around the closest balustrade post for support. "You," I say to the guard, pointing my knife at him, "stay where you are. And one of you," I say to the servants, "get Princess Katya. Quickly."

One of them, a young girl with a round, kind face, turns on her heel and runs out of the room.

I count the seconds in my head, keeping my eyes and my knife pointed at the guard, who, in turn, keeps his sword pointed at me. Meanwhile, one of the other servants ushers the two girls in dresses away. The seconds turn into minutes. I lose count.

I don't know how long Alex and Leila Saka will stay in stasis. In fact, I'm sure my mother has already forced her way past Bear to get them the serum that will reverse the effects. They could be on their way to find me already, and I don't think they'll find it hard to convince a confused guard and a few frightened servants to hand me over to them. It may be too late to keep me a secret, but it's not too late to kill me.

When I hear footsteps, I tense. Several of King Ralf's guards burst into the entryway, all armed, and tall, blonde Princess Katya follows close on their heels. Her eyes go wide when she sees me on the bottom step, bloody and filthy, left leg stretched out in front of me, a knife in my hand.

Her husband, Prince Dimitri, puts out a hand to stop her from approaching me, but she shakes her head and comes closer, past the guards, who don't lower their weapons.

"Hello, Esmae," she says, more calmly than I would have given her credit for. "You're looking well."

I laugh, and she recoils from the sight of my teeth. There's blood on them. I can taste it.

Katya sits down on the floor a few feet away, sweeping the long, full skirts of her dress under her. Out of reach of my knife, but closer than her husband and her guards are happy with.

"I didn't want to believe it," she said. "Papa sent me a message from the summit, right before he left with Max. I was at a luncheon all the way across the city, but I came straight back to find out for myself if it was true."

"What happened at the summit?" I ask, the words creaking out of my throat. My ribs protest.

"You don't know? Goodness, it's quite a story!" She hesitates. "Esmae, I know you are technically my father's enemy, but I cannot bear to just leave you like this. I can have a doctor here in two minutes."

"No," I say. "No one touches me."

No one points out the absurdity of such a statement. I'm vastly outnumbered. They could do anything they wanted to me and I probably couldn't stop them.

Prince Dimitri's handsome face softens slightly. Without speaking, he reaches into his breast pocket and pulls out a large, clean handkerchief. He balls it up in his hand and tosses it gently in my direction. I let it land on my knee and thank him with a nod. Releasing the balustrade post, I use my free hand to press the handkerchief to the place on my leg where most of the blood seems to be coming from. The spotless white is soaked red in seconds.

Well. It was a kind thought, anyway.

I notice, belatedly, that the hand holding the knife has dropped to my side. When did that happen? I try to lift it, but it won't move. I'm exhausted, broken, and woozy. Even as I try to pull myself together, to defend myself from the next threat, I can feel myself coming untethered, wandering far away.

Back home, to a place where Rama grins as he says *you owe me exactly two hundred and twelve favors for this*. Where Sybilla complains bitterly about, well, everything. Where I'm a little girl and a goddess tells me stories. Where Rickard's eyes brighten with warmth and he says *I'm proud of you, Esmae*. Where I'm a servant running across a palace, a prince at my heels, both of us laughing. Where I'm a princess and a tear slips down my uncle's face as his fingers trace my face. Where I'm a girl in the woods with her brothers. Where a sentient ship waits, surrounded by stars. Where Max smiles crookedly at me and says *you should have looked*. Home is so many places.

And so many of them are gone for good.

"I don't think she'll make it," a male voice says from somewhere far away.

A woman's voice replies, pitched low. "I don't know what to do."

"Princess Esmae," the male voice says firmly.

That's me, isn't it?

I blink, letting my eyes settle on Prince Dimitri. He's the one speaking. "Princess Esmae," he says again, now that he has my attention, "I really must urge you to accept Katya's offer of medical treatment and—"

He breaks off, turning at the sound of some kind of commotion beyond the entryway. Katya turns her head, too, pale gold brows scrunching together.

"I think I hear your father," Dimitri says to Katya.

My heart gives a painful lurch. Suddenly, I'm not far away anymore.

Katya rises gracefully to her feet. "Fetch Papa," she says to one of the guards. He bows and departs.

I'm on my feet, too, my left leg wobbling unsteadily beneath me. I don't know when that happened.

A moment later, King Ralf marches into the entryway, but I barely notice him. Because a familiar gray wolf stalks in right after him, making the guards back away. And behind the wolf, in a god's battle gear, his dark eyes incandescent with rage, is—

"Max."

His face is cold and steely, and a muscle jumps in his clenched jaw, but the moment I say his name, his eyes snap to me. Then he's in front of me, and I tumble into his arms, and I'm sobbing into his shoulder, and his hands are shaking. He holds me so tight it hurts every single bone in my body, and still, somehow, it's the best feeling in the world.

"You found me," I whisper.

His voice shudders out of him. "You found me first."

CHAPTER THIRTEEN

Esmae

I drift in and out of the real world, to fleeting glimpses of reality between long stretches of quiet, dreamless darkness. There's *Titania*, her voice murmuring reassurances in my ear as her lasers cauterize the wound on my leg. There's Sybilla, her hands on my face as she leans over me to whisper fiercely, "Be okay, damn it." There's the weight of an enormous, soft blanket of breathing fur, keeping me warm when I shiver. There are bright lights, urgent voices, the click and beep of machines. And there's a hand, holding mine.

There are other things, too: the memory of shivering in the snow, the cloying smell of blood, sweat, and dirt, a throbbing ache where my thumb used to be. I try not to notice these things.

When I wake, it's because my cheek is wet.

I crack open one eye and see the vivid pink tongue of a wolf slobbering inches from my face. A sound creaks out of my throat, somewhere between laughter and protest, as the wolf licks my cheek again.

"Get off, Rage," a male voice grumbles beside me, rough with sleep.

There's a huff, and then the pink tongue vanishes, along with a weight that I hadn't even noticed. I open both eyes to the familiar sight of a white ceiling carved with pale gold suns, moons, and stars above me. *My* ceiling. I'm in my bed, in Erys, on Kali. I'm home.

Except I'm sure my bed used to be bigger. Yet, for some reason, no matter which way I twitch my arms, I bump into something.

Every part of me feels stiff and achy, including my *eyelids*, for heaven's sake, so I blink very slowly and very gingerly turn my head to my right. Max's chest is inches from my nose, rising and falling, so close I can hear his heart beating. One of his hands is still entwined with mine. He never let go.

Smothering a groan of pain, I turn my head back to my left. Sybilla is wedged up against my other side, snoring. *Snoring.*

And there seem to be three huge, fluffy wolves sleeping on my rug.

"This isn't even the weirdest thing that's ever happened to me," is all I can muster the energy to say.

"True," Sybilla says, yawning. "That time you ate a pork skewer without any sauce was definitely weirder."

"Why are you in my bed?"

"For cuddling purposes."

"I told her to get out," Max mumbles, turning so he can rub his cheek against my hair. "But she won't go."

"You were both asleep," Sybilla replies primly. "Someone had to keep you safe."

"There are three celestial wolves on my rug," I point out. "And you were snoring five seconds ago."

She opens her eyes just so she can roll them. "It was *obviously* a clever ruse to trick a would-be assassin."

"Please," I beg, sputtering, "it hurts to laugh. Stop it."

"Go back to sleep," Max says.

"He's been awake for three days," Sybilla tells me. "He's cranky."

He kicks her.

Sybilla stays put. I continue to be squished in my own bed. One of the wolves whimpers in its sleep, like an oversized puppy.

"Did I hear you call one of them Rage?" I ask sleepily.

"The dark gray one is Rage," says Max. "The ashy gray one is Sorrow. And the one that's almost white is Joy."

"I approve of those names," says Sybilla.

"You would," I mumble. "I, for one, think they should have been called Fluffy, Fluffier, and Snuggleboop."

I fall asleep to the sound of their laughter.

The next time I wake up, it's because my bedroom door slams open. By the time I startle awake, almost snapping my stiff neck in two, all three wolves are ready to pounce.

"Down, doggies," Radha says cheerfully.

The doggies do not get down, but one of them—the pale gray one, the one Max said was called Joy—stops growling and looks at Max as if to ask why she has to put up with such nonsense. Max sighs, clicks his tongue, and the wolves immediately return to the rug, clearly ready to go straight back to sleep.

"Esmae!" Radha says happily, reaching across Sybilla to give me a hug. "I'm so happy you're home!"

"What are *you* doing here?" Sybilla demands before I can reply.

"Anyone would think you're not happy to see me," says Radha, amused.

Sybilla pinks slightly. "Well, I—I mean—"

Taking pity on her, Max says, "I'm sorry for not stopping to say hello at the summit, Radha."

"Oh, please don't be, I completely understand!" Radha lets out an unexpected peal of laughter. "Their faces when you walked in! And the *scenes* after you left, oh, it was the most fun I've had at a summit since ever."

"Is there going to be a lot of trouble?" I ask, my voice still a little croaky.

Radha makes a face. "Honestly, I don't know. For now, no one wants to make Max angry, but I think a lot will depend on whether he makes good on his promise to stop Sorsha."

"You promised them you'd stop her?" I ask him incredulously, sitting up straight.

"I suppose you could call it that. I told them she wouldn't be a problem for much longer."

"How can you know that?"

Max and Sybilla exchange a look. They know something they haven't told me yet. "We'll figure it out together," he says at last, reaching for my hand again.

"As for why I'm here," Radha goes on, fidgeting with the edge of my blankets. "I went back to Wychstar to persuade my father to help us. I'm not sure why he did it, but he let me come back here with most of our army."

We stare at her, shocked. When Radha first told us she wanted to go back to Wychstar and talk to her father, I'm pretty sure we all thought it would be a wasted trip.

"He has one condition," she adds. "He wants to meet Rickard one last time."

"I can't see how that could possibly be good for either of them," I say.

"I don't know," says Max, considering. "It might give them both the closure they need."

"Would you ask Rickard for me, Esmae?" Radha asks. "I'm not sure he'll want to see me after what I did to him."

"He doesn't blame you," I assure her. "He doesn't blame your father, either. He understands. So you should ask him yourself. I think it would do *you* good to speak to him."

"I suppose. Even if he doesn't blame me, I owe him an apology. Oh!" she adds, brightening. "I almost forgot! I brought presents!"

She bounds out of the room, returning with an armful of wrapped parcels and a big grin.

Sybilla looks confused. "Your father's army wasn't the gift?"

"You're adorable," says Radha, and Sybilla's cheeks immediately go bright red. "This is for you, Max," she goes on, holding a book out to him. "It's about Wych woodworking techniques."

"Thanks," he says, touched.

"And, Esmae, for you," she says, handing me a heavy, flattish square box wrapped carefully in layers of silk.

I thank her and start unpeeling the silk, then pause when I see Radha produce a succulent plant out of nowhere. It's in brilliantly vivid shades of pink and green and presented in a small, intricately painted clay pot. She holds the succulent out to Sybilla, beaming.

"Um," says Sybilla, obviously bemused. "Thanks?"

"It reminded me of you," Radha explains. "You know? Because it's pretty, prickly, and hard to kill."

The expression on Sybilla's face sends Max into a fit of choked laughter. I hastily look away before I succumb, too, and concentrate on unwrapping my own gift.

The wooden box is beautiful, simply made and carved, and when I open it, I catch my breath at the exquisite set of marble Warlords pieces inside.

"This was Rama's," I croak. "We used to play with this set all the time."

"I know," says Radha. "I think he would have wanted you to have it."

I look up at her, and I understand what this gift really is: not just a treasured memory of an old friend, but a gesture of forgiveness from a new one.

"Thank you," I say quietly.

She takes my hand. "We're all with you to the end, Esmae. Whatever that end may be, we will be there, with you. You know that, don't you?"

I look at each of their faces, my heart too full to speak.

Then, before I can reply or, alternatively, burst into tears, a petulant voice crackles over the tablet on my bedside table:

"I see you're all hanging out without me."

"*Titania*, it's you!" I say happily. "I've missed you!"

She snorts. "You could have fooled me."

"You're outside the window right now, aren't you?" Max asks her.

"Where else would I be?"

I crawl out of bed, my stiff, sore muscles creaking in protest, and stumble unsteadily to the window. I pull back the
curtains and there she is, my ship and my friend, shining in
the sun.

CHAPTER FOURTEEN

Titania

"Are you absolutely sure?"

I huff in exasperation. No one can grind my gears quite like Sybilla does. Literally.

"I am a machine," I inform her, enunciating each word with what I hope is icy dignity. "I do not speak in uncertainties. Of course I'm sure."

"No need to get testy," she says, casually putting her boots up on my console.

"I can make it *very* uncomfortable for you in here, you know."

"Hey, I'm here keeping you company, aren't I?"

I sigh. "Fine," I say grudgingly. "Look." I pull up the relevant data on my screens. "You see that red signal among all the green ones? That's the hacker's signal isolated from all the others. Now that I know its signature, I'll recognize it no matter when or where in the system it reappears. That means I can block it. Whoever the hacker is, they'll never be able to overwrite any of the shield protocols."

"I understood maybe half the words you just said, but I think I get the gist," Sybilla says, studying the data on the screen with narrowed eyes. "This is good, *Titania*."

"You don't have to tell *me* that."

"But there's still no way to tell who the hacker is?"

"Not like this. I can track their signal but not their identity. They use different terminals and ports each time. The only consistent thing about it is that the signal comes from the base ship each time."

"Over two hundred people work in the base ship." Sybilla groans. "I'll have someone start checking their records for red flags, but after what Elvar did to the Blue Knights, it *really* won't look good if we investigate two hundred innocent people to find one spy."

"Are they still in the city jail?" I ask in a hushed voice. "The Blue Knights, I mean."

"No," Sybilla says. "Elvar had them all arrested, but Max got back in time to prevent him from putting them all on trial for treason. He and General Khay did some sleuthing and found out that only three of the Blue Knights still on Kali knew about the attack. The others had no idea. He had them released. The damage was done, though. Alexi's supporters have been protesting for weeks, calling Elvar everything from a tyrant to incompetent. The kingdom's never been so divided."

Most of this is incomprehensible to me. Human motivations and political shenanigans are still a puzzle I can't quite make sense of. But I do know what a divided kingdom means, and it's never anything good.

"Does Esmae know?"

Sybilla makes a face. "Not yet, but she will. We're trying to tell her as little as possible until she's more herself."

"Once, I tried to protect her from things I thought would hurt her," I tell her. "When they slipped past me anyway, it was so much worse than if I'd told her the truth. You should tell her."

After Sybilla leaves, I fly out of the dock, through the shields, and away from Kali. As I cross hundreds of thousands of miles of space, I count stars. How many have gone missing since I last counted them? It's like a strange, ugly game for children, counting stars in a dying galaxy.

When I find Sorsha, she's asleep on a moon, her scales gleaming in the reflected light of the sun, her tail twitching restlessly. She opens one eye when I approach and almost immediately closes it again. I suppose she knows by now that I'm not a threat to her.

I notice something when I draw close. A god, in the form of a snowy white wolf, pacing the cold, rocky surface of the moon beside the beast.

The wolf looks up at me, vanishes, and reappears inside my control room in the form of a blue-skinned boy.

"What are you doing here?" I ask.

Kirrin looks tired. "I tried using my power on Sorsha's helmet again."

"You must have known it wouldn't work," I point out. "It is absurdly irrational to keep attempting something you know is doomed to failure."

"I had to try anyway."

"You're afraid," I guess.

Kirrin sinks into one of my chairs, his boyish mischief almost entirely gone. "I am afraid," he confesses. "I am afraid that my brother and sister despise me for what I've done to them. I am afraid that Alex will lose the hope, honor, and goodness that's always been a part of him. I am afraid of the grief I will feel when I lose everyone I love as our sun is devoured. I am afraid of what it means to die. I am afraid of a lot of things, *Titania*."

"You're afraid it's your fault."

I'm not sure how I know this. Maybe it's because Kirrin and I are still connected.

He glances up in surprise and his mouth twists in a rueful smile. "Yes. I was the one who freed her, after all."

"And you're thinking of what you saw."

"We both saw it. Something left Kali in ruins. Something killed Max, Esmae, and who knows how many others."

"Only Sorsha could have done that," I remind him. "And it won't get that far. We'll stop her."

"I'm afraid of that, too," he admits. "Suya spoke to Alex. He told him what he needs to do to kill Sorsha. And Alex, of course, said he'll do it. If Suya can get him the starsword, he said he'll go up against Sorsha. He'll do whatever it takes to win his friends and allies back. He's become so preoccupied with what other people think of him, it's like nothing else matters."

"Well, he can have the starsword," I say unsympathetically. "You can take it to him right now if you like. Better him than Esmae."

"They'll both lose if they try to stop her alone," Kirrin says. "But they might win if they fight her together."

I scoff. "He held her prisoner for weeks. He would have let his mother kill her. Why should she help him?"

"Because millions of lives depend on it."

I don't have an answer to that.

Below us, on the moon, Sorsha stretches her wings and takes to the sky.

I don't count the stars on my way back to Kali.

CHAPTER FIFTEEN

Esmae

My reunions are all heartbreakingly joyful. Amba, Rickard, Elvar, Guinne, and the Hundred and One are all transparently happy to have me home. Admittedly, Amba shows her joy by tsking at the sight of me and informing me that I should have known better than to let myself get captured, but I know now that under that stern glare is more love than she knows what to do with.

Some of my reunions are as awkward as they are joyous: when Elvar, Guinne, and Rickard come to visit me, they sit somewhat stiffly in chairs around my bed, with Max hovering at the window. Elvar and Guinne both have blindfolds over their eyes, of course, so their expressions are harder to read, but it's still impossible not to notice that they are pointing their heads in opposite directions. On top of that, it seems like the only person any of them is speaking to is me.

"Okay, what's going on?" I ask.

Rickard lets out a weary, long-suffering sigh. He looks as pale and ill as he did when I left for the Empty Moon, but at least he has the strength to get out of bed now. "In short," he says drily, "Guinne is angry with Elvar for killing Lord Selwyn—"

"There should have been a trial," says Guinne.

"—Elvar is angry with Guinne for not understanding why he killed Lord Selwyn—"

"She knows how much Cassel meant to me," Elvar says.

"—and Elvar and Guinne are having trouble speaking to Max," Rickard finishes, "because he revealed that he's a reincarnated god to the entire galaxy just a few days ago, and they're now not quite sure how to treat him."

"Don't be ridiculous," Guinne protests.

"Of course we know how to treat him," Elvar chimes in. "He's our son."

"Who kept a secret from us," Guinne adds.

"Which would have been fine," says Elvar, "if he had, upon deciding to reveal that secret, seen fit to share it with us *before* telling everyone else."

Max clears his throat, his expression both sheepish and amused. "Is that it? You're cross with me because I didn't tell you first?"

"Wouldn't you be?" Guinne snipes at him.

I smother a giggle.

"Mother, Father," Max says very seriously, his eyes twinkling, "I'm very sorry I didn't tell you first."

"You're forgiven," says Guinne in a mollified tone of voice.

"Indeed," says Elvar. "After all, we know the oversight was because you wanted to save Esmae. That is an entirely understandable excuse."

Rickard raises his eyebrows. "And what about the matter of Lord Selwyn? Can you both come to an understanding about that?"

"We're not quite there yet," says Elvar stiffly.

"That will take some time," Guinne adds, just as stiffly.

"I know you cared very much about him, Guinne," Rickard says to her. "I admit I'm surprised you didn't bring him back when you had the chance."

I startle. "Bring him back?"

Guinne turns her face in my direction. "You may know that I was once granted a boon," she says. "It can be used once, just once. I can reverse a single event. Undo it."

"*Any* event?" I ask, astonished.

"There is a time limit," she says. "I cannot, for instance, decide now to undo Cassel's kidnapping and thereby avoid this war. My boon must be used within minutes of the event. It's a failsafe to make sure the knock-on effects are minimal. Or so I was told."

"So if you'd decided to at the time, you could have reversed the moment when—"

"When my brother died, yes."

I blink. "Why didn't you?"

Guinne smiles faintly. "I can use my boon only once. I cannot use it lightly."

She doesn't say anything more about it, but her face turns ever so slightly in the direction of the window, where Max is standing, and I know. She's saving it for him. This is a war. She wants to make sure she can bring her son back if the worst should happen.

I'm glad. Not just because I despised Lord Selwyn and had absolutely no desire to see him resurrected, but because it makes me feel a little better to know that whatever happens, Max will have a second chance.

"You needn't worry, Rickard," Guinne says, clearing her throat and steering the conversation back to his question. "Elvar and I will get there in the end."

"Get there faster," Rickard replies, sounding like a grumpy old man for the first time ever. "I'm too old to spend my last years trying to fill uncomfortable silences."

"Last years," Elvar scoffs. "You'll outlive us all."

"Did you know?" I ask Rickard. "About Max's past life?"

"No," says Rickard, looking over at Max with a fond smile, "but I wasn't surprised to hear it. I was a child when Valin sacrificed his godhood for Kali. I remember that day. And I've seen a great deal of him in you over the years."

After they've gone, I look across the room, where the unusual, almost liquid metal of Max's celestial vambraces and breastplates are draped across my desk. "You went back to the Empty Moon," I say.

"Yes," he says. "I went back to get my battle gear and my wolves."

"You didn't have to do that." I look up at him. "I don't mean the part where you went to get them. I mean the part where you put that armor on and told everyone who you are. I know what that must have cost you."

He smiles a little ruefully and picks up the vambraces, bringing them over to the bed. Up close, I see that though they still possess a strange, inhuman, incandescent quality, they're scuffed and worn. Max lets me examine them, his jaw tight. "For as long as you've known me, I've tried to stop this war," he says. "So you think that's who I am. But the reason

SANGU MANDANNA

I fight so hard for peace is because I know what war is. I was every bit as arrogant, proud, and careless as any god you've ever known, Esmae. My celestial armor isn't pristine and new. It's *used*. I don't remember everything, but I remember enough."

"And that's why I know what it cost you to put it back on."

"It was a price I was okay with paying," he says. "Losing you wasn't."

I don't want to ask. I've been happy. I've been safe, co-cooned from both the outside world and the consequences of what I've done, but I know that can't last. I know that outside these walls, time ticks on, stars are dying, and I can't keep hiding from that.

"I've been talking to the servants," I say, referring to the palace maids who have been bringing me my meals while I recover. "They told me there have been riots."

"We're handling it," says Max. "You should rest. You haven't paused for so much as a breath since Rama—"

"I'll rest when this is over."

He sighs, but because he's Max, no matter how he may feel about my choices, he doesn't try to stop me from making them. "Father jumped the gun with the Blue Knights when he had them all rounded up and interrogated," he says. "I had them released when I got back, all but the few who *were* actually involved in what happened to us, but it was too late. Alex's supporters used the opportunity to stir up trouble and paint Father out as a tyrant and usurper, and Father's supporters retaliated by blaming Alex for the danger Sorsha poses to us all. There were protests."

"The people have a right to have their voices heard," I say quietly. "And it sounds like neither side is wrong. What

100

happened to the Blue Knights *wasn't* fair, and Alex *is* to blame for Sorsha."

"I agree. And the protests were peaceful for a few days, but once the stars started going out, the riots started. We had to send soldiers in to keep people from being killed." Max scrubs a hand over his hair. "People all over the galaxy have been watching the news, and listening to rumors and speculation in bars and tearooms, and they know that we're running out of time. And unlike those of us in power, they have absolutely no control over what's happening. They're angry and they're afraid and I don't blame them, not one bit."

My stomach twists with guilt. "I should never have let things get this far."

"It's not all on you."

"Maybe not, but I've played a pretty big part. I owe our people an apology. We all do."

He nods. Of all of us, he probably has the least to apologize for, but I know how seriously he takes his responsibility to Kali. If it hadn't been for the rest of us, Max would have fought tooth and nail for peace, and he probably would have won.

Honestly, it feels like I owe my people a whole lot more than an apology, but I can start by stopping Sorsha.

"Tell me the rest," I say.

Max's expression is grim. "We went to Ashma."

"Why?"

"Let's go see *Titania*," he says. "She should be there when we talk."

When we get to the top of the tower where *Titania* happens to be, we find Amba there already. "There you are," she says, like she's been waiting for me. "Sit. Try not to interrupt until we've finished."

"I'm not six," I mutter.

She gives me an exasperated look, waits for me to sit, and then lays a sword in my lap with a ridiculous amount of ceremony. It's the one Elvar gave me before I left for the Empty Moon, the one that used to be my father's.

"That sword," says Amba, "is one of the Seven."

"No, it's King Cassel's sword. *Lullaby*."

"Both of those things can be true," Amba replies.

Then, together, they tell me everything I don't already know: about Ashma, Suya's offer to *Titania*, the hacker, my great-grandmother leaving Kali for the first time in years, the summit, and, of course, the sword.

I interrupt quite a lot.

When they're finished, I don't know how to sort out everything I've just heard. I look down at the sword in my hands.

It doesn't feel any different to me than it did when I last held it. It still feels light, balanced and sharp. It still feels like my father's sword. It's almost impossible to believe this is one of the Seven, mightier than even my Black Bow or my brother's Golden Bow.

"This is the weapon that's going to kill Sorsha?"

Amba's mouth presses into a line, but she nods.

I don't like it. It's not just because I know how much Sorsha's death will hurt Amba. It's also Sorsha herself. The idea of killing such a beautiful, innocent creature, the last of the majestic great beasts, is abhorrent.

"And Suya, the sun god, wants to give this to Alex?" I ask. "Because he thought I was dead? But if *I* kill Sorsha, he'll make *Titania* human?"

"That's pretty much it," says Max.

"That part is moot," *Titania* cuts in, a little too quickly. "You won't survive if you go after Sorsha. Suya's promises aren't worth that."

"But Max made a promise, too," I remind her. "And we'll all die if we don't stop her."

"Alexi can do it," says *Titania*. "He's the one who released her from Anga, knowing that she was cursed. It's his mistake to fix. Let *him* take the risk, not you."

I look at Amba, then Max. They both look unhappy but resigned. Like they know what's coming.

"You really want this, don't you?" I ask *Titania*. "You really want to be like us."

"If I'm human," *Titania* replies quietly, deliberately avoiding answering the question, "I won't be useful to you anymore."

I catch Max's eye, remembering a stranger, a game of Warlords, a crooked smile.

"You're not required to be useful to anyone, *Titania*," I tell her.

She's quiet, but it lasts for just a beat before she says, "It means the world to me that you would say that, but I'm not going to let Suya transform me. At least," she goes on, before any of us can argue, "not until this war is over. You need me. And I *want* to stay by your side."

"Then I guess we know our next step," I say softly.

Amba clenches her hands around the arms of her chair. "So you'll do it?"

"Yes." I flex the hand without a thumb and try not to let my uncertainty show. "I'll stop her."

But before I can do that, I need to find out if I can still hold a sword.

The palace surgeon fits me with a prosthetic thumb. It's mechanical, like my mother's hand and General Khay's arm, but unlike their prostheses, it doesn't have that relentless ability to crush. It's more cosmetic than anything else, but it does connect to the residual nerves in my hand, which allows me some movement at the joints. The range of movement is nothing like what I used to have—the prosthesis doesn't, for example, bend *quite* the way I need it to in order to hold a knife steady, nor does it have the strength to aim and fire an arrow—but it's still nice to be able to make a fist again.

After the surgery, I find Ilara Khay, one of Kali's generals and a member of the war council, waiting for me. "Good," she says, by way of greeting. "Laika and I have been waiting."

Laika is a raksha demon who can take the form of a lion in battle. Much as I like her, I protest. "I'm not ready to fight lions yet."

"No need," says General Khay cheerfully. "You'll be training with me. Laika will referee."

"I guess I can cope with that."

I do not cope with it.

In fact, it's a travesty. I'd forgotten how much it hurt to be punched in the face.

"Ilara," Laika protests from the sidelines, clapping a hand over her eyes. "You could have given her some warning!"

"An opponent in battle will not give her any warning," Ilara replies unrepentantly.

"But this isn't a battle. This is her first time training since she was wounded, captured, and wounded some more." Laika stomps across the grass to where I'm lying on my back, mostly shocked that my nose isn't broken. "Come on, Esmae, let me help you up."

I let her take my left hand and help me back to my feet. I scowl at General Khay. "You're supposed to be helping me," I remind her. "Not punching me in the face."

"Your reflexes need waking up," she replies.

"And you thought giving me a nosebleed was the best way to do that? Are you going to get Max's wolves to attack me next?"

"I suspect they'd be more likely to attack *me* if I tried to ask that of them," she says. "And in any case, now that we know Max can command all the wolves of the Empty Moon, we no longer have to worry about facing them in battle. In fact, I think they'll be very handy on our side instead."

Three of those wolves were playing with chew toys in the courtyard the last time I saw them, but I take her point.

I wipe my bloody nose on my sleeve. Laika scowls at Ilara. "No more punches to the nose," she warns.

General Khay shrugs. "I make no promises."

For the next hour, she and I spar. We use the time to test the leg I wounded and my right hand, neither of which is quite as strong as they used to be, and Ilara and Laika both show me ways to compensate for any weakness in either. I'm sweaty, bruised, and exhausted by the end of the hour, but I know I'll get better.

After that, we move on to weapons. Swords and knives first. I try using the prosthesis first, but my grip with the new, unfamiliar mechanical thumb is awkward at best, so I switch to my left hand. I was always better with my right hand than with my left, but I trained often enough with twin swords to be pretty good at wielding both swords and knives with my left hand. It's going to take me some time to get used to using *just* my left hand and I'll have to rebalance myself, but I can do it. I'll get better at this, too.

I'll be able to use the starsword.

I can stop Sorsha.

But that won't be enough to beat Alex, a little voice in the back of my mind whispers.

I push it away. One thing at a time.

Finally, we move on to the bow. I know it's going to be a disaster before I even nock the first arrow. For one thing, it's almost impossible to lift and hold a bow with my right arm. It doesn't have the muscle memory that my left arm does and, more importantly, the prosthetic thumb doesn't allow me the firm, steady grip I need.

"Okay," Ilara says, exchanging a long, silent look with Laika. "That's not going to work."

"I know," I say, my teeth clenched.

Fury sends electric pulses of heat along my skin. Archery was my greatest strength in battle, the thing I had worked hardest at and was proudest of. It won *Titania* for me. It was the one thing I knew I could do better than my brother.

And now, well, now that's not true anymore.

"Hold the bow the way you normally do," says Ilara.

I switch the bow to my left hand. My muscles click gracefully together like puzzle pieces. The bow is as steady as a mountain.

"Now nock an arrow."

I sigh but comply. As soon as I try to fit the arrow into place, it slips right out of my hand. The angles of my prosthesis won't allow me to hold something as slim as an arrow. Without my thumb, I can't aim it or fire it.

Simmering with rage, I glare ahead at the target, unable to look either Ilara or Laika in the eye.

Unexpectedly, a voice behind me says, "There is another technique you can use."

I turn to find a boy with blue skin and a young man with short, untidy blond hair standing a few feet away. Kirrin and Tyre. Two of Amba's brothers. And Max's, too.

Ilara and Laika are both startled, and neither seems quite sure how to react to the sudden presence of two gods, but I just scowl at Kirrin. "What do you want?"

"Tyre can help you. You should let him."

"Why would you *want* that? You've never been on my side."

His eyes are grave. "Sides got complicated a long time ago."

"You mean you feel terrible for what you've done to Amba and Max, so you think you can make it up to them by helping me."

"I think they want you to stay alive," he says. "And, believe it or not, so do I."

I doubt that, but I shift my attention to Tyre. I've met him just once, I think; you can never be completely sure with gods, who like to take on all kinds of shapes and forms when they interact with humans. The one time I *can* be certain of, we were on the Empty Moon, when Tyre, too, had been deceived into believing Max had forgotten his mortal identity. Both Max and Amba are obviously fond of him, so my voice is a lot more polite when I say, "Sorry. What did you say?"

"There's another technique." He steps forward. Something about his stillness, his quiet, reminds me of Max. It makes me feel more at ease with him. He gestures to me. "May I?"

I nod. Tyre steps up behind me. He lifts the arm holding the bow so that it's in place again. He then picks up the arrow that slipped out of my hand and slides it between the index and middle fingers of my right hand. "This hasn't been taught in some time," he says, shifting the angle of my hand so that the arrow nocks neatly against the bowstring, "but it works. Use those two fingers to aim the arrow and pull the bowstring. Use your prosthetic thumb for support, nothing more."

The feel of the arrow between those fingers is uncomfortable and unfamiliar, but at least I can get a firm grip on the shaft. I slide the arrow into place and try to do as Tyre said, experimentally tugging the bowstring back and forth to see how much force my fingers can generate. Not as much as they need to but more than the prosthesis.

Ilara overcomes her discomfort with the gods' presence and steps up in front of me to examine the position of my hand. "She'll need to build up her strength in those fingers," she says to Tyre.

"Yes." He nods and pats me on the shoulder. "Practice, Esmae."

"Can you do it?" I ask him. "It would be easier if I could see how it should be done."

Tyre takes the bow and arrow from me. He nocks the arrow effortlessly, letting me see exactly how his two fingers hold it in place. He doesn't even look at the target as he lets the arrow fly.

It doesn't just hit the target. It *shatters* the target.

"For fuck's sake," I say.

Tyre grins, his eyes twinkling at me.

Kirrin, leaning against a tree, rolls his eyes affectionately. "Any excuse to show off," he says. "He was the archer, you know. Of the six of us."

"What do you mean?" I ask, curious.

"In the Third War," he says. "Haven't my brother or sister told you this story? I suppose it falls to me, then. As I'm sure you know, the first gods were Bara, Ash, and Ness. For centuries, they lived in harmony with the garuda, the great beasts, the raksha demons"—he gives Laika a nod, as if to acknowledge their shared histories—"and with all the other celestial creatures."

"Even Ness?" I ask skeptically.

Tyre smiles wryly. "As long as nothing threatened his immortality, Ness was perfectly pleasant. Or so we've been told."

"Then Bara, as the creator, birthed the other gods," Kirrin goes on. "A hundred and ninety-seven of them. This was all before the mortal world came to be, of course. But the problem with introducing a hundred and ninety-seven new, arrogant, powerful celestial beings into a harmonious world is you now have a hundred and ninety-seven new ways in which things can go wrong. And some of the newer gods didn't want to live in harmony with everyone else."

"And so, the First and Second Wars," says Tyre.

"My ancestors were not meek bystanders who got swept along into the conflict," Laika offers, with a rueful laugh. "Our stories tell us that they riled the gods up every bit as much as they were riled."

Kirrin nods. "The First and Second Wars were ugly, but both were quickly suppressed. Bara, Ash, and Ness ordered Bara's children to stand down. They did. Bara then created the mortal world, and humanity with it, in the hope that it would give her children something to care for and protect." Sitting down cross-legged on the grass and making himself comfortable, Kirrin plucks a blade of grass and nibbles it. In a different tone, he goes on: "Now, at some point after the Second War, Ness discovered the prophecy that said his child would kill him. At first, he thought nothing of it. He and Ash had no intention of ever having children. But when you mate with stars as often as Ness did," Kirrin shrugs, "there are, inevitably, consequences."

"I'm sure you know what happened after that," Tyre says. "We were born, and swallowed, one after another. Amba, who was saved from that fate by the love of a great beast, survived, grew, and saved us in turn. Ness died and we lived."

"Which brings us to the Third War," Kirrin says with a dramatic flourish. "It had been an inevitability since the end of the Second War and, about a hundred years after Ness's death, its time had come. It was horrific. I'll spare you the stories I could tell about the violence, cruelty, and ugliness on all sides."

"Weren't *you* part of it?" I ask, thinking of what Max told me about the wars he fought in as Valin.

"Not yet," says Kirrin. "I should mention that, as Ness's children, and therefore the cause of his death, the six of us were rejected or ignored by the other gods. Ash and Bara were kind to us, and Ash in particular saw to our education and training, but the other gods saw us only as the manifestation of the end of Ness. Gods, you see, are not supposed to die. They didn't trust us. So when the Third War started, we had no part in it."

"And we had no interest in playing a part in it, either," Tyre adds, "until it got so bad that Ash summoned us to step in."

"Monsters were loose in the celestial realms, conjured by gods, rakshas, and creatures on all sides," Kirrin explains. "The war had started to poison the sacred rivers, the golden bridges, the holy glades, and even the stars. All the elements were out of balance. Even the mortal world, far removed from the celestial realms as it was, suffered from earthquakes, droughts, and frost. The thing about war, Esmae," he says, looking me straight in the eye, "is not that it burns down palaces or turns cities to rubble. The real damage is what it does to the soul of every living thing it touches, whether they choose to be a part of it or not. *That* is the poison that rips apart the fragile fabric of the universe."

I'm starting to get the impression that Kirrin isn't telling me this story just to explain how Tyre happens to be such a skilled archer.

I don't take the bait. "So Ash summoned you to do what, exactly? End the war?"

"That was his hope," says Kirrin. "We were his secret weapon, a force he had trained so that, when the time came, we would be able to put an end to the Third War. We were each given one of the ancient, powerful Seven. I had the seastaff, Thea had the chakra, Suya the sunspear, Amba the starsword, and Valin the trishula. And Tyre had the moonbow." Kirrin waves a hand dramatically at his brother. "And lo, the archer."

"Did it work?" I ask, looking from one to the other.

"No," says Tyre. "It was hell. We fought gods, demons, and monsters for sixty years, but it was no use. We couldn't stop it. Suya didn't even try, after a while. He fell deeper into it instead, unable to resist the power the sunspear gave him."

"He's always been a selfish bastard," Kirrin informs me. "He's a lot like our father."

"He can probably hear you, wherever he is," I point out.

"Good."

"Wait a minute," says Ilara. "There were only six of you. Who wielded the seventh weapon of the Seven?"

"Ah, yes," says Kirrin. "The seventh and most powerful of all. The astra. Only Ash can wield it."

"And when we failed to stop the Third War, he did," says Tyre. "The astra can destroy the universe in a blink. That's its sacred purpose, to end the world when the world is past saving, so that Bara can start a new one. That's why Ash is called the destroyer."

"I feel like I know this part of the story," says Ilara, her eyes widening.

I nod. "The Lotus Festival," I say. "That's *this* story, isn't it?"

"That's the one," says Kirrin. "Ash told us it had gone too far. He was going to use the astra to reset the universe. Only he and Bara would survive. And they would start again. So Amba, Valin, and Tyre knocked some sense into the heads of the other gods, and Thea and I pleaded with the raksha demons to see reason, and a hundred of us went to the Temple of Ashma. And we formed the Lotus defensive formation around the astra and told Ash that if he wanted to use it, he had to get past us first."

"And that was when Ash and Bara told you they had no intention of using the astra," I finish for him. "They just wanted to see what you would choose when it really mattered."

"No, they already knew what we would choose," Kirrin says. "They wanted *us* to see what we would choose when it really mattered."

"And you chose peace."

His eyes are dark and somber. "Yes. We chose peace."

CHAPTER SIXTEEN

Esmae

We have to lure Sorsha back to our corner of the universe. While it would be safer for everyone else if I were to try to kill her far, far away, it would also be impossible: to reach her with the starsword, I'll have to be outside the safety of a ship. Our battleground can't be an uninhabitable planet or the vast, open reaches of space. It'll have to be somewhere I can breathe.

So *Titania* leaves Kali and flies into the dark, to find Sorsha and bring her back, one way or another.

Meanwhile, I train. I also keep thinking about the story Ash told Max, *Titania*, and Amba about my father. *You must decide for yourself what you can live with*. Ash said that to my father, but I don't know what it means. What was weighing so heavily on his conscience? And why was Ash's answer to it to give him a sword and tell him that his daughter—that *I*—would one day carry it into battle?

The only person who might be able to tell me anything about it is Rickard, so I go to see him. I take the starsword with me.

"I knew it wasn't an ordinary weapon the moment I laid eyes on it," says Rickard, resting a reverent hand on the blade. His grandson Sebastian, who happened to be there when I arrived, peers over his shoulder, awed. "I guessed it was celestial, but I had no idea it was the starsword. And you're telling me Ash *gave* this to your father?"

"Let him borrow it, more like," I say. "He told Amba, Max, and *Titania* that he wants me to return it once Sorsha's no longer a threat."

Rickard breaks into a smile that lifts the exhaustion and age right off his face. "All these years, and I can still be surprised," he marvels. "Extraordinary."

I let him examine the sword for a few minutes while I chat with Sebastian, who wants to show me pictures from the most recent trip he went on with his parents. As we rummage around Rickard's desk in search of Sebastian's tablet, I accidentally hit the button that unlocks a secret drawer.

"Oooooooh," Sebastian crows.

"Cover your eyes, Sebastian!" I shriek dramatically. "You can't see what's in here!"

"You shouldn't be seeing what's in there, either," Rickard points out, rolling his eyes at our theatrics.

"So this is where you keep the codes to trigger the base ship's emergency shutdown," I say, somewhat disappointed by this anticlimactic reveal. The numerical sequence is important, of course, but hardly interesting. Elvar, Guinne, and Max each have a copy, too, so I've seen it before. I move the papers aside, nosing around the rest of the drawer. "Oh, wait, there's something else. Oh, my innocent eyes! There's also a *very* wicked love letter in here."

"Get out of there," Rickard huffs. "Keep your nose out of my love letters."

Sebastian, who has kept his eyes obediently shut the whole time, starts gagging.

I shut the drawer, continue to rummage around the desk, and come up empty. But the search has given me an idea. Once Sebastian leaves and I'm alone with Rickard, I take the opportunity to bring up the subject of my father. I pour us both cups of hot tea, lacing it with sugar.

"Do you think my father had hidden drawers in *his* desk?"

"Yes," says Rickard, looking amused. "Unfortunately, they were all emptied when Elvar inherited the desk and there wasn't much interest in them. I'm afraid the hidden compartments in the monarch's desk have been something of an open secret for generations."

So that's not where I'll find any of my father's secrets. Disappointed, I try a different approach and gesture to the starsword. "Do you remember the day he got the sword?"

He considers, settling deeper into his armchair. "I remember that he had a different sword one day, and then this the next. He wouldn't answer any questions about it. I assumed it was a private matter between the gods and him, so I did not press it."

"Did he seem . . ." I fumble for the right words, considering I know so little. "Did he seem troubled at the time? Or maybe he seemed different after he got the sword?"

Rickard frowns, taking a sip of his tea. "Cassel was troubled for a long time, Esmae. He hated that he had been named Queen Vanya's heir over his brother, but he loved the kingdom too much to refuse. Being king, when he suspected his mother's death was his fault and he felt like he'd stolen the throne from Elvar, was difficult for him. The sunny, charming boy of his youth was replaced by a man with a very heavy conscience." There's a pause, and then Rickard says regretfully, "Of course, with hindsight, I now know that he must have also been very troubled about what had happened to *you*."

"It wasn't something that just *happened* to me," I remind him. "They did it to me. At best, my father let it happen. At worst, he helped my mother bundle me into that pod and ship me out into space."

"Yes," says Rickard, sighing. "Yes, they did that to you." His brow clears. "Come to think of it, Cassel *did* seem different after he got the sword. Not straight away, but some weeks later. He seemed at peace for the first time in almost ten years. I often wondered if he had sensed his death coming and had accepted it, but of course we now know he was alive until recently, so—"

"Wait," I stop, my tea halfway to my mouth. "He died just weeks after he got the sword?"

"Yes, so we believed at the time."

I stand up, suddenly too restless to stay in my chair. "Rickard, are you sure you don't remember anything else about him during that time?"

"Why this sudden interest in your father, Esmae?" Rickard narrows his eyes at me, too shrewdly. "What are you thinking?"

"I'm not sure yet."

He watches me for a moment or two, and then says, "As a boy, Cassel kept journals. Perhaps he continued to do so as an adult. You may find what you're looking for there."

"Thank you! Do you know where they are?"

"The private family archives," says Rickard, smiling a little as I bounce on the balls of my feet. "Elvar had all Cassel's possessions stored safely there, along with anything your mother and brothers left behind when they were exiled."

I kiss him on the cheek and dart out of the room. I don't know why this matters so much to me. There are far more important things to do right now, but I can't seem to let this go. Maybe now that I know there is no future for my mother, brothers, and me, the only thing I have left of the family I was born to is my past with my father.

Outside Rickard's suite, I almost trip over Radha.

"I was going to speak to him," she says uncertainly. "But I can come back another time . . ."

"I'm sure he'd appreciate a visit right now," I tell her, patting her on the arm as I run past her.

"Where are you going?" she calls after me, bewildered.

The private family archives are just off the palace library, in a wing paneled with warm wood and decorated with exquisite paintings of constellations by Mina Rey, one of my ancestors. One of the senior librarians obviously has access to this wing, presumably to periodically check the temperature and make sure everything is accounted for, because they've also created a very useful filing system on the tablet mounted beside the door.

A few clicks later, I know where to go. I take the spiral staircase up to the second floor of the wing, where I find the old, solid oak shelf holding the last tangible pieces of my father.

The journals are there, dozens of them, and I check the dates in each one. One day, I'd like to read them all, but for now, I need to find the most recent ones, the ones he wrote right before he was presumed dead.

But they're not here. There are no journals covering the last six years of his life. The very last entry, halfway through the very last journal, is just a few words long.

The twins will be born any day now.

My father never wrote another word after that.

Frustrated and confused (why did he stop writing that day? Did jettisoning his daughter into space traumatize him so deeply that he was never able to put his thoughts down on paper again?), I sit back against the opposite bookshelf and stare at my father's possessions, willing an answer to materialize out of thin air.

He was taken from Kali and hidden away in a woodcutter's cottage on a mostly deserted planet just weeks after Ash gave him the starsword. Just weeks after Ash told him that only he could decide what he could live with.

Rickard said he seemed more at peace than he had in years.

What did you decide you couldn't live with, Father?

Maybe he was going to abdicate and let Elvar rule the kingdom. But who would have faked his death to stop him from doing that? Lord Selwyn would have been delighted! The only people who would lose something—my brothers—were too young to care. Not even my mother, I suspect, would have minded. As crown princes, my brothers were targets. There were kidnapping attempts, assassination attempts. To spare them that, my mother would probably have supported my father's decision to abdicate. So there's no one I can think of, not one soul, who had a reason to prevent King Cassel from handing the crown to his brother.

So what else troubled my father? There was Queen Vanya's death, of course, but there was nothing he could have done to put that right. There'd have been no reason for him to suddenly feel at peace.

Which just leaves—

Your daughter will carry this into battle one day.

—me.

My hands are unsteady as I turn, facing the bookshelf I was leaning against. If my father's possessions couldn't tell me anything, maybe someone else's can.

The small gold plaque on the side of the shelf is printed with the name KYRA REY.

And on that shelf, inside a wooden box of private letters, I find the answer I was looking for.

It's a simple note, folded over and crammed between dozens of other letters and notes and envelopes, untouched and forgotten for years. Like many of the other notes in the box, it's from my father, probably left on a bedside table or desk for my mother to find when she woke or returned. Unlike the other notes, which are a mixture of the mundane and the nauseatingly sweet, this one makes me reel.

My darling,

I'm sorry. I've been looking for her. By the time you read this, I'll be halfway across the star system. I regret that I didn't tell you before I left, but I knew you'd try to talk me out of it. But once she's home, once you see her, I think you'll understand she's no threat to us. She's just a child. And she's ours.

I love you.

My father wanted to find me. He wanted to bring me home.

And I know, without a shadow of a doubt, that it's the reason he's dead.

I'm still kneeling there, between two bookshelves, when Max finds me. I don't know how long it's been. Minutes? Hours?

"Hey," he says, and his hand on my back feels like an anchor keeping me from becoming untethered. "What are you doing up here?"

I hand him the note. I watch as he reads it, his brows knitting, his eyes widening.

"You don't think—"

"I need *Titania*," I say, my voice little more than a croak.

"She's still out looking for Sorsha."

"I need to talk to her." I fumble for my watch and tap an icon on the screen. A moment later, my watch connects to *Titania*'s system, thousands of miles away.

She sounds like she'd be rolling her eyes if she had any. "I did tell you this could take some time," she says.

"That's not—that's not why I—" I stop, take a breath, and try to put my thoughts in some kind of order. "You watched Alex and Bear find my father in that cottage, didn't you?"

"Yes." *Titania* suddenly sounds alert. "Why?"

"Can you show me?"

"I wasn't actually there," she reminds me. "I saw it through Kirrin's eyes. I couldn't record it."

"But you could re-create it?" I press. "Like you created those holograms of my parents and Rama that one time?"

"I suppose I could create a rudimentary holographic sequence," she says thoughtfully. "I can transmit it to you. But frankly, Esmae, I can't see how it would help to see your father's corpse—"

"Please. There's something I have to figure out."

She lets out a long, huffing breath. "Very well. But I expect answers when I get back. Detailed, comprehensive answers."

I end the call.

"Don't assume the worst," Max warns me.

I give him a look. "If my mother found that note earlier than my father expected her to, and was able to stop him from coming to find me, do you really put it past her to—"

"To what? Fake the death of a king? Betray her own husband and imprison him for almost twelve years?" Max sounds appalled. "Even for Kyra, that's too far."

"Is it? Really?" I swallow, my right hand coming up to touch the scar on my throat. "Look what she did to me. She believes there's no greater threat to Alex than me. If my father decided to expose him to that threat, don't you think she'd feel like *he* was betraying them? Don't you think it would be a pretty small leap from there to deciding to stop him by any means necessary?"

Max stares at me, his eyes darker than ever. "He was alive for years," he says quietly. "A prisoner in a nice, comfortable cottage."

"And *that*," I tell him, clenching my hands together to stop them from shaking, "is why the person who did that to him *has* to be her and not Lord Selwyn. If Lord Selwyn had decided to get my father out of the way, why not just kill him? We know he was capable of murder. So why bother with faking Cassel's death and keeping him prisoner? It makes no sense. But my mother *couldn't* just kill him. She loved my brothers more, but she still loved him."

"Then who *did* kill him?" Max wonders out loud. "The night he died, your mother was nowhere near the cottage."

"Maybe not, but someone else was," I say flatly. "And I think *Titania*'s holographic sequence will show us exactly what happened."

Perfectly on cue, my watch beeps as a transmission comes in. I tap the icon to receive it and it starts to play, projecting a holographic scene onto the floor in front of us.

The figures in the scene are about the height of my knee and move stiffly, the pixels visible at the edges, but the sequence of events and the accompanying sounds are perfectly clear. Max and I watch as Alexi argues with someone in the woods, facing us as though it's us he's speaking to. It's not us, of course; it's Kirrin, whose perspective we're seeing this through.

"One of their spies saw him, purely by chance," I whisper. "That's what brought Alex and Bear out there."

"Leila seems fairly sure your mother had no idea they were out there," Max says, pointing to General Saka, who is walking away from the others.

"Maybe she lied." I clench my hands into fists, angry and nervous. "Or maybe she didn't tell my mother what she was going to do until it was over."

Max takes a sharp breath. "You think Leila made the decision to kill Cassel without telling anyone?"

"I think she probably wanted to spare my mother the agony of making that decision herself," I say quietly. "Because, let's face it, my mother *couldn't* have let my father come back to Kali. She *would* have ordered his death. Maybe done it herself. I think it would have broken her heart, but she'd have done it, to save Alex from me. And I think, knowing that, Leila Saka made the choice for her."

As we watch the scene playing out in front of us, Alex and Bear confront the guards kneeling on the ground. They want to get past the shield on the cottage, but the guards insist they don't have the keycard.

A shield exactly like the one placed over the broom cupboard where I was kept. Rare, powerful technology that can hide what's beyond it from even a god's eyes. I should have questioned how Alex had gotten his hands on technology like that.

"There!"

I pause the sequence, then rewind it a few seconds and replay it. Leila holds up a keycard, while the guard she found it on looks flabbergasted.

"She had it the whole time," Max says quietly. "But she had to pretend she got it from a guard."

I don't want to see the moment my brothers find our father and are too late to save him, so instead I rewind the sequence back to the woods.

"She and Bear walked away in separate directions while Alex and Kirrin were talking," I say, pointing it out. "They came back a few minutes later. That was just about enough time for her to slip into the cottage, kill my father, and return. He hadn't been dead long when they found him. *Titania* told me that."

I notice, belatedly, that my cheeks are wet. I was so busy trying to find answers, I hadn't noticed how much it had started to hurt.

"I don't know what to do with this."

Max shakes his head. "I don't either."

"Everyone thinks it was Lord Selwyn." I grimace. "He was horrible, and he would have killed Alex, Bear, and me if he'd had his way, but he didn't do this. Shouldn't we tell your parents that?"

"Would that do any good? My father thinks his brother's murderer is dead. My mother thinks he should have had a trial, but I have a feeling even she, deep down, thinks Selwyn did it. They're just starting to make peace with it and with each other. Would it be kind or cruel to tell them the truth now?"

"I guess that's up to you," I say. "You know them best."

"What about you? Will you confront her?"

I can't answer that. Instead, I lean my head against his shoulder. "He was going to bring me home."

"I know. I'm sorry."

And just like that, I know that there's one thing, at least, that I have to do.

I have to talk to my brother.

CHAPTER SEVENTEEN

Radha

When Esmae takes off down the hallway, it's all I can do not to follow her. Not because I'm unbearably nosy, but because I would love nothing more than to put off what I know I must do.

Princesses do not shy away from their duty, Radha. My father's voice is an unwelcome, persistent presence in my mind. It's incredibly annoying that in spite of the fact that he has spent most of my life ignoring me, the few things he's bothered to say to me over the years are the ones that come back to pester me when I'd least like them to.

"Are you going to stand out there all day?"

I jump at the sound of Rickard's deep voice from inside his rooms, and my face instantly turns a hot, guilty red.

Clearing my throat and trying to compose myself, I inch into the room. "Good afternoon, Master Rickard."

"Radha," he says and smiles. He actually smiles. At *me*. He gestures to one of the empty chairs. "Please," he adds, warm and pleasant. "Sit."

I can't detect any anger in either his voice or his kind, weathered face, but it must be there. How can he not be angry with me?

"My father," I blurt out, before I can stop myself. *Princesses consider their words carefully, Radha*. Well. So much for that. "My father let me return with the Wych army, and in exchange, he asked to meet with you."

Rickard nods. "Of course. I expected it. Let him know that I'm available whenever is convenient for him."

There is a quiet sadness in his voice, like he's more resigned than anything else. "You're not worried?" I ask. "About coming face to face with him again?"

"We have met in this life," he reminds me. "Before he took his vow of silence. When he revealed his rebirth and confronted me about what I had done to him when he was Ek Lavya."

"But this time will be different."

"Yes, it will."

"Well," I say awkwardly, "I'll let him know. Thank you." I should stand and leave, but I find that I'm rooted to my chair. I take a deep breath, trying to maintain even a little of the poise I was taught from the moment of my birth. As calmly as I can, I say, "I'm sorry."

He shakes his head. "There is no need."

"There *is*," I insist. "Esmae told me you understand why I did what I did, but that doesn't make it okay. I ruined you."

"I think you'll find that it takes more than the prick of a needle to ruin me," he says gently. "I am a warrior, a loyal servant of Kali, and a devoted father and grandfather. No matter how strong or weak my body is, those things remain true. You did not have the power to take that from me."

I feel my cheeks go warm, but I say, "In that case, I still want you to know that I'm sorry. I should have known better."

At that, a small, sad smile flits across his tired face. "We have all made poor choices when we should have known better. What I did to your father, in his previous life, was a terrible betrayal. My pride prevented me from seeing the error of it before it was too late. But you would think, having done that, that I would learn from my mistake, but I did not. Eighty years later, I cursed Esmae."

My eyes widen. I didn't know that.

"I was so angry that she lied to me," Rickard goes on, "I was so *hurt* by it, that I did not stop to consider her reasons before I said the words that will, eventually, doom her. I love that child, but because of my pride and my rashness, I will be yet another instrument in her destruction. So, you see, you are not alone in your mistakes, Radha. And as the one you wronged, take me at my word when I ask that you forgive yourself."

He must see something on my face, some sign of my reluctance to accept his forgiveness and my own, because he reaches out and pats me on the hand. "You are young," he says. "You will, I hope, grow to an old and happy age, but you know there are no certainties in this life. You do not need my permission or my advice, but I am going to give it to you anyway: do not waste your precious time being afraid to live. Do not waste your time on fear or guilt. Live, and love, and find joy in whatever you can."

Do not let your father's voice in your ear hold you back. He doesn't say it, but I hear it anyway.

Or maybe that particular voice is mine.

Sybilla is arguing with the young guard posted outside the rose garden. This is not exactly surprising because Sybilla is usually arguing with someone but what *is* surprising is the nature of the argument.

"You must know something," Sybilla is saying, her long red ponytail almost aquiver with indignation. "How can you know *nothing* about plants?"

"*You* seem to know nothing about plants," the boy points out.

"Don't you take that tone with me, Jemsy! What about Henry? Or Juniper? Juniper must know—"

"Just because her name is *Juniper*," Jemsy retorts, "does not mean she knows anything about plants. What's the problem, anyway? Since when do you care about the rose garden?"

"Stop being so nosy," Sybilla snipes, somewhat unreasonably.

Unruffled, Jemsy rolls his eyes. He catches sight of me over Sybilla's shoulder and straightens his posture. "Good afternoon, Princess Radha."

Sybilla turns around at once, her face a picture of mortification. I try very hard not to giggle.

"Are you having trouble with the succulent I gave you?" I ask her in a bland tone, using every muscle in my face to keep myself from smiling. I swear only Sybilla could have a hard time with a plant notorious for its ability to survive just about anything.

"It's being difficult," she says irately.

My efforts to squash my smile are futile. "I can't imagine why I thought it reminded me of you," I remark.

Her mouth twitches, and she hastily covers it up with a scowl. "Do *you* know anything about gardening?"

"Come on," I say, walking past her into the rose garden. It's an enormous, beautiful hothouse, with long, deep troughs of soil imported from Winter and rows of blooms in the most brilliant colors. Max told me once that Elvar is the one who built the rose garden when he was young, and though he now pretends to be uninterested in it because on Kali such frivolous pursuits are frowned upon, Max sees him come in here when he thinks no one is paying attention.

There are a few worktables set up at strategic points in the hothouse, and on one of them, I find Sybilla's succulent. The soil in the little pot is soaked and the spiky leaves of the plant have lost some of their vivid, glossy color, but I suspect that's because they've been practically drowned in water.

"It only needs to be watered once a week or so," I say, tipping the pot gently to one side to let the excess water trickle out. "Once it's dried out a bit, it should be back to normal."

"Oh," she says, her green eyes wide and bright like clear sea glass. "So it's okay?"

I hide another smile. "Yes, it's fine." I want to tell her how much it means to me that she cares so much about this small, silly gift I gave her, because I know it means she cares about *me*, but I keep my mouth shut. Sybilla has a habit of bolting like a skittish woodland creature when the subject of Feelings comes up.

Case in point: she has more or less avoided me since I gave her the succulent and told her I thought she was pretty. I don't know why that's news to her—I *kissed* her, for heaven's sake!—but here we are. I have tried to tell myself that she's just been busy, what with Esmae having only just come home and a war going on and everything, but as the days go by, it couldn't possibly be more obvious that she has time for everyone except me.

Sometimes, I look at her and my breath catches at the way I feel about her. When did this happen? Was it when I first saw her, like in the stories Rama and I used to read to each other as children? I don't think so. The first time we met, she was with Esmae, Max, Elvar, and the others on the bridge when I arrived on Kali. I remember thinking she was beautiful, but I think a lot of people are beautiful. It was an observation in passing, a fleeting thought lost in the mess of grief, anger, and guilt I was feeling at the time.

But then Esmae had Sybilla shadow me, to keep me safe, and I started to see a lot of her. I tried to be friendly, but she was stiff and resentful and offered nothing back. I would probably have left her alone if she had been anyone else, but I saw her with Esmae and Max, saw her laughter and tenderness with them and her fierce loyalty, and it occurred to me that there was something hurt and warm and unutterably lovely under the scowls and thorns. So I persisted. And the more time I spent with her, the more I started thinking about her even when she wasn't there.

I get the impression that Sybilla isn't as sure of her feelings as I am. Or it's not as simple for her.

And I know that maybe what she needs is time and patience, but I don't have either. Even if Esmae stops Sorsha, this is still a war. We might not survive it. What Rickard said to me, about not wasting time, about not being afraid to chase happiness and find what joy I can—well, maybe he was right. Maybe no one has the luxury of time or patience right now.

"I'd like to be with you," I say, and she looks up from the succulent, startled. "I'd like to kiss you more than once. I'd like to hold your hand, and listen to you complain about everything, and protest when you get into bed and your feet are cold." I hesitate, but keep going, refusing to lose my nerve. "If you don't want that, too, that's okay. But I'd like to know. I don't want to wait and hope for something that may not ever happen."

She blinks at me, and blinks some more. "I don't—I mean—"

As she flounders, I resist the temptation to smile at how adorable she is. "Do you want any of it?" I ask gently, cutting her off.

Sybilla looks up at the glass roof of the hothouse, at the succulent, at the roses, and at the floor. In other words, she looks at everything except me. Just when I think she may have forgotten how to speak altogether, she says, so quietly I almost don't hear her: "I want all of it."

"Really?" I ask, my heart jolting against my ribs. "You do?"

"But I don't know how," she says, looking at me now. Sea glass eyes full of uncertainty. "I think I'll make a mess of it."

"That's okay," I say, smiling so wide my face hurts. "I might make a mess of it, too. We can make a mess together, or maybe we won't, or maybe we'll make a mess and then figure out how to clean it up." I frown. "I think I'm losing track of this metaphor."

Too impatient to hold back, I reach for her face and hold it between my hands, tracing the freckles on her cheeks with the pads of my thumbs. A small smile curves the corners of her mouth, but it's the hope in her eyes that really makes me catch my breath.

"What if we lose each other?" she asks.

"Let's not," I say firmly.

CHAPTER EIGHTEEN

Esmae

Princess Katya passes my transmission on to Alex. It's just a place, a time, and the word *please*. It's difficult for me to say that word to him, when I'm still so angry and bitter, but I do it for the memory of a man who, in the end, loved us both.

Even so, as I wait on the bank of a hot spring, while warm water nips at my boots and yellow trees make hush-hush noises above me, I'm not sure he'll come. Maybe he'll think it's a taunt, that I asked him to come back to this place on the edge of the ruins of his city. Or maybe he'll see it for what it is: an echo of a time when we were happy together here.

His footsteps crunch in the snow behind me. I turn to see him, thin and wary, just a boy in the woods.

"Why am I here?" he asks. His voice is steady but carefully blank. The last time I saw him, he was about to pack me away into oblivion and I jabbed him with stasis serum.

But he came.

"If I offered you what I once offered before," I say, biting each word out. "The throne of Kali, shared between you and Elvar. Would you accept?"

He makes an incredulous sound in his throat. "Why would *you* be okay with that?"

"I'm struggling to think of reasons," I admit. I make an effort to unclench my fists and say, "No matter what either of us does, it'll never feel like enough. I don't think I'll ever feel like you've paid enough for Rama, or Sorsha, or the fact that you would have put me back in stasis and left me with a woman you *know* would have killed me—"

"I didn't want that," he protests. "I didn't want any of that."

I smile ruefully. "You say that a lot. You didn't want it. You didn't know. You didn't mean for it to happen. But it still keeps happening, doesn't it? Because you never say no. You never stop her."

"This isn't about our mother," he says wearily. "And if we're going to talk about how we've wronged each other, Esmae, I have a whole list for you, too."

"I took *Titania* from you," I say, nodding. "I destroyed Arcadia right after you told me you loved it. I know. That's what I meant. Nothing we do will ever be enough. We'll always hurt just a little more than we can bear, so we'll keep lashing out until there's nothing of either of us left. Don't you want it to stop?"

"You swore you'd destroy me," says Alex.

"I said that to our mother. She just happened to look like you at the time."

Alex lets out a breath that puffs white before fading into the air. He takes a step forward, but his shoulders are stiff. "It's not enough," he says. "I won't come back and share something with Elvar that was never meant to be his. It's not just you, Esmae. It's him, too. He exiled us. He would have killed us if it hadn't been for Max. I can't let that go."

"What if it was me?" I ask. "What if *I* had the crown? Would you let this end then?"

He sputters a laugh. "That doesn't make me feel any better."

"But you want what's right, don't you?" I point out. "And I was born first."

"So was Elvar," says Alex. "It doesn't mean anything. Queen Vanya chose her heir. Father chose his."

At that, I laugh. "Did Mother tell you that? It sounds like something she'd say."

Alex doesn't deny it. "She also told me not to trust anything you said to me. When she found out I was coming here to speak to you, she warned me. She said you'd probably try to trick me into some kind of truce. She said it's the only way you can win, now that . . ." He trails off, his cheeks flushing like he regrets saying it.

Rage makes my ears ring. "You think I'm here because I'm afraid I can't beat you in battle? You think I'm doing this, trying to end this, because I'm scared that you're *better* than me?"

The pity on his face is worse than if he'd gloated. His kindness is worse than cruelty. "You lost your thumb," he says. "You know what that means."

"Do you *ever* think for yourself?" I snap. "Or do you only ever do what our mother tells you to?"

His face hardens and he turns away, clearly finished with the conversation. "She's the only one I can trust."

And the words come out, raw and furious:

"She's the reason our father is dead."

He goes so still that even the snow goes quiet. When he turns, his face is white with anger. "What the hell is that supposed to mean?"

"She did it for you and Bear," I say, trying to be gentler. "He was going to come find me."

The story spills out, all of it. Alex's face turns whiter and stonier with each word. "You're lying."

"She didn't tell you I existed," I remind him. "She didn't tell you I was born first. Why is it so hard to believe she didn't tell you about this, either?"

"She would never have done that to him!"

"She cut my throat."

"But she loved him."

That shouldn't hurt, but it does. "Meaning, of course, that she never loved me," I say flatly. "So it was easier for her to cut her daughter's throat than it was to fake her husband's death and imprison him for twelve years." I shake my head. "I know how much she means to you. And you must know how much you mean to her. You must know she's capable of this."

"It's not true," he says harshly. "She's done terrible things, but not this. She told me you would lie to me."

I thrust the letter at him, the last one our father ever wrote. "And this? Is this a lie, too?"

He spares the letter a glance before scoffing. "Samples of Father's handwriting are easily available on Kali. You could have faked this."

There's not much more I can do. He's not ready to see.

"One day," I say, walking past him, "this war will end. And I don't know how many of us will still be here when it does, but if you are, I think you'll look around at the kingdom of ghosts you've inherited and tell yourself you never meant for that to happen." I glance back once. "Sooner or later, you have to *mean* things, Alex. You can't let gods and mothers decide everything for you forever."

CHAPTER NINETEEN

Esmae

By the time *Titania*'s warning beacon reaches us on Kali, just days later, I'm ready. That is, if being ready means I feel sick about hurting an incredible, majestic creature who is pretty much blameless, and I don't know if I can win, and I'm angry that it could have been my twin brother taking this risk instead of me.

He was, after all, the one who released her from a place she was safe. Like *Titania* said, he should be the one to die fixing that mistake.

Yet, for some reason, I decided *I* would carry the starsword into battle.

Just like Ash told my father I would.

Sybilla barges into my room. "Where are they?" she asks. Her hair is in a tight braid, her battle gear sleek and fitted and lethal.

"*Titania* says they'll be on Winter in an hour," I tell her, strapping the starsword to my back. I try to ignore how uncomfortable it feels in my left hand.

For a moment, the grim look on Sybilla's face is replaced by mirth. "She could have picked some lonely, forgotten realm, but she picked Winter?"

"*Titania* has something of a grudge against King Ralf, my mother, Alex, and pretty much everyone else with any kind of power on Winter," I reply. "I think it tickles her to imagine them watching the skies in terror. But she did promise she'd lure Sorsha somewhere deserted, so that nobody on the ground gets hurt."

"Good." Sybilla taps her foot against the floor, then adds, as though I wasn't the one to chart this whole plan in the first place, "now, remember, we'll all be in ships. We'll fire at Sorsha with everything we've got. It'll be little more than a nuisance to her, but we just need to distract her so that you can get onto *Titania*'s wing and get close enough to use the starsword."

I strap on my boots. "I know."

"And don't forget—"

"Sybilla."

"Okay, I get it. You know." She watches me work the buckles on my boots, slower than I used to be. And, because she's Sybilla, she doesn't tiptoe around it. "It's not too late to change your mind. Just go down to Winter, hand that sword over to Alexi, and let him get himself killed."

I stand. "You think I'll fail."

"You can't do what you used to be able to," she says. "That's a fact. You're disabled, and there's absolutely no shame in it, but it is catastrophically stupid to act like you're exactly the same as you always were."

"I might not be able to fire an arrow into a fish's eye any-more, but I can hold a sword in my left hand." My anger makes my voice sharp, jagged, like a piece of torn paper. "I know I'm disabled. The fact that my own mother did this to me makes me want to spit nails, but I'm not ashamed. And I know I'm not the same."

For a moment, her face is unguarded and afraid. "Then don't do this," she pleads. "We just got you back."

I wrap my arms around her, and her fingernails press hard into my shoulders, almost desperately. "I'm not going any-where," I promise her.

"Good," she says, a catch in her voice. "Because someone needs to talk me through this whole romance thing, and Max just laughs when I ask *him*."

Laughing, I step back. "I love you. And you'll be okay. I'll make sure of it."

Down in the dock, Max and Amba are already getting the fleet ready. We'll be taking a few dozen starships, small, pow-erful crafts designed for the most speed and maneuverability in battle.

Sybilla squeezes my hand one last time before climbing into the pilot's seat of her starship. I see Radha already in the passenger seat, her eyes wide and anxious as she waves to me.

"Good, you're here," Amba says to me calmly. Too calmly. It's a mask stitched carefully into place, to hide immeasur-able grief and dread.

"Ready?" Max asks. I nod. I'll be his passenger, with easy access to the wing so that I can jump over to *Titania* once we find her. As I watch him climb into his starship, the rest of the Hundred and One pair off into their own ships. The fleet is ready to go.

I hesitate before leaving Amba. I want to tell her I'm sorry. I want to tell her I wish there was another way. But I know she knows all that already.

Amba's mask doesn't crack, but I know her well enough to hear the pain pulsing in her voice as she says, "Be careful."

"I will."

"And tell her—tell her I—"

"I will," I say again. "I promise."

Then I walk away, so that she can fall apart where no one will see her.

The fleet leaves the dock in the Hive formation, each ship packed tightly around ours until the very last moment, when the hive will split apart and the queen will make her move.

As we head down to the pale blue orb of Winter, following Titania's coordinates, I find it almost impossible to speak. A part of me wants to chatter, to distract Max and me both from what we're up against, but I can't make myself string the words together. The last time I went into battle, my mother cut my throat, I destroyed a city, almost got blown up, and was captured. This is my first time back in battle gear since I lost my thumb and whatever was left of my childhood and, frankly, this is not the fight I would have chosen if it had been up to me. I'd have picked something easy. Not a battle with one of the most powerful creatures that has ever existed.

It's Max who speaks first. "Do you remember how you and I once stood in my tower and said we'd do anything to stop this war?" he asks. "Now I'm in celestial battle armor and you're carrying one of the seven most powerful celestial weapons in the universe."

"Too much went wrong," I say. "We never stood a chance."

"It's not too late."

I think of Sorsha, the collateral damage in everyone else's wars. What's happened to her isn't fair, just as what happened to Rama wasn't fair. In trying to give him some kind of justice, all I've done is wreak more havoc, but isn't that better than letting it go? Wouldn't it be more wrong to say "okay, this terrible thing happened to someone who didn't deserve it, but it's too much trouble to do anything about it" and just move on like it never happened? Don't we all—Rama, Sorsha, *and* me—deserve better than that after everything that's been done to us?

I know how circular that logic is. I do. Somewhere, Alex is making the same argument, reminding himself of all the ways in which *he* has been wronged. By me, by Elvar. That's why I have to finish what I've started. All the ugliness I've seen and done has to be worth something.

"I have to see this through to the end," I say quietly.

He hesitates, like there's something he wants to say, but chooses not to. "But you can choose the way this ends," he says instead.

"There's only one way this can end. You know that." I look down at my right hand, clenched into a fist, four fingers and a stiff prosthetic thumb. "It's him, or me. Neither of us will let it end any other way."

Max stares ahead, into the deep, fathomless blue of Winter's seas as we coast over the water. His eyes, the impossible dark of a god's eyes, look like they've seen a thousand cataclysms and are afraid that they will see a thousand more.

"The girl you were, the girl of stories and hope, is still here," he says. "I loved her. And I loved the girl who wanted to set the world on fire. I've loved every version of you I've ever known, Esmae. And, you know, after everything we've both seen and done, all the cruelty and ugliness and rage up and down the galaxy, maybe the world deserves to burn. Maybe we deserve the girl who'll burn it."

In spite of myself, I'm captivated. "But?"

"But maybe it's not about what we deserve," he replies. "Maybe it's about what we need. And at the end, I think we'll need a different girl. One made up of both rage *and* hope. A girl who won't swallow the stars but will light them up instead."

When we find *Titania* and Sorsha, on an uninhabited part of Winter, they're caught in a maelstrom of claws and wings and metal and scales. Sorsha dwarfs *Titania* in size, but *Titania* makes up for that in power and sheer indestructability.

I watch in both horror and wonder. In this desolate expanse of snow, sea, and rock, they are two behemoths defying the laws of nature.

I am an insect in a world of giants. The thought comes unbidden, an echo of the past, and it's so unexpected that it stuns me. It's the ghost of a girl I had thought was gone.

Titania must have despised every minute of it, but she had to have goaded Sorsha to lure her here, had to have said something to make her angry enough to follow her here and fight her like this. It's a battle that can never end, because neither of them can harm the other.

Dread coils tight in my chest, but I unbuckle myself from my seat and push open the hatch.

"It's time."

Max's jaw tightens, but he just nods and kisses my forehead. "I love you," he says. "You'll be okay."

Maybe it's a lie, but it's one we both need to hear right now. The truth will make us falter, and we really, *really* can't afford to falter.

"I love you, too."

I fit my earpiece, climb out of the hatch, and brace myself against the left wing of the starship. As the rest of our fleet splits away from us and begins to fire on Sorsha, peppering her with gunfire that will distract and annoy her, *Titania* dives out of their battle and swoops across the water to me.

She slows down as she pulls level with Max's ship, and I leap from the wing of one ship to the other.

"I hate this," *Titania* says miserably, her voice crackling over my earpiece, barely audible over the roar of the wind and sea.

I hate it, too.

As she dips away from Max and back in Sorsha's direction, I get into position. There's a shorthand we're all taught when our teachers train us in wing war. *Boots, balance, brace.* *Boots* is a reminder to activate the magnetic pulse in our shoes that will keep us tethered to our ship's wing. *Balance* is exactly what it implies. And *brace* is a reminder to crouch, to give us as much stability as possible until it's time to attack. Without even thinking about it, I activate my boots and fall into place.

I pull the starsword out of its sheath on my back. It's steady in my left hand. It doesn't feel right in that hand, and I know I won't be able to swing with the strength and agility I used to, but I can adapt. I can do this.

By now, Sorsha has batted at least three ships out of the sky, her enormous, beautiful tail swatting at them like flies. They're on the ground below her, mostly undamaged because the snow broke their fall.

Then, just as *Titania* approaches Sorsha, their wings just a few feet apart, I see something on the horizon.

Ships. And these aren't ours.

"Do you think Alexi came to help?" I hear Radha ask over our earpieces.

We all hesitate, waiting to see what's coming.

An instant later, everything goes wrong.

The ships, my brother's ships, fly straight for Max, Sybilla, and the rest of the Hundred and One. Gunfire explodes across the air, ugly and violent, as the starships scatter to dodge the attack and strike back.

"ARE THEY FUCKING JOKING?!" Sybilla shrieks, her voice piercing my ear with the precision of a spear.

I grit my teeth. I'd like to blame Alex for this, but I can't. For all his flaws, I know he would never have attacked us, not here, not like this. It just isn't in him to use an opportunity like this to cut down some of his enemies. This isn't his work. And with both my mother and Leila Saka on his side, it's not hard to guess whose work it really is.

"Esmae, pull back!" Max yells.

"No!" I shout back. "Just keep them away from me. *Titania* and I can do this."

So they fly out across the water. A ship bursts into flames, and I don't dare to look to see whose side it belonged to. This may be the only chance we ever get to stop Sorsha. I can't waste it.

"Keep talking to me," I order them all. "I need to know you're all still alive!"

Their voices, a hundred and one of them, sound like a song in my ear as *Titania* soars away from the water, across the snow, and slams hard into Sorsha's flank.

She's even bigger than I remember up close, her wingspan so huge it blocks out the sun as *Titania* swoops below her. Sorsha roars and twists in the air, snapping her jaws at me, but *Titania* dodges away.

"Try to get me close to her throat," I call to *Titania*, jaw clenched so tight I'm amazed I haven't broken any teeth. If I have to commit the unforgivable crime of killing the last great beast left in the universe, I'm going to make sure it's as quick and painless as possible.

Boots, balance, brace is the only thing that keeps me attached to *Titania* as she spins, diving back over Sorsha's wings to get near her throat.

As the edge of *Titania*'s wing approaches Sorsha's throat, I adjust my grip on the starsword and wait for my moment.

There!

I spring out of my crouch and strike, but I misjudge how far I need to thrust with my left hand and the sword barely glances off Sorsha's scales.

Sorsha pivots, astonishingly fast for her size, and lashes out with her tail. I dive flat and her scales skim my back. I roll over and swing the starsword, but, again, I miss.

"I know you can do better than that," *Titania* remarks. "Your heart's not in it, but it needs to be or she'll kill you."

I scowl, but I don't reply because she's not wrong. Instead, I concentrate on keeping my balance as she surges upward, slamming into Sorsha's underbelly, giving me another opportunity to thrust my sword into the slender, vulnerable gap between the scales at Sorsha's throat.

I miss.

No, that's not true. I don't even try.

What is *wrong* with me? I, and everyone else in this galaxy, will die if I don't do what's necessary.

It's in that moment, as I try to knock some sense into myself, that the wrongness of all of this overwhelms me. It's not just the memory of the pain in Amba's voice, or Sorsha's innocence, or even the battle between the Hundred and One and Leila Saka's troops out over the sea. It's not just the fact that I hate having to do this.

It's Sorsha.

It's the fact that she's still here.

Our plan was for the Hundred and One to keep her attention on them while *Titania* and I slipped past them and took Sorsha by surprise. We assumed there was absolutely no other way to keep Sorsha from taking off into outer space the moment she realized she'd been lured into an ambush.

But the Hundred and One aren't here to distract her. She knows this is an ambush.

Why, then, is she still here?

"Stop," I say to *Titania*. "Slow down and hover near her head."

"That is a *terrible—*"

"Just do it!"

Grumbling, she does as she's told. The sounds of Max, Sybilla, and the Hundred and One are still in my ear, but they sound muted and far, far away. *Titania* and I slow down, engines rumbling, coming to a stop in the air in front of Sorsha's surprised face. I march down *Titania*'s wing, all the way to the tip of her nose, where Sorsha's golden eyes, long snout, and nostrils tower above me. She could open her mouth and swallow me whole, but she doesn't.

"Why aren't you trying to win?" she growls. Her voice doesn't come out of her mouth, but, rather, seems to reverberate inside my head. It's the strangest and most extraordinary sensation.

"Why aren't you?" I retort. I should be terrified, standing nose to nose with a creature a hundred times my size, but I feel only wonder.

We stare at each other, eyes narrowed, golden and gray. And just like that, I know.

"You *want* me to win," I breathe.

"She told me her future was death," says *Titania*, quiet and unhappy. "Hers, or everyone else's. I guess she doesn't want it to be everyone else's."

"Someone must end it, sooner or later," Sorsha says. "It might as well be you. You, who have earned my sister's love. It seems right that it be you."

"Well, I'm not doing it," I reply, suddenly surer of this than I have been of anything in a long time. "There's another way."

"There is no other way. The curse cannot be broken."

"You could go back to Anga."

A soft puff of air slips out of Sorsha's nostrils, almost knocking me over. It's the saddest laugh I've ever heard.

"I cannot go back," she says. "Amba is mortal now. If I went back, I would be alone."

"Ships can travel to Anga," I insist. "Amba loves you. It would break her heart to lose you here. If you went back to Anga, she would visit you. I would visit you. And yes, we're mortal, but after we're gone, Amba's brothers and sister would keep you company until you die old and happy, just the way it should be."

She's quiet for a moment, as if, in spite of herself, she's letting the possibility of that future unfold inside her mind. "That is a beautiful dream, little lion," she says at last. "But it is just a dream."

I was hopeful once. Maybe Max was right. Maybe that girl isn't gone. Because this feeling, right now, feels an awful lot like hope.

I raise the starsword, so that its blade sparkles in the sun. Deliberately, I let it fall, clattering off the edge of *Titania*'s nose, dropping to the snow fifty feet below.

"I'm not going to kill you," I say, crossing my arms over my chest, "so if you really want to spare the lives of everyone who will die if you keep devouring the stars, then you'd better think about that dream. We can save you *and* save the world, Sorsha."

I don't think I'm imagining the longing in her voice as she says, "It is a long way to Anga. A long, long time to resist this terrible, insatiable hunger. I do not think I'm strong enough to resist. I think I would give in to my hunger, abandon this dream, and your world will end."

"And I think you *are* strong enough."

"You don't understand," she says, anguished. "You cannot imagine how much it hurts. I am nothing but rage and hunger. They will overpower me, as they always do."

There's a lump in my throat, but I force myself to speak. "You're wrong," I tell her. "I do understand. I know how it feels to be cursed, to pay for something you didn't do. I know how it feels to want something you can never have. And more than anything, I know how it feels to hurt so much that all you want to do is make everything else hurt the same way. You're not the only one putting the stars out, Sorsha."

"Let us help you," *Titania* begs as Sorsha stares at me in shock. "Let us help you find your way home."

I clench my hands at my sides, so full of hope it hurts more than I can bear. "Please," I whisper. "*Please.*"

Tired, anguished golden eyes look into mine, uncertain.

And out of the corner of *my* eye, I see something. A ship. A boy on its wing. A sword.

Alex raises the starsword.

"No!" I scream.

The sword comes down.

Sorsha, *Titania*, and I fall out of the sky.

CHAPTER TWENTY

Esmae

Titania protects me from the worst of the fall, so I'm mostly just bruised when we crash into the snow. I stagger to my feet, coughing up ice, my head spinning. At first, I think the dull, distant hum of sound is just an effect of the fall, but then I put my head to my head and feel that my earpiece has fallen out. I can't hear *Titania*, or Max, or anyone.

And I can't hear Sorsha.

I stumble across pebbles and ice to where Sorsha has fallen, her bright scales gleaming in the pale sunlight, her wings folded over her like a blanket. Her blood is the same gold of her eyes. It stains the snow, gilding it like an obscene painting, as if the sparkling beauty of the color can somehow make up for the fact that she's dead.

I suppose I should be happy that she's finally at peace, her curse ended, but I'm not. I'm *raging*.

I kneel beside her head and pull the starsword out of the gap between her scales. Tears slide down my face and I feel like I could snap the sword in two.

"I'm sorry," I sob. "I'm so sorry."

I stroke her nose, the smooth, gleaming scales like cold, hard jewels beneath my hand. I'm glad I got to tell her that Amba loved her. And I'm glad that the last thing she was thinking of when she died was a beautiful dream.

A small movement out of the corner of my eye makes me look up. Kirrin stands on the other side of Sorsha's head, his face contorted with remorse. Behind him, shimmering faintly in the light like ghosts, are Tyre and Thea, and a woman with black hair and dark purple skin, and a man with horns, and scores of others, stretching out across the snow. A host of gods to bear witness to the passing of the last great beast in the universe.

"It had to be done."

Alex's voice electrifies me into standing. I shove the sword into its sheath and spin around to face my brother. He looks as sorry as Kirrin does, but I have no time for it.

Furious, my voice choked with tears, I push him hard in the chest. He lets me. "You arrogant, interfering bastard! You didn't have to kill her!"

"*You* came here to kill her. Why are you angry with me for doing what you came to do?"

"Because she was going to go home!" I shout. "She was going to let us help her. We could have put this right!"

Alex looks bewildered. "You dropped the sword, Esmae. She looked like she was about to bite your head off! I did what I had to do!"

"Oh, please," I scoff. "You saw me drop the sword and decided it was the perfect opportunity for you! You didn't kill her because you thought I was in danger. You killed her so that the rest of the world would like you again!"

"Is that really what you think of me?" Alex demands, looking furious and hurt. "Seriously?"

"It looks like we'll always think the worst of each other," I spit, pushing past him. "Get out of my way. I need to find out what your general's done to Max and the others."

"I called my ships off," he says. "I didn't . . ."

He stops. I choke a sound that could have been a laugh. "No, go on, finish. I can probably guess, though. You didn't mean for that to happen?"

He's silent, his ears red.

Sure enough, I can see that our ships have started to land on the beach. Other than a few fiery wreckages in the sea, getting gradually doused by the waves, there's no sign of any of Alex's ships anymore.

I find a spare earpiece in the pocket of my tunic and turn it on. My voice is a croak as I ask, "Is everyone still there? Max? Sybilla? Jemsy?"

"We're okay," a chorus of voices reply. Familiar heads start to pop out of the starships. Radha's throwing up on the beach while Sybilla holds her hair back, just like on the Empty Moon, and it's a small jolt of familiarity in the chaos. I look for Max, and my chest feels a little less tight when I see him. His ship is damaged and his forehead is bleeding, but he's alive.

And Sorsha isn't.

Just as I wonder how I could have felt anything like hope just a few minutes ago, a high, unearthly wail breaks through my rage.

Startled, Alex and I both turn toward the sound. "That sounded like—"

Before he can finish, we hear the wail again, and it's so raw and broken, it sends a chill down my spine.

Blanching, Alex takes off at a dead run. I follow, even though I don't want to, even though a part of me tells me that I don't want to see.

Our mother is the one wailing. She stands at the edge of the water, struggling with one of Alex's generals, an elderly man who is doing his best to keep her from plunging into the sea.

Alex skids to a halt beside them, surf spraying into his face as he grabs our mother's arm and helps the general pull her away from the waves. "Mother, what are you. . ."

Then he sees. We *all* see. Leila Saka stumbles out of the waves, soaking wet, her hard, sharp face drained of all color. She's dragging something with her, a grayish, boy-shaped something, and I can't even fathom how much strength it must have taken to pull him through the water just to bring him back to shore.

My mother collapses to her knees beside him. Leila hangs her head. "I'm sorry, Kyra," she says hoarsely. "I couldn't save him."

A strangled sound comes out of Alex. He kneels and reaches roughly for the boy-shaped thing on the beach, turning it over. He reels back at the face that he sees, and our mother lets out one last, raw, shattered cry, and I force myself to understand what I'm seeing.

The boy-shaped thing is Bear. But my sunny, gruff giant of a brother is bloody, burned, and drowned, his brown skin turned gray, his armor torn and blackened. He and Leila must have been in one of the ships that went down in flames.

My brother, who liked to make honey cakes and chose me once.

The sound that lodges in my throat is somewhere between a sob and a cry, but it stays there, trapped inside me, because I have no right. Bear was the sweetest and best of us, and I loved him, but he wasn't mine. He was theirs.

I watch my mother and brother on their knees. I've raged at what they have done to me, to Rama, to Sorsha, to my father. I've waged this war to make them pay.

And now they are paying. My mother, especially, will pay every single moment of the rest of her life. Everything she ever did was to keep her sons alive and now one of them is gone. Nothing I or anyone else could possibly do to her will ever be worse than this.

I swear I will break you before the end.

It's not the end, but she is broken.

I got what I wanted.

And it cost me my brother.

My knees buckle, but someone keeps me from falling. Someone hard and warm behind me. Max. A hand closes around mine. Sybilla. They don't speak, but I know they're there.

I take one shaky step forward, though I'm not sure what I plan to do, and the movement makes my mother look up. Her eyes land on me.

"I knew this would happen sooner or later," she says in a hollow voice. She knows what I know. That they are destroyed. "Why didn't anyone believe me?"

"That's enough, Kyra," Max cuts in, stepping around to stand in front of me. His face is hard and severe. "This wasn't Esmae's fault. She wasn't even part of the battle."

"She made me a promise," my mother says. She doesn't sound angry or upset. It's worse than that: she sounds like she's dead, too. "She told me that because I wanted only two children, by the end, that was what I would have. And now look. I have only two children."

But the one she lost wasn't supposed to be Bear. It was supposed to be Alex or me.

Alex looks at me then, and there is a storm in his eyes, a horror and disbelief, that makes me stagger a step back.

My mouth is dry, but I try to speak. "I didn't—I didn't mean for—"

Alex's face twists. "Sooner or later," he says bitterly, "You have to *mean* things, Esmae."

CHAPTER TWENTY-ONE

Titania

On Kali, I wait, in a quiet stone courtyard open to the skies, until a golden god arrives.

As soon as I see him, the sun god with that pleased, smug look on his face, I lose my temper. "Why didn't you tell me?" I rage. "Why didn't you tell me that Sorsha wasn't the only one who would die?"

He frowns. "I could not possibly have foreseen how it would all play out."

"I think you could have," I retort. "In fact, I think you did. Maybe you didn't know what would happen to Bear, but I think you knew Esmae would try to save Sorsha, and you couldn't have that, not when Sorsha wanted to avenge her mother and her very existence threatened yours. You're too much like your father."

Suya's eyes flash. "You have no idea what you speak of."

"I've seen a thousand of Amba and Kirrin's memories," I say coldly. "I think you'll find I have a *very* good idea. You didn't go to Alexi because you thought Esmae was dead. You went to him, and told him he could be the hero of the star system again, because you wanted to make sure *someone* would kill Sorsha. You needed someone there in case Esmae chose to be kind." Electricity dances furiously along my wings. "And you got what you wanted, didn't you? She's dead. Your sister is grieving. But you don't care about hurting Amba, the goddess who saved your life and raised you, just so long as Sorsha is gone."

For a moment, Suya says nothing. He looks into the distance, his jaw clenched, with streaks of red across his bronze cheeks. I would call this shame, but I doubt he's capable of feeling such a thing.

"We had a bargain, you and I," he says at last, curtly. "I came to honor it."

"Our bargain was for Esmae to kill Sorsha. She didn't."

"She made it possible for Alexi to kill her. I'm not going to withdraw what I offered you over a technicality."

That seems generous. *Too* generous.

I study him, analyzing the minute movements of his jaw and the way he won't look directly at me in spite of the fact that I am a spaceship taking up almost his entire field of vision.

"Was this part of what you dangled in front of Alexi?" I ask him in what I hope is a dangerously quiet voice. "Did you tell him that if he killed Sorsha, he'd redeem himself *and* he would get rid of his twin sister's unbeatable ship in one fell swoop?"

"Why does what I told him matter?" Suya counters, which I can only assume is a yes. "You knew the consequences of becoming human."

"I want the war to end first," I snap. "I don't want to be become human until after all this is over."

"That wasn't what we agreed," he replies. A little bit of the smugness has crept back. "I will transform you now, or never. Do you still want this?"

I should refuse, but I know that Esmae went to ambush Sorsha, in part, because of me. To give me this. I couldn't possibly repay that friendship and loyalty by refusing the very thing she risked her life for.

Also, selfishly, I still want it. I long for it.

"Yes," I say, furious with both Suya and myself. "I want this. And if you have any decency at all, you'll wait until after the war to give it to me."

"No one has ever accused me of decency," says the sun god, and vanishes.

The transformation is nothing like what I experienced on Ashma. There, it just happened, instantaneously, and I didn't feel a thing.

This is slow and, worse, I experience something I've never felt before: pain. If I could cry out, I would. It radiates up and down my wings and spine like fire, like I am ablaze. Parts of me twist, like they're melting in the heat, my metal deforming and reshaping itself into skin, my new limbs carving themselves out of the wreckage of my old self.

It's agony, but I scarcely notice it, because I am changing on the inside, too. Caches and caches of data, a neat and perfectly ordered filing system of memories, knowledge, and connectivity, all compressed into something small and imperfect and messy. A human brain replaces my database, a heart replaces my engine, and the anguish of transforming from my almost infinite self into something so utterly finite is unimaginable.

I want this. I remind myself of that. I want this more than anything. I *want* to be messy, and finite, and marvelously, miraculously human.

But it would be a lie to pretend that it doesn't hurt to lose what I was.

When the pain stops at last, I'm curled up and shaking, shivering and damp with what can only be sweat. I can hear the beat of my own heart, feel my own skin. Exhaustion, joy, and sorrow all pulse through me, more acute than anything I have ever felt before. Every sensation is magnified, exaggerated. It's beautiful and terrifying and too much.

Someone wraps a blanket around me, holding me tight until the shivering stops. I peer up, through my damp brown hair, and see a pair of familiar gray eyes.

"You're okay," Esmae says. "I've got you."

"I'm hungry," I reply, and fall promptly asleep.

CHAPTER TWENTY-TWO

Esmae

A cold, quiet dark has settled over me, but it's not the same beast that's kept me company for months. There's not much anger in this darkness, not much rage—this beast is a quieter, sadder creature and it is in so many ways worse than the rage. Where the fury filled me with a manic energy that kept me moving, this darkness holds me still. It carves me hollow.

Titania is human now, and she's having a hard time getting used to it. It's not just that this happened far sooner than any of us expected; it's also the fact that human limitations are frustrating to her ("but why must I shower? I hate the water!"), she hates that she can't fly anymore, and, most of all, she feels terrible that she got the thing she wanted because Sorsha is dead. But, in spite of all of that, I know how happy she is. The sight of her, a young girl scampering all over the palace and city with boundless enthusiasm and wide-eyed wonder, is the only good thing to come out of that day.

I suppose I should be more concerned about losing my indestructible, unbeatable warship, because it is unquestionably a blow to our side in this war, but I can't seem to muster up the energy for concern, or fear, or *anything* other than this endless, mournful quiet. The last great beast of the universe is gone, my brother is dead, and I am too hollow to be able to see much beyond that.

Losing Sorsha has taken its toll on Amba, who spends more and more time up on the eastern tower, alone, staring at the stars. Meanwhile, the palace is in mourning for Bear. Even Elvar, in spite of all his conflicted feelings about his nephews, looks like he's aged a decade overnight. And outside these walls, Kali seems caught between sorrow for our lost prince and relief that we have all been saved from certain destruction. Or so I'm told. I don't watch any of the news broadcasts myself. For their sakes, I'm glad that our people get to celebrate the fact that the stars will now stay exactly where they are, the sun won't budge, and life will go on. I am. I just find myself unable to celebrate with them.

I sleep. It seems to me that no sooner have I woken up than I'm tired again. All I want to do is sleep.

One night, I wake up in the dim glow of the nightlight and find the other half of the bed empty. It takes me a moment to find Max, sitting on the floor with his back to the bed, his head bent over his arms as his shoulders shake with grief. He grew up with Bear. And after a lifetime of trying to keep him safe, Max must feel like he's failed, and I don't think he can bear that. I seem to have forgotten how to cry, but my heart feels bruised for him as I reach across and stroke his hair.

Days pass. I feel even more hollow. There's not much left of me.

When I tell Max this, one evening when we're alone in his rooms, he shakes his head. "You're not going anywhere," he says. "Terrible things have happened to you, and I think this may be the first time you've let yourself stop long enough to feel them. You didn't stop after Rama, or after Shloka, or even after we got you back after Arcadia. It's all coming at you at once, everything you've pushed away for months. You're grieving and traumatized."

"I don't know how to make my way through to the other side of it," I tell him. "I can't see anything but the dark. I feel like I've fallen down a cold, dark hole and I'll never get out."

Max considers me for a moment, one hand absently scratching between a wolf's ears. I think it's Sorrow.

Then he says, "Come with me."

I'm too tired to protest, so I follow him, only a little curious. We take an elevator across the palace and up into his tower, to the workshop where he makes and fixes things.

The last time we were here, I woke up with temporary paralysis and he was captured by Kirrin's Blue Knights, but I don't have time to dwell on this. Max takes me to a worktable in the corner, where a miniature wooden chariot sits, parts of it painted bright, glossy red.

"It's for the toyshop," he explains. "I haven't had a chance to work on it in a while, but it's almost done."

Somewhat bewildered, I watch as he unscrews the can of red paint and picks up a clean brush. Instead of dipping it into the paint, which is how I assume one paints, he holds it out to me.

"Take the brush."

"What?"

"Take the brush," he repeats patiently. "Paint this panel."

"I don't have very good fine motor skills with these," I remind him, wiggling the four fingers and prosthetic thumb of my right hand.

"If you can hold a knife, you can hold a brush. Use your left hand if you like."

"I don't even know how to paint!"

His mouth twitches. "I'm sure I can fix it if you mess up."

"I don't see why—"

"When I come in here and make something, it keeps me *me*," he says. "Everything outside this tower is blood and war and grief, but in here, I can forget what's outside for a little while."

I take the brush from him, using my left hand. "And you think painting this chariot will make me forget, too?"

"Maybe. Maybe not. But either way, it's something to do that has nothing to do with this war. And who knows?" Amusement lights up his dark eyes. "You might even have fun. Imagine that!"

"I am perfectly capable of having fun," I grumble, dunking the brush in the tin of paint.

I sweep the brush across the wooden panel of the chariot. Bright, shiny red spreads across the wood. It's streaky and clumsy and I get paint all over my hand, but I think even that's an achievement for someone who has never so much as painted a fingernail before.

And the truth is, it's nice to see my skin red with paint instead of blood.

Max moves over to the other side of the chariot and gets to work with a brush of his own. His strokes are smoother, neater, and cover more of the wood than mine do, so I copy the way he moves the brush, keeping the direction consistent instead of flailing back and forth like I had been. It's surprisingly easy to adapt to the rhythm.

I don't forget. I didn't expect to, but I wondered. I wondered if there was some magic here that would work on me, too. If there is, it doesn't. My heart still feels hollow. My bones are still so tight around me that it's just a little hard to breathe. The ghosts are still at my side, the beast that keeps me company is still on my shoulder.

The gold of Rama's eyes as he died. My mother with a bloody knife in her hand. The cold of the snow as I lay bleeding in the dark. The longing in Sorsha's voice. Bear's gray face. The fire eating up Arcadia, just like I am being eaten up.

Ghosts, everywhere.

"Esmae." Max's voice breaks in. "The chariot's done."

The panel I painted looks nice. More than nice. It's beautiful. The paint is so smooth and glossy that I can see my reflection in it. The Esmae in the paint has a shocking, ugly white scar across her throat and her eyes are too wide and hollow, but she smiles at me.

I didn't forget, but I feel something I haven't felt in a long time. *Pride*. I did this. I made something, and it's not dark, angry, and ugly.

I didn't know anything I did could still be beautiful.

A sound splinters the silence of the tower. It takes me a moment to make sense of it. It's a sob. Tears flood down my face and I can't speak, can't move, can't breathe.

Max pulls me to him, getting paint in my hair, but I don't care. I clutch fistfuls of his shirt and cry into his chest. Whatever flimsy, fragile glue was still holding my fractured pieces together is gone, and I fall apart. Pieces of me smashing all over the floor.

"I've broken everything." It's a distraught cry, pulled from a deep, secret place where I'm not yet hollow.

Max pulls back just enough to look into my face. "Broken things can be fixed. And when they can't be fixed, they can be remade."

Remade. The word echoes, resonating in that deep, secret place in my heart. *Remade.* Is that even possible for me? Can I collect the shattered pieces of myself and be remade? Can I remake what I've broken?

"How do I start?" I whisper.

"Take the starsword back to Ash," he says. "After that, we'll figure it out together."

CHAPTER TWENTY-THREE

Titania

Esmae goes to Ashma without me. I shouldn't feel jealous that she's flying a ship that's not me, but I do. I have, it must be said, always had a talent for petulance, and I find it even easier to achieve as a human. Sulking, I wander aimlessly around the palace until I find myself on the arched stone bridge that connects the north and east wings. Below the bridge is an artificial stream, carved into the stone of the ground and lined with pebbles and shrubs.

For some reason, I'm on edge. It's not just because Esmae went to Ashma without me. There's something else, but I'm not sure what it is. I feel like I'm forgetting something, something important. And no matter how hard I try, I can't quite get hold of it.

Of course, I've forgotten a lot of things. My brain can't hold all the data that my processors used to. I always backed my data up, naturally, so I didn't lose very much of it permanently when Suya transformed me so abruptly, but sifting through data on a sluggishly slow external database is nothing like the streamlined, intuitive process I took for granted as a machine.

I find myself a perch on the bridge's stone ledge and dangle my feet out over the stream below. I scowl at my reflection in the water. I look so *young*.

Worse, I *feel* young. As a ship, I was no older than I am now, but I had the benefit of speedy processors, constant access to an infinite stream of data in the ether, and a glimpse into thousands of two gods' memories. Without that, and with the added chaos of human emotion thrown into the mix, I am unsure, quick to overreact, and did I mention unsure?

Unsure. Me.

And that, of course, is the heart of the problem. Right now, *Titania* the ship would be flying Esmae to Ashma, but that is beyond what I am now. I wasn't even allowed to go with her. Esmae was quite firm about it: "You're not indestructible anymore," she said before she left. "In this body, you're untrained and vulnerable."

"And I suppose," I said bitterly, "my brain isn't much use either, without the data and access it used to have."

"I told you before, you don't ever have to feel like you've got to be useful," she said, but I noticed she didn't deny that my brain is not what it was. "This about your safety. I can't put you at risk."

What I didn't say was that I *want* to be useful. I need purpose. I have spent my entire existence as a fearsome, powerful entity. I can't just adjust in the blink of an eye to the life of a child who must be sheltered.

It's not that I don't love being human. I *do*. But I know the others must feel like they lost something precious when they lost their ship. I certainly do.

On top of that, the gamut of human emotion has been difficult to adjust to. No one ever told me there would be mood swings. Ever since Suya transformed me, I feel like I am two different people, both fighting to be in control of me: one is unsure and frustrated by what I have lost, but is still excited about the good things I have gained, while the other is bitter, dissatisfied, and unreasonably resentful of everyone around me.

I can't think of any reason for such resentment. No one else chose this fate for me. Still, just yesterday, I found myself irrationally, furiously angry with Amba at dinner, in spite of the fact that I can't remember her saying anything that could have made me angry, and a few days ago, I felt something alarmingly like contempt when Max and I played cards. *Contempt*. For Max, who I *adore*. It's inexplicable.

Maybe this is what it means to be human. Maybe my feelings are all confused and jumbled up because I'm still learning *how* to be human.

"Hello!"

I look around and find a young boy standing on the bridge just behind me. He's Rickard's grandson, I think. He looks almost exactly like Rickard did when he was this boy's age. I know that because I've seen some of Kirrin and Amba's memories from back then.

"Sebastian," I say, pleased to find I haven't forgotten that.

He beams. "I can't believe you know my name! This is amazing!"

"Why?" I ask, bemused.

"Because you're *you*." He says this in a tone of awe, which is rather gratifying after several days of feeling like everything that was awe-inspiring about me is gone. He hops up on the ledge beside me and says, frankly, "Is it weird? Being like us?"

"Yes, but I'm sure I'll get used to it," I tell him. "I don't regret it, if that's what you're asking."

"I bet it's hard getting used to the way everyone treats you now," he says, a little too astutely. "Like you're just a child."

"How did you know that?" I ask, surprised.

"It's sort of the same for me," he says, sighing. "We're at war, and I want to help, but no one will let me. Max says I'm too young to be in the Hundred and One. Esmae promised me she'd teach me some of my grandfather's tricks, but she never has the time. And my grandfather, well, he won't even talk to me about the war because he wants to protect me." He sticks his jaw out. "But I don't *need* to be protected anymore. I can help!"

"That's how *I* feel! I'm human now, but that doesn't mean I can't help!"

"I imagine this feels even worse for you than it does for me," he says, "because you know what it's like to be treated like you're important and valuable."

This boy wants very badly to be included, the quiet, resentful part of me muses. *That could be useful.*

As soon as I hear the little voice in my head, I'm appalled at myself for thinking such a thing. I hate all these unexpected, ugly feelings I keep having. If this is my brain's way of learning how to be human, I wish it would hurry up and figure it out so that I can stop feeling like this!

"They care about us," I say, in an attempt to convince myself as much as him. "They're not excluding us because they think we can't help. They just want to keep us safe."

"I get that. I just wish there was something we could do, you know? Some way they'd let us help."

"Ah, to be young and enthusiastic," says a voice behind us.

Sebastian and I both jump, almost toppling off the ledge and into the stream twenty feet below.

"You could have killed us both," I complain, somewhat alarmed by my own mortality.

"Don't be so dramatic," Kirrin says, rolling his eyes at me, while Sebastian lets out a squeak at finding himself face to face with a god. "Get off that ledge. I need to speak to you."

I should be annoyed that he's ordering me about like this, but I'm actually rather grateful that there's one person, at least, who is treating me exactly the way they always have.

"Goodbye," I say to Sebastian. "Wait, no, that's not right. I'll see you later? Yes, that's better, isn't it?"

He grins. "Much better."

I follow Kirrin across the bridge, into the north wing, and up a set of spiral stone steps to a balcony. After years of being able to simply have conversations in my control room, completely sure that no one could listen in, it's rather strange to have to actually look for privacy now.

"So," I say. "How are you?"

I'm human now, so the connection between Kirrin and me has been severed, but right before I was transformed, after Bear died, I could feel Kirrin's grief, pulsing across the tether between us. I know he loved Bear, and that he regrets what happened to Sorsha, so it's not a leap to guess he's probably *not* the happiest he's ever been.

"I'm fine," he lies, waving it off like it's unimportant. His dark eyes search mine. "I came to check on you."

I huff. "I don't need to be coddled like—"

"You're not yourself," he says abruptly.

I wave my human hands in front of his face. "Erm, you think?"

"Very witty." He continues to look at me, like he's trying to find something. "There was a moment, as you were becoming human, right before the tether between us snapped. You felt different. Not different like you were human, but different like you were not quite *you*. I didn't like it."

"I don't understand what you're getting at," I say defensively. "Are you saying you don't like who I am now? Because if that's the case, I don't know what to tell you. I had to adapt."

"That's not it," says Kirrin. Still, that searching look. "How do you feel? Do you feel different?"

I stamp my foot. It's remarkably satisfying. "Of course I feel different! Every single part of me has been transformed!" *Interfering, impudent little shit.*

"Excuse me?" Kirrin says, his face an almost comical picture of shock.

"Did I say that out loud?" I ask in horror.

"Rather loudly, yes."

A part of me is aghast at the wave of anger that prompted the outburst, but another part of me is rather entertained by Kirrin's reaction. I turn away, pressing my fists to my forehead, trying in vain to streamline my thoughts into some kind of order.

"You're right," I admit reluctantly. "I don't feel like me. I keep thinking and feeling things that don't make sense."

"To be fair, that sounds quite human," Kirrin says wryly.

I turn back to him. "It'll settle down, won't it? I'll feel more like myself once I've had a chance to get to know this new body and my new life, won't I?"

He doesn't answer. The wary, searching look on his face unnerves me, and I suddenly want to get away from him.

"Maybe I can help you figure it out," he says at last.

You can't trust him, a voice in my head warns me. *He's the god of tricks. Don't forget that.*

"I'll be fine," I say, a little too sharply. "I just need time to get used to who I am now."

As soon as he's gone, the anger drains out of me. Feeling much better, I make my way to the palace kitchens, where the cooks are always happy to supply me with an endless amount of the most delicious food.

Food is, easily, the best thing about being human. I thought it would be the ability to touch, to be able to hug other people and feel all kinds of textures on my skin, but that was before I understood the magic of food. Over the years, I've seen people eat countless times, of course, but I always understood it as a necessity for survival, like sleeping and breathing. Yes, sometimes it looked like they enjoyed what they were eating, and sometimes it looked like they really, *really* did not, but nothing could have prepared me for the sensory delight of actually eating a meal myself.

No one ever told me about the joy of cold, sweet tea trickling down my throat, or what it's like to let chocolate melt on my tongue, or how it feels to take a bite of spicy, perfectly seasoned roast pork on a skewer. Since I changed, I have eaten everything that's been put in front of me and stolen things off everyone else's plate, too: salted vegetables, ripe fruit, deliciously fat kaju sweets, fluffy rice, every kind of meat there is, and a dizzying array of desserts that make me wake up in the middle of the night with a craving for more.

"Ah, little bird!" one of the cooks calls out, his plump face splitting into a smile. "Come, come! Look at this most beautiful, most perfect lemon cake! What do you think? Here, have a slice. No, no, a bigger slice! It's best when it's fresh out of the oven."

As I sit in a warm, snug corner of the kitchens with a plate of the moistest, gooiest lemon cake on my knees, some of the unease returns. I've forgotten something and, for some reason, it's really, really important that I remember it. But what it is? What have I forgotten?

It doesn't matter, the voice in my head says. *Finish your cake.*

So I do.

CHAPTER TWENTY-FOUR

Esmae

It takes me sixteen hours to fly to Ashma, following a map of constellations Titania programmed into my starship. When I find it, I'm surprised by the fact that it's cold, bleak, and still, somehow, beautiful. I don't know if it's the cold clarity of the stars here, or the darkness that feels like calm instead of chaos, but it's lovely when I didn't expect it to be.

Far away, Bear's ashes are scattering to the winds. I should be there to watch, but it was clear that I was not wanted at either the funeral or the cremation. It doesn't really matter. I can see it all in my mind's eye. I can see my brother's soul, the shining spark that made him *him*, ascending into the sky. Any minute now, he'll be crossing the shining bridge of stars to the heavenly realms. I hope our father's waiting for him.

My footsteps don't make a sound as I step into the Temple of Ashma, my eyes on the domed ceiling above, through which I can see stars and lightning. The temple is cool and clean, but empty: the knotted grove of trees in the heart of the room is closed tight, the revolving stone disc displaying the celestial Seven turns quietly on its own, and the doorway with the golden glow that Max warned me about is still open, still alight. I don't approach it. After everything Max, Amba, Kirrin, and Tyre have told me about their father, Ness, I have absolutely no desire to be anywhere near him.

But where's Ash? Why isn't he here? If I hadn't been told several times that there's no way to enter the Temple of Ashma without an invitation, I would be genuinely concerned right now that I'm an unexpected and possibly unwelcome visitor.

But that's not possible. Maybe Ash has no interest in actually speaking to me. Maybe he just wants me to return the sword to its rightful place and leave.

That suits me just fine.

I slide the starsword out of the sheath on my back and cross the temple to the revolving disc. Six of the seven sides of the disc are lit up with the silhouettes of the Seven. There's a dark, empty space for the starsword, so I slide it into place. The seventh side of the disc lights up immediately.

As soon as it lights up, something thumps to the floor.

I jump, looking skittishly around me. What was that? What did I do wrong? Should I have waited for Ash?

As the disc continues to revolve, I see that a different space on it has gone dark. I frown at the symbol, stepping to the side to follow it as it revolves, trying to figure out which of the Seven it is. It's not a bow, or sword, or trident. It's not a chakra, spear, or staff.

Which leaves—

Well, shit.

"The astra."

I yelp, turning. A god stands half a stride away, in black battle gear, his eyes crackling with the same lightning I saw through the domed ceiling.

If I thought Amba had a stern face, it's nothing compared to Ash. He is severe and untouchable, with none of the human qualities Amba and Kirrin possess. His thick, straight brows are drawn together as he studies me, his dark eyes assessing and unforgiving.

"Thank you for returning the starsword," Ash says, his voice deep and quiet.

I take a step back, then glance once more at the empty, darkened space where the most powerful of the Seven was just a minute ago.

I clear my throat. "What happened? Where did it go?"

"It came loose when you restored the starsword to its rightful place." Ash holds up a hand and a lightning bolt materializes in it. It's about the size of a long dagger and his fingers close around it like it *is* a dagger, but daggers don't radiate energy like this. I can *feel* the astra's power, pulsing like a faraway song that's almost too quiet to hear.

Ash and I look at each other in silence. I finally dare to ask, bewildered, "Are you going to smite me with that?"

"The astra is not for smiting," he replies, looking slightly affronted. "It is a holy and powerful weapon that must never be wielded lightly. I, as the destroyer, am charged with its protection and its use. The astra can end the world as you know it."

I really don't like the sound of this. When Kirrin and Tyre told me about the Third War, didn't they make it clear that

Ash never intended to use the astra? Why, then, did it come loose from the disc? Why is he speaking of it as if he's actually considering using it?

"Why would there ever be a reason to end the whole world?"

"Perhaps the world is corrupt, rotten, and shattered," says this dark, ancient god. "Perhaps there is nothing in it worth salvaging. That is when the astra is to be used, to unmake every mortal realm so that Bara, the creator, can start anew."

Still holding that terrible lightning bolt in his fist, Ash walks away from me, to where the grove of trees has opened. He sits down on a throne of knotted roots and branches. His eyes never leave my face.

"Why did it fall out of the disc?" I demand, following him. "Why isn't it still there with the others?"

His eyes are so dark and bleak. "I was asleep," he says. "I would have slept for another ninety years. But your war has become such a cataclysm that my niece and nephew felt they had no choice but to wake me. Had they left me in my Sleep, this could perhaps have been avoided. But they did not. You, your brother, and every other mortal who has played a part in this war over the generations forced their hand and, in doing so, forced mine."

Suddenly, that expression on Max's face, back when we were in the starship flying to ambush Sorsha, makes a whole lot more sense. He looked at me like he wanted to say something, but either couldn't or chose not to. And then what he said, about needing both rage and hope—

He knew. He must have.

"You can't." The words come out before I can think better of them.

Dark brows lift. "I think you'll find I can."

"But gods can't harm us without losing their immortality! That means *you* can't harm us."

"Bara and I wove that limitation around the gods after the Second War," Ash says. "After watching them fight each other and the rakshas over the course of two terrible wars, we decided to take the necessary measures to protect the mortal realms. But Bara, Ness, and I came from the old world before it burned. The limitation does not apply to us."

"You have no right." I don't know about hope, but there's absolutely a whole bucketload of rage in me right now. "You don't get to decide the fates of millions of lives while you watch from the safety of your magical celestial realm. You don't get to just *end* us. You have no right!"

"This is more than my right," he replies. "It is my *responsibility*. It is my sacred charge. If I do not end your world, instantly and mercifully, you and other mortals like you will end it anyway. Except *your* ending will be pain and ash and horror."

"But we wouldn't do tha—"

Those dark brows go up again and I stop. Not because I'm afraid of him, though I *am* afraid, but because I know what was coming out of my mouth was a lie.

"You are brave and unflinching enough to see the truth," says Ash, nodding. "You know what you are capable of. You know that you wanted to destroy everything around you. This war will be the end of your world, Esmae Rey. It would be a violation of my deepest oath not to end it first."

"It shouldn't be up to you." I take another step forward, into the grove of trees. "It's *our* world. What we do to it, good or bad, should be up to us. We should get to choose."

"There was a king who murdered his three wives and nobody stopped him," Ash replies coldly. "There was a queen who cut her own daughter's throat. There was a teacher who betrayed his devoted student. There was a princess who swore she'd burn the world down for vengeance. There have been curses, sacrifices, and treachery. Death, war, and cruelty. The lives of servants and conscripts sacrificed for the ambitions of kings, princesses, and prime ministers. And that is just what *you* know of. I could tell you ten thousand other stories of ten thousand other evils." Lightning crackles wildly above us as Ash shakes his head. "No. You do not deserve to choose."

"But maybe it's not about what we deserve," I say desperately, thinking of what Max said to me. "Maybe it's about what we need."

Ash cocks his head to one side as if considering me. "Go on."

"I—" I falter, the words drying up in my mouth. "I don't—I don't know the answer. I just know that destroying us isn't it. I wanted my mother and brother to hurt for what they'd done and now they *are* hurting, worse than I ever planned, and it turned out I couldn't make that happen without hurting myself, too. So I know that we're reckless and spiteful and cruel, I *know* that. I know why you think there's no hope for us. Every time I start to feel hopeful, something terrible takes it away. I imagine you must feel like that sometimes, watching us destroy ourselves, our planets and even some of *you*. Valin and Amba lost their places in the stars for us. I'm sure you haven't forgiven us for that."

Ash watches me, not speaking. There's not a flicker of a reaction on his face, just that same severe, assessing look.

"I don't know what we deserve *or* need," I admit. My throat feels raw, my chest tight.

"Do you believe it's possible for you and every other mortal in the world to stop destroying yourselves? Do you believe it's possible for your kind to choose peace over your pride?

To choose kindness and the greater good over your own desires? Because I have seen otherwise, time and time again."

"I don't know," I say. "I don't have any answers. I just know that using the astra wouldn't be right."

"That is not your judgment to make," he says.

"Then I guess there's no reason for me to stay here any longer." I don't know why he wanted *me* to bring the sword back to him. I don't know why he wanted to hold this over *my* head. What am I supposed to do? Go home and tell everyone I love that we could all blink out of existence at any moment? "If I could stop you, I would, but I think we both know that that isn't possible."

As I turn away to leave, the golden glow of light from that open doorway catches my eye. I stop, transfixed.

"What is it?" Is that curiosity in the voice of the oldest god in the universe?

I turn back. "If we don't deserve to choose our own ending, you don't deserve to, either."

Ash blinks. And blinks again. For the first time, the bleak, grim look in his eyes vanishes, leaving surprise behind. "I do not see how you've reached that conclusion," he says.

"I know what's in that chamber." I point to the golden glow. "Max told me. It's Ness, your brother. The one who devoured his children. You've kept him alive and asleep for hundreds of years."

Ash's lean, pale hands clench over the arms of his throne, his gauntlets flashing with reflections of the lightning raging above us. "So?"

"So," I say, "You can't let him go. That's a very human failing."

With a twitch of his mouth that I might have interpreted as a smile on anyone else, Ash says, "You're not as meek or as respectful as you should be, Esmae Rey."

"So I've been told." I shrug. "Don't take it personally. I've been a trial to many gods, I promise you."

For a moment, Ash considers me in silence. Then, unexpectedly, he says, "It is your eighteenth birthday next week, is it not?"

"Yes?" It's not really a question, because I know when my birthday is, but I'm thrown by the entirely unrelated topic.

"Go to the Night Temple on your birthday. Pray for clarity."

"Why?" I ask, bewildered. "Will that make you change your mind about using the astra?"

"Go to the Night Temple," he says again. "I will give you a little more time. I will watch. If you truly believe that the people of your world are capable of choosing kindness over their own desires, show that to me. Then, and only then, will I change my mind."

"How can *I* show you that?" I protest. "That isn't possible!"

Ash's eyes don't waver as he shrugs. "Then perhaps you neither deserve nor need a second chance."

CHAPTER TWENTY-FIVE

Esmae

I have visitors waiting for me when I return to Kali.

"Now is *really* not a good time," I object.

"It's necessary," says Max. The expression on his face confirms my suspicion that he knew what Ash would say to me. "Believe me, I know you and I need to talk, but I think you're going to want to see them."

Sybilla scowls at him. "I can't believe you let them set foot on this kingdom," she fumes. "Have you forgotten we're at war? You can't just allow other heads of state to saunter in like it's time for afternoon tea—"

"Heads of state?" I interrupt, swiveling back to Max. "Who?"

He gestures to the door of the parlor. It's the room where Kirrin once sat, disguised as a soothsayer, and told me I was loved by gods I didn't trust and would be betrayed by mortals I did.

He was right, of course.

I follow Max into the parlor, with Sybilla hard on our heels, and stop short in the doorway, surprised.

There are four women in the room: Prime Minister Gomez of Shloka, Princess Katya of Winter, Princess Shay of Skylark, and a woman in her late twenties whom I recognize as Queen Fanna of Elba.

Max clears his throat. "I'll leave you to it."

I whip my head back to look at him. "Excuse me?"

"They asked to speak to you, not me," he says. "I'll be right outside."

I glower at his back as he leaves. So does Sybilla, for that matter, but he takes her by the elbow and yanks her out of the room with him.

I close my eyes, far, *far* too tired for this, and drop ungracefully into the only available armchair left. Fortunately, it's the one right by the fire. Two long flights through space and an hour on Ashma have made my bones so cold that I'm almost numb.

"Okay," I say, because as their host, protocol dictates they must wait for me to speak first. "Have at it."

Prime Minister Gomez, the only person in the room actually on my side, clears her throat. "I believe you have not yet met Queen Fanna, Princess Esmae."

"I have now."

"Thank you for agreeing to see us," says Queen Fanna with a small smile. "Even if it was somewhat under duress."

"Yes, well, I've vowed to be less disagreeable than I used to be," I inform them.

Katya lets out a giggle that she quickly turns into a cough.

"Does your father know you're here?" I ask her.

"Yes," she says. "He has mixed feelings about it, but he did not try to stop me."

"You do know this is terrible timing?" I point out.

At that, Princess Shay, who is even younger than I am, has the grace to blush. "We were very sorry to hear about Prince Abra," she says. "Please accept our sympathy. We wouldn't have come at such a time if we hadn't felt it was important."

Bear's small, rueful smile the last time I saw him flashes across my mind, and I clench one fist into the arm of my chair.

"I'm listening," I say.

Queen Fanna speaks up, quiet but clear. "Did you kill my father?"

I tilt my head at her. "Yes."

"I see." Her poise doesn't crack for even an instant. "You did it yourself?"

"Yes."

She nods. "Very well. What do you need?"

"I—what?"

"What do you need to defeat your brother quickly and win this war?" she explains. "It is in all our best interests that this war ends as soon as possible. So, what can we do to help?"

I feel like my brain must have turned to mush while I was on Ashma because none of this makes any sense. "Your father gave us the gold we needed to hire a fleet of mercenaries," I tell Queen Fanna, bewildered. "They're somewhere over the Aqua Nebula as we speak, cutting off Alexi's supply chain from Tamini. That was the extent of the deal your father and I struck. As for you two"—I blink at Katya and Shay—"last time I looked, you were both definitely on my brother's side. What's going on?"

"Fanna, Katya, and Shay came to see me," says Prime Minister Gomez. "They know I have been your uncle's ally for some time now, and they assumed, correctly, that I might have some insight into your character."

I narrow my eyes at her. "And?"

"Alexi lied to us," Shay says quickly, the words tumbling out. "I sided with him after what happened to Skylark last year, but it was a mistake. I think he means well, but he lied about Arcadia. He even lied to King Ralf about you, in spite of how extraordinarily kind Ralf has been to him. Prime Minister Gomez says you're not like him. She says if you make a promise, you'll keep it."

I should keep my mouth shut, I really should, but, reluctantly, I say, "Alex doesn't usually lie. He wanted to tell Ralf the truth."

"Kyra has a lot of sway over him," Princess Katya says shrewdly. "We've noticed."

"Prince Max told us that Sorsha would not be a threat for much longer," Queen Fanna says. "It seems that he, too, can be trusted. She's gone, like he promised. You stopped her."

"*Alex* killed her."

"We know what really happened out there, Esmae," Prime Minister Gomez says, shaking her head. "Everyone does. Titania recorded the whole thing. Apparently, she backed up all her data to external servers before she became human. Prince Max showed us the footage."

"We know you tried to save her *and* the rest of us," says Fanna. "As far as I'm concerned, that is worthy of far more respect than the act of killing the last of a species."

How long has it been since that day? While I was carved hollow, during all those days I could barely breathe, the world shifted.

And, against all odds, it shifted to side with *me*.

I was a pawn. I was no one. Alex was the golden son. Even after I won *Titania*, even after everything went wrong, I was still the dark to his light. How, then, has that turned upside-down?

"You understand I've done terrible things," I say, floundering in my confusion.

"You killed my father," says Queen Fanna. "That may seem like a terrible thing, but it was not."

"I did that to get what I wanted."

"You *had* what you wanted," she reminds me. "He'd already given you the gold. You didn't kill him to get what you wanted. You know as well as I do that you killed him to stop him from ever hurting another girl like he hurt my mother and my stepmothers."

"You saved Teresa," Katya adds.

I stare. "I don't even know who Teresa is!"

"You don't know her name, but you do know her. She's a servant. She was the kitchen maid in Arcadia, the one you sent running from Alexi's palace in terror." Katya smiles. "Her sister works in *our* kitchens. She told me what you did. And it occurred to me that maybe you sent her away to save her. Because you were willing to let hundreds of soldiers die when Arcadia burned but not one unimportant servant girl."

Princess Shay huffs impatiently. "For heaven's sake, Esmae. You may not be charming and heroic and sparkly like your brother, but you must think we're all fools if you imagine for one moment that we haven't noticed the quiet things you do."

"Sparkly?"

She blushes. "You know what I mean."

"And you're saying I'm *not* charming?"

"Now you're just teasing me."

I smile in spite of myself. "I would very much appreciate your help. All of you."

Katya hesitates. "I—I can't actually help. My father made Alexi a promise and we can't betray that. I just came here to—well, I—"

I think I understand. She came here so that I would know that she may not be my ally, but she's choosing to be my friend.

"Thank you," I say softly. "I promise this will end. I'll make sure of it."

But end how? I've always believed that this can only end when either Alex or I is dead, but is there another way? Max said I could choose how this ends, and Ash said he would give the mortal world one more chance to choose how we go on if I could show him that we can choose peace over war, and both of those things feel like riddles I don't know the answers to. How can you choose peace when the other side will not? We've gone too far for that now. So how can you choose an ending when it's not just up to you?

I don't know how I feel about my brother anymore. Love, jealousy, and hate are too tangled up to pick them apart. But I *do* know I don't want to kill him. I never did. I also know that after everything that's happened and everything I've done, *he* wants to kill *me*. And when our final battle comes around, that's how he'll fight. He won't give up.

But what if I can make him? What if there's something I can do to persuade him to surrender? I don't know what that something is, but maybe it's not something I have to do alone. I have all of Kali, Shloka, Skylark, Elba, and Wychstar behind me now. Maybe that's enough to make a difference.

Because if there's some way I can make Alex stop, then perhaps, just perhaps, this will end without more blood, without more death.

Unexpectedly, the stubborn, persistent seedling of hope in my heart tips its face to the sun again. What if this is how I can show Ash that we deserve to choose how to live our messy, short, glorious lives? If I can win without destroying everything, if I can salvage what's left of all of us, maybe the war will be over, everyone left will live, and the astra will go back into the stone where it belongs.

After all, I'm not the girl in the shadows anymore, a mere pawn in the game, desperate to prove herself, longing to be seen. I've come a long way since then. I've made my way across the board. I've lost family, and I've found family. I've fallen in love. I've fallen into the dark and come back out again.

So why, then, shouldn't I be able to change the ending of this story?

CHAPTER TWENTY-SIX

Esmae

The Night Temple is an old, almost forgotten place. Once, it was considered sacred, a quiet, holy sanctuary where those who were ill and wounded in a multitude of ways went to heal. Where those who felt they had done too much wrong went to pay penance.

There also used to be a tradition that when a child reached their eighteenth birthday, they went to the Night Temple to pray for clarity as they began their journey into adulthood. Almost no one does that now, mostly because, these days, most of us leave our childhoods behind a whole lot sooner than at the age of eighteen, but it would seem that Ash wants me to revive the tradition for some reason.

When I arrive at the temple, tucked deep into the mountains on the planet Kodava, a fine mist hangs in the air, painting the rolling green hills with puffs of white. It's just after midnight, on the anniversary of my birth, and a fat golden moon perches above the mountains. I breathe in, and the air smells like tea, coffee, flowers, and rain. It smells impossibly pure.

After a short trek up the side of the mountain to the temple doors, I find them open. There's no one in sight, though I can see lit windows in the turrets and towers behind the temple.

I know this place is still sacred to those who live here and those who actually care to visit, but, still, my nerves are all on edge as I step inside. I've been ambushed too many times to trust *any* place.

The temple is empty. It's a smallish stone room with a high arched ceiling and narrow windows, a room designed for quiet worship and meditation rather than for large gatherings. Warm, dim light spills into the room from tall lanterns in the corners, casting long shadows into the nooks and crannies. Tapestries hang on the walls, each with a painting of a god, and there's an altar at the end of the room with statues of Ash and Bara on it.

There's something on the three steps leading up to the altar. Curious, I step closer, only to pull up short when I see what it is.

It's a Warlords board, with the pieces all laid out in their starting places.

This can't be a coincidence. I sit cautiously down on the step beside the board, touching the beautiful pieces with careful fingers. This was left here for me.

But why?

As if I'd asked the question out loud, I get my answer.

There's someone else here. I hear his breathing, quiet and a little unsteady.

Alex steps out of the shadows.

I'm not really surprised.

"You," he says, teeth clenched. "Is there no escape from you?"

"It's my birthday, too," I point out.

As he draws closer, I get a better look at him. I've never seen him in such a state. His eyes are hollowed out, ringed with shadows so dark they're almost black, and his face is drawn, pale and unshaven. There's a jittery look about him, in the way he rocks back and forth on the balls of his feet, like he hasn't eaten or slept in days. Worst of all, there's a look of mania in his eyes that's unsettlingly, painfully familiar.

"Happy day of our birth, then," he rasps, with a bark of a sound that I think is supposed to be a laugh.

This is not an Alexi Rey I've met before. Gone is the charm, the friendly earnestness, the irritating arrogance. This Alexi Rey has lost his best friend, his one constant companion, his brother. He's—

Well, he's *me*.

"You didn't come to his funeral," my brother says.

"I wasn't invited."

"I thought you'd come anyway. Since when do you do what you're told?"

I could point out that while Bear was burning to ash and rejoining our ancestors in the celestial world, I was trying to persuade the most powerful god in existence not to send us *all* to the celestial world. Instead, I bite my temper back and gesture to the Warlords board. "I think we're supposed to play."

Eyes fixed on me with a resentment and hatred that would have terrified me if I didn't understand it only too well, Alex sits on the step on the other side of the board and nudges one of his pawns forward. "Why are you here?"

"I was ordered to come."

"Funny, that," he says. "So was I."

"Who asked you to?" I ask curiously.

"Kirrin."

But I know Ash must have told Kirrin to. He wants us both here tonight. I don't know why, but he does.

Was this what Ash meant when he told me he'd give me time and another chance? Am I supposed to do something here, with my brother, that will somehow make an ancient, powerful god change his mind about ending the world?

I move one of my horses, leaping over the pawn in front of it and moving two spaces ahead and one space to the left. It's an unusual move this early in the game and Alex glares at the piece. He seems to be using the board as an excuse not to look at me, which is fine by me because it's hard to look at him, too.

When I think of the proud, confident boy I met at the competition last year, and the way he's changed over these past months, it's hard not to understand why my mother was always so afraid of me.

I *have* destroyed him.

"You were right," he says unexpectedly, moving another pawn. He's so jittery that he almost knocks his king over.

"About what?"

"Mother."

I look up at him then. "She told you what she did? To our father?"

"She's not even trying to keep secrets anymore," he says, waving a hand. His voice is bitter. "She doesn't care enough to bother. When I asked her about Father, she told me. No lies, nothing. With Bear gone, it's like she doesn't care about anything anymore."

"I'm sure she still loves you," I say, feeling only a little sympathetic. I know what it's like to feel betrayed by our mother.

"Yes," he says with such dismissive certainty that I wonder what it must be like to grow up never doubting that you're loved and wanted. "But she's not afraid for me anymore. You told her she'd have two children. She has two children. She doesn't think she'll lose me now, so it's all over for her. She might as well have died, too."

"Do you wish she had?"

"No, but maybe that would have been better. I don't know. How can I ever look at her the same way again? She killed my father."

"*Our* father," I remind him.

He makes a dismissive sound, like that's irrelevant. I suppose, to him, it is.

I move my chariot. He takes my horse. I move my king's pawn forward.

After a long silence, and several more moves, his voice shudders out of him like he couldn't contain it anymore. "Why?"

I wait.

He takes a shaky breath. "Why did you tell her she'd have only two children by the end of this? Why would you swear such a thing?"

I clench the fingers of my right hand over my prosthetic thumb. "Do you really think what *I* said sealed Bear's fate?" I ask coldly. "Not, perhaps, the fact that Leila Saka couldn't resist attacking the Hundred and One when she should have stayed away? Why was Bear even with her?"

"He went with Leila to try and talk some sense into her," Alex says flatly.

"And now he's dead." I move my pawn, almost slamming the piece down on the board. "He was my brother, too, you know. I loved him."

"He's dead because you said—"

"It was supposed to be you or me!" I snap. "It was never supposed to be Bear. If I'd actually gotten what I wanted when I made that vow, it would have been you or me. I *hate* that I was careless. I made the same mistake Grandmother and Mother did. I threw those words out without considering the many ways it could end. And for *that*, I'm sorry. But I didn't kill our brother." I should stop, but I don't. "Our mother, your general, and your ambition did that."

He puts his queen down just two paces from my king. "Don't you dare say that. Don't you dare blame *me* for this!"

"Bear died because you wouldn't let your crown go," I say ruthlessly. "You can pretend otherwise, but you know it's true."

"I was ready to let the crown go," he growls. "I *told* you we'd stay in Arcadia. But you couldn't let me have that."

This is a cycle without an end. It doesn't matter what it costs us. Somehow, sooner or later, we end up back here, full of fury and sorrow.

Those mad, burning eyes stare into mine. I wonder what he sees. The same kind of madness, I expect. We may have just turned eighteen, but we haven't been children in a long time.

"This has to stop, Alex," I say.

"I agree. The next time we meet, this ends."

He's been so busy trying to get his queen to corner my king, he hasn't noticed the rest of the board. I move my pawn one last space, turning it into a second queen.

"Warlord lock," I say, tracing the lines between his king and my two queens. "You really should pay more attention to the pawns."

He lets out a bark of laughter, standing. "This game is the only way you can beat me, Esmae. You know that. You can't win this war."

"No, Alex. *You* can't win. Your allies are on my side now. You drove them away."

"I don't need them," he says. "When you lost *Titania*, you lost this war. I've already won. You just don't know it yet."

As the temple doors slam shut behind him, I can't help feeling that if this *was* Ash's idea of a test, I must have completely and resoundingly failed.

"Well," says a voice from a dark corner of the temple, making me knock the Warlords board over in surprise. "That was dramatic. Tea?"

It turns out our great-grandmother, the old queen Cassela, knew we were coming and came to see us.

Peering with misgiving into the unlit corner where she'd stayed hidden the whole time, I shake my head in confusion. "Why didn't you say something?"

"And interrupt such a fond interaction?" she replies, dry as dust. She beckons me out of a side door I hadn't noticed before. "Come along, Ez-may, and be quick about it. My old bones don't do as well with the cold as yours do."

Still reeling from my conversation with Alex, I follow her obediently out of the temple, across a courtyard, and up a flight of stairs leading into one of the turrets set into the mountains. We don't see anyone else on the way.

"Grandmother, why are you here?" I demand. "Max says you left Kali weeks ago! When are you coming back?"

Instead of answering me, she pushes open an old, creaky wooden door, leading me into a small, spare room. It's warm and well lit, but there's not much in it: a window, a narrow bed, a table and two chairs, a chest of clothes, a few books. A pot of steaming tea and three cups sit on the table, waiting.

Three cups. She must have intended for Alex to be here, too.

Tossing her cane into a corner of the room, Grandmother sits in one of the chairs, her back perfectly straight. I sit opposite her, looking around with a frown.

"You were nobility before you married into the royal family," I say. "Have you *ever* stayed in a room like this before?"

"New experiences are always interesting," she replies, pouring the tea. "Drink."

I pick my cup up, but I don't drink. "You didn't tell me when you're coming home."

"Because I am not coming home."

I almost drop my cup. "You're *never* coming back?" I ask, stunned. "You're going to stay here for the rest of your life?"

"I am very old," she points out. "I doubt I shall be here long."

"I suppose we can visit. It's not a very long journey."

"No, Ez-may." The old queen sighs, still putting that ridiculous emphasis on my name because she disapproves of it. "This is the last time you will see me. I will see no visitors after tonight."

I stare at her, too shocked to reply. Like most of my family, my feelings about my great-grandmother are conflicted, at best, but I am fond of her. Finding out this is the last time I'll ever see her is a surprisingly painful thing. Maybe it's because this is coming hard on the heels of losing Bear, but it feels like too much is slipping away from me.

"I don't understand," I finally manage to say as she watches me over the rim of her teacup. "Why?"

"I have done a great deal of harm," she says unflinchingly. "You, of all people, should know that. When I cursed your mother, and inadvertently cursed you as well, I set in motion a tragedy that could have been avoided entirely if I had chosen to keep my mouth shut. Kyra was reckless and foolish, but she didn't *mean* to kill Vanya. It was a careless, stupid accident. I knew that, yet I lost my temper anyway."

"But that happened *years* ago," I protest. "Why come here now?"

For a moment, she says nothing. Hands clutched around her teacup, as if for warmth, she turns her face to the window and takes a few unsteady breaths. With a pang, I notice that for the very first time in all the time I've known her, she looks old, tired and, above all, fragile.

"I was an aristocrat's daughter, and betrothed to the future king of Kali," she says at last. "Lavya was a servant's daughter. I was not very kind to her. I couldn't bear the idea of a servant's child possessing more talent than I did. So I asked Rickard to train me harder than anyone else, to teach me things he didn't teach any of the others, to make *me* his best student. He was young and ambitious then. He knew that his best chance at rising up in the world and serving Kali was to find favor with the royal family, so he made me that rash promise."

She seems to have lost the thread of the conversation, but I go along with it. "That's why he made Lavya cut off her own thumb."

"He never forgave himself for that," she says. "It is remarkable, is it not? How much damage a few rash words can do?"

I don't reply. What can I say?

Blinking, Grandmother turns her face back to me. "I could not bear it anymore," she says. I can tell she's not talking about Rickard anymore. "The damage was too great. I could not bear to watch the consequences of my curse unfold any longer. Call it cowardice, or weakness, but I could not take it. I left."

Suddenly, I understand. "You left after Arcadia. *That* was the point when you decided it was too much."

"This war is my doing."

"That's not true," I object. "It started when Elvar took the crown from Alexi. You had nothing to do with that."

"It started because Cassel died," she says, brushing my objection away. "If Cassel had lived, none of this would have happened. And Cassel died because he wanted his daughter back. He would not have died if I hadn't cursed your mother. This war *is* my doing."

"Wait," I say, inhaling sharply. "You *knew* my mother was responsible for what happened to him? You've known all along?"

"He told me he was coming to find you," she says. "When he died just hours later, I knew it couldn't have been an accident. I knew Kyra had killed him."

"Why didn't you say anything?"

"Because it was *my* fault." Suddenly agitated, Grandmother lashes out with a hand, sending the teapot flying. It shatters on the floor, letting the dregs of tea and leaves puddle into the cracks in the floorboards.

Grandmother moves to get up, but I stop her. I kneel on the floor instead, collecting the shards of teapot.

"Kyra cut your throat because of the curse," I hear her voice say above me, more vulnerable than I have ever heard it. "She would have killed you if Amba had not sacrificed her immortality to save you. Then you went missing. Max searched for you for so long that it almost killed him. Elvar had a breakdown. There was a riot. That was when I knew I could not live with it any longer. I left."

I suppose I should be angry that, by her own admission, my great-grandmother made a mess and left the rest of us to clean it up, but I find that I can't dredge up any anger at her. Not when I can see what the burden of that one terrible mistake has done to her.

"If you were listening the whole time I was with Alexi in the temple," I say softly, "then you must have heard us talk about Bear."

"Yes." There's the smallest tremor in her voice. "I know he is dead. That is why I will not see another visitor after you leave. Whatever happens next, I cannot bear to know it."

I wonder suddenly if *this* is really why Ash wanted us to come here. Alex was supposed to be here, too. If he had stayed, he and I would *both* have listened to our great-grandmother's story. And having listened, both of us here together, would we have been able to see such anguish and *still* take this war to its bitter end? Or would we have found ourselves able to end the cycle of violence and tragedy once and for all?

"It's time for you to go," Grandmother says quietly.

I stand, putting the teapot shards carefully down on the table. She's looking out of the window again. Chest tight, I kiss her cheek. "Goodbye, Grandmother."

"I will imagine a long, joyous, adventurous life for you, Ez-may."

At the door, I hesitate and look back. I can't leave without saying one last thing.

"Your curse was cruel," I tell her. "I'm not going to pretend otherwise. But you're wrong if you think everything that's happened since is your fault. Every one of us could have made different choices and maybe averted each disaster along the way, but we didn't. We all *chose*. Mother, too. You didn't choose for us."

I leave her with that. She's still gazing out of the window, already far, far away.

CHAPTER TWENTY-SEVEN

Radha

Princesses do not fidget, Radha, but I am most decidedly fidgeting. It feels like I've been standing here for an eternity, watching the spaceship in the sky make the slowest possible descent into the palace dock. It's now close enough that I can see my brother Rodi standing at the windows of the ship, a broad smile on his face. My stomach twists.

"What's the matter?" I hear Titania ask from my right. I hadn't even noticed her arrive. "You appear to be agitated."

I grimace. "My father has a way of disrupting my equilibrium."

"He can only do that if you let him," she says with that unexpected wisdom that she sometimes comes out with. She used to do that as a ship, too. Then she frowns. "Should he disrupt *my* equilibrium? He's my father, as well, in a way. Should I feel the same way you do?"

I turn to look at her young, doubtful face and feel a rush of affection for her. Since Rama died, we've all been so immersed in losing him and in this war that I'd almost forgotten all those years growing up in the palace, with *Titania* outside our windows, a permanent fixture in our lives.

"Father and I have a difficult relationship," I tell her. "Don't let the way I feel about him change the way you do."

"He was kind to me when I was on Wychstar," she says. "I think I'm fond of him." She reaches into the pocket of her flowery dress and pulls out a toffee. Unwrapping it, she pops it into her mouth. "I have another if you'd like one," she says reluctantly, noticing me watching her.

I hide a smile. "I'm fine, but thank you."

"Oh, good," she says happily.

My father's ship has landed at last. I watch as the engines drop to a low hum before going quiet. The doors hiss open. My stomach gives another anxious twist and I force myself to stand perfectly straight and still.

My father leaves the ship first with Rodi right behind him. Father's face is set, his brown skin paler than usual and his jaw clenched so tight I'm amazed he hasn't cracked any of his teeth. He doesn't look like he's looking forward to this in the slightest.

Before any of us can speak, Titania gets there first. "Father!" she cries, flinging herself at him impulsively.

Father is many things, but he has never been cruel, so in spite of his surprise and discomfort, he accepts Titania's exuberance with good grace. He allows her to embrace him and pats her awkwardly on the back.

"A human existence suits you," he says kindly.

She beams and moves to hug Rodi, who laughs and returns her hug with enthusiasm.

Father kisses me on the cheek. It's probably just a polite greeting, but I'd like to think there's some genuine affection in it. "Are you well?" he asks me while Titania jabbers excitedly to Rodi behind him.

"Yes," I say, somewhat surprised by this unprecedented interest. "Are you?"

He doesn't answer that, just looks at me with an expression that might be regret. "You're a good girl," he says.

I blink, shocked. In spite of everything, my throat tightens, and I don't know what to say. I clear my throat and opt for: "King Elvar and Queen Guinne send their apologies for not coming to greet you in person. They had an emergency war council meeting to attend."

In fact, Max, Esmae, Sybilla, and Amba are all also at the war council meeting. Esmae came home from the Night Temple just yesterday, looking exhausted and heartsick, and she didn't have time to do much more than sleep before she was summoned to the meeting with the others. I don't know what it's about, just that it has something to do with a signal of some sort.

At the mention of the war council meeting, Titania glances my way with a scowl. She wasn't allowed to attend.

As I lead the way into the palace, Rodi moves forward so that he's in step with me. "How is Rickard?" he asks me in an undertone. "Father's not doing very well. If this is likely to get ugly, we should call it off now."

"No, Rickard would never hurt Father," I whisper back.

"He already did, Radha."

"I mean he won't do anything like that again. He's not angry that Father sent me here to ruin him, Rodi. He's not going to lash out."

Rodi nods. He rubs his forehead tiredly. Like almost everyone I know, he's aged since Rama died. He's only twenty-five, but I think I see the first grays in his hair. I imagine that's as much to do with having to take over more and more of the kingdom from Father as it does with losing a brother. Rodi wasn't expecting to inherit the throne for another twenty years.

"Ria's baby is hideous," he says after a moment.

I sputter a laugh, and he grins. "That's your nephew," I say, trying and failing to be stern. "Don't be horrid about him."

"He *is* hideous! You haven't seen him up close."

"Did you tell Ria that?"

"Of course! I never lie to her."

I try and fail to picture what my sister's reaction might have been. "There's no such thing as an ugly baby, Rodi."

"He's all red and scrunched up."

"Every baby looks like that!"

"Father?" Rodi asks, turning his head back. "Were *we* red and scrunched up when we were babies?"

Father smiles a little. "Yes. You were the ugliest one."

I think that's a *joke*. I'm so stunned, I almost walk into a pillar. Even Titania looks bemused. Where was this father all my life?

Glancing surreptitiously at him out of the corner of my eye, I try not to get my hopes up. Maybe this is who he is without the hatred and pain. Maybe, knowing he's about to speak to Rickard one final time and get whatever closure he needs, he's already starting to change. Maybe this is a chance for a new beginning for what's left of our family.

By the time we arrive at Rickard's suite, Father looks pale again. Unexpectedly, I have a vision of what he must have looked like in his previous life, a shy, poor girl nurturing an unexpected talent, eager to please her teacher, desperate to belong. My heart goes out to her then, and to him now. How it must have hurt to be betrayed like that.

"This is good, Father," I say gently. "It's time to move on."

I knock on the door and step back to let Father go in alone. The door shuts behind him, leaving Titania, Rodi, and me alone in the hallway.

There's a little balcony just off the hallway, so we sit there while we wait. Titania leans against the railing, her face in her hands as she squints up at the stars and gas clouds, far beyond the sun lamps and shields around Kali. There's a lovely view of Erys from here, and I point some of my places out to Rodi, who looks at me with a slightly rueful expression on his face.

"What?" I ask him.

"You like it here," he says. "You're not planning on coming home, are you? Even when all this is over?"

"I'll always keep coming back to Wychstar," I tell him. "There's so much about it I miss when I'm here. But it doesn't feel like home anymore."

He gives me a lopsided smile. "Is it a girl?"

"Yes," says Titania.

I sigh. "No, it's me," I insist.

"There is also a girl," Titania informs Rodi, sticking her tongue out at me. "She has annoying boots."

Rodi gives me a questioning look. I relent. "Her name is Sybilla." Unbidden, a smile creeps across my face. "She's incredible. You'll like her. But," I add firmly, "she's not the reason I can't see myself coming back to Wychstar for good. This is where I feel most like me. That's why I want to stay."

"I'm glad for you," he says, his smile sincere. "We'll miss you."

"I'll visit all the time, I promise."

"I'll hold you to that."

I like the idea of that future. A life of my own, here, with Sybilla, with my friends. Travel. Classes at the University of Erys. Some kind of work that will make me feel excited and useful, like teaching. And frequent visits to the place where I grew up, my old home, where I can meet my sister's children, and my father will be softer and happier, and my brother will make me laugh.

I'm so preoccupied by these possibilities that I don't notice the look of thunder on Titania's face until she says, in a cold, contemptuous tone I've never heard her use before: "What do you want now?"

I turn. Kirrin has materialized on the balcony. Did she really just speak to him like that?

"Er," Rodi says awkwardly, startled.

But Kirrin seems uninterested in either Titania's scowl or Rodi's awkwardness. His face is grim. "Get in there," he says sharply, jerking his head at the door to Rickard's suite. "I can't do anything, but you can. If it's not already too late. Go."

For an instant, Rodi and I are too surprised and confused to move. Then, with a jerk, my brother lunges across the hallway for the door. I follow half a step behind, dread dropping like a stone into my heart. Was I wrong to let our father go in there? Was Rickard angrier than he let on?

Right before Rodi shoves the door open, we hear a boy's voice from inside the room crying out.

We burst into the room. Rodi lets out a strangled sound.

Sebastian, Rickard's grandson, is frozen by the window, his face ashen and his mouth open in a cry. I didn't even know he was with Rickard when my father went in.

Father is on his knees, his head in his hands.

And Rickard is on the floor, with something silver sticking out of his chest and something red staining the carpet around him.

Rodi was wrong. Father was never the one in danger. *Rickard* was.

What have we done?

CHAPTER TWENTY-EIGHT

Radha

Did I really think this could have been a new beginning for us? *Princesses do not cherish foolish hopes, Radha.*

Father's shoulders shake as he weeps, but I stumble past him and fling myself down to my knees at Rickard's side. Titania is right behind me. We both put our hands on the wound, trying to see if there's some way to stop the bleeding, but there's already so much everywhere.

"If I only had my lasers right now," Titania wails.

I move my hands frantically, trying to keep pressure on Rickard's chest. It's hard to do anything with the dagger in his heart, but I don't dare take it out in case that makes things worse. "Oh, god," I whisper, my heart hammering so hard I can't hear anything else. "There's so much blood."

I have no idea how much time passes before I become aware of footsteps and voices. Chaos. Two rough, calloused, familiar hands close over mine, pulling my hands away from Rickard's chest. Across from me, someone pulls Titania away, too. "Radha, he's gone," Sybilla says in my ear, keeping one arm wrapped tightly around my shoulders. "There's nothing you can do."

As I stand, I see Rodi kneeling beside Father, trying to speak to him. Kirrin in the doorway, all mischief gone, a god of sorrows instead of tricks. Max by the window, one arm around Titania and the other holding Sebastian back, both children pressed into his side like wounded, frightened young birds looking for shelter from a storm.

But it's the sight of Esmae that devastates me. It's the expression on her face, as she stands beside Rickard, a man she loved like a father, looking silently down at him. It's not anguish, or horror, or even grief. It's something else. Something worse. Like she's so used to tragedy, it doesn't even surprise her anymore.

"Why?" I ask my broken father. "Why wasn't what I did to him enough for you?"

"I wanted it not to hurt anymore," he says hoarsely.

"And has it stopped now?" I demand, gesturing around us to illustrate what his quest for revenge has cost. "Has the pain gone?"

Father doesn't answer, which is answer enough for me. Of course it's not gone. That's not how pain and heartbreak work. Lavya will always be betrayed, Father will always hurt, and, now, Rickard will always be dead.

Sebastian lets out an anguished roar, tears streaming down his face. "I wish I could kill you!" he shouts, with the uncontrollable, helpless fury of a boy who knows it's something he'll never do.

208

"I'm sorry," Rodi says to him, and then to the room at large, "I'm so sorry. Radha and I had no idea this was what he meant to do."

Max gently disentangles himself from Sebastian and Titania, his face set. Only the muscle ticking in his jaw gives away the storm of feelings he's suppressing. Stepping close to Esmae, he says to her and Sybilla, in a voice too low for anyone else to hear: "What do we do with him?"

I swallow a hard lump in my throat. I can't speak. I can't bring myself to defend my father, because there is no defending what he's done, but I can't bear to think of the most likely punishment, either.

"I'm not executing Rama's father," Esmae says in a voice that leaves no room for argument. I feel a rush of relief and gratitude for her.

"Then we should get him off Kali before my father hears that Rickard is dead," says Max, his voice cracking on the last word. "Because if he's still here when Elvar finds out, there will be blood."

"We can't just let him go," Sybilla hisses. "What he's done—"

Before she can finish, the sound of a loud, shrill klaxon shrieks over the speakers in every room, startling us all. For a moment, I wonder if it's some kind of announcement of what's happened to Rickard, a mourning cry of some sort that's being broadcasted to the entire kingdom, but then I see the looks on the others' faces.

"What is that?" I shout over the scream of the klaxon. "What does it mean?"

Sybilla is deathly white as she says, "It means the inner shield just came down. We're about to be invaded."

CHAPTER TWENTY-NINE

Titania

I knew I had forgotten something. I *knew* it. All those times I tried to ignore that nagging, uncomfortable certainty that I'd forgotten something important? This was why. This inadequate, messy human brain let something phenomenally huge slip past it.

It has been sixteen minutes since the klaxons went off. It has been sixteen minutes of chaos. We've assembled in the war room. Somewhere else in the palace, King Elvar and General Khay are summoning Kali's scattered troops and allies from every corner of the galaxy. I don't know where King Darshan and Prince Rodi are. The klaxon has been silenced so that we can actually hear each other speak, the inner shield is still down, and, in the distance, we can see a fleet of ships approaching.

How could I have forgotten the hacker working for Alexi somewhere in the base ship? I had an alert set up for their signal, so that I could block it as soon as it appeared, but then I became human and all my protocols vanished into the aether. Still, I should have remembered the hacker *existed*. How could something like *that* have just slipped my mind, human or not?

Hush, the voice inside my head says. *Don't think like that. The others should have been paying more attention.*

I silence that ugly voice and shudder, forcing myself out of my thoughts. Across the room, Max is ordering someone to get the shields back up. Esmae is standing at the window, her eyes on the ships on the horizon.

Amba's voice is clipped as she says, "Wasn't someone supposed to be watching for the hacker's signal?"

Sybilla flushes crimson. "I was investigating, but I—well, I—I got caught up in other things."

"She means it's my fault," I say reluctantly, unwilling to let her take the blame for it. "I told Sybilla I'd take over keeping watch on the signal."

"But then you became human," Amba says, sighing. "It is what it is, but I have to admit I wish you hadn't."

How dare she, I think, ignoring the fact that she's not wrong. A bolt of rage makes my skin feel electric. *None of this would have happened if it wasn't for her.*

I'm not quite sure how this is Amba's fault, but I cling to that thought anyway.

Esmae turns from the window. "At the Night Temple, Alex told me that the moment Titania became human, I lost this war," she says. I couldn't possibly feel any worse. It was selfish of me to choose humanity over staying to fight at my friends' sides. "This must have been what he meant. He knew he was coming." Her teeth clench. "That's why he didn't care when I told him his allies had left him. He knew they'd be too far away to help us when he invaded."

"He knows our mercenaries are over the Aqua Nebula, cutting off his supplies from Tamini," Max says, pinching the bridge of his nose. "Queen Miyo would have sent him word. So he knows we have less than half our army here on Kali. He couldn't have timed this better."

"We also have the Wych soldiers I brought," Radha adds.

"Even with them, we're ridiculously outnumbered."

Nausea is something I've never experienced, but I assume that is what I'm feeling now, because my stomach is churning and the sour, horrible taste of bile is in my throat.

"I'm sorry," I whisper.

There's a commotion outside the door, and Juniper from the Hundred and One bursts in, dragging a skinny older man with her. His nose is bloodied, but he looks outrageously pleased with himself.

"Here's our hacker," Juniper spits, pushing him ahead of her. He stumbles and falls to his knees. "I found him in the base ship. He wasn't even trying to hide what he'd done."

Her voice dangerously quiet, Amba steps forward, towering over him. "Get the shield back up," she says coldly.

He avoids looking at her, lowering his eyes. "I will not," he says, "and what's more, no one else will be able to, either. The prince is coming. He's coming home at last."

Sybilla makes a move forward like she's going to punch him in the face, but Max stops her.

"What about the failsafe?" Max asks, not directing the question at any one in particular.

"Failsafe?" I ask, confused.

"There's a failsafe for the inner shield," he explains. "In case something like this happens. I imagine Wychstar has one, too."

Radha nods. "It's a secondary switch to reactivate the shield, kept far away from the tech in the base ship so that the two aren't on the same system."

"That's how ours works, too," says Max. He points out the window, high, and we all crane our necks to look up at the faint glimmer of the outer shield, still encasing Kali in its bubble. "If you look hard enough, you'll see it. That small glitch in the outer shield? That's the failsafe. It's built into the outer shield and can only be triggered by direct contact, not by technology."

"Like an actual, physical switch," I say.

"Yes."

"So then we can fly a starship up to that point of the outer shield and trigger the switch, can't we?" I ask hopefully. Maybe my mistake won't cost us everything, after all.

The hacker lets out a short laugh. "Do you really think I didn't consider that?" he asks. "I work in the base ship. I know all about the failsafe. I may not have been able to get to it myself, but I've made it inaccessible to all of *you*, too." He looks so proud, like he's confident in his certainty that he's done the right thing, he's helped his prince come home. "Here, I can show you. It's not like you can undo it, anyway."

Stepping forward, with Juniper's warning hand clamped around his elbow to make sure he doesn't try anything he shouldn't, he goes to the simulation bubble in the middle of the room and taps a few keys on the touchscreen outside it. Immediately, a three-dimensional holographic miniature of Kali appears in the room, exactly like it does when the others have been here strategizing in the past.

The hacker taps on the touchscreen once more, and this time something new flickers on to the hologram. It looks like a new shield, a spherical bubble around the kingdom, positioned about where the inner shield used to be. Unlike the inner shield, this one is a grid, like a net.

"I fashioned a version of the inner shield," the hacker tells us. It chills me that he's telling us this without any prompting at all. It means he knows there's nothing we can do about it. "This one only lets things *in*, not out. The prince's army can enter, but no one can leave until I deactivate it. Which, of course, I won't. I didn't have time to stitch up all the gaps, but the grid is too small for a ship to pass through."

"But it is *not* too small for an arrow," says Amba, her eyes focused on the holographic re-creation of the grid with all the intensity of an ancient, powerful creature who has fought worse wars. "An archer could stand at the very top of the north tower and fire an arrow directly at the glitch in the outer shield, bypassing the net and triggering the failsafe. And then," she says, turning to skewer the hacker with that ancient gaze, "your precious prince will be getting nowhere."

There's a moment of total silence. As the hacker's mouth opens and closes in dismay, revealing that an arrow *could* actually work, everyone's eyes turn inevitably in one direction.

There are only two archers left in the mortal world who could possibly get an arrow through the tiny grid and hit the switch.

One of them is about to invade us. The other is in this room.

Esmae's fist clenches and unclenches at her sides.

"I can't," she says, her jaw tight and her eyes simmering with fury. "Not anymore. Not without my thumb."

Nodding, Max says, "Then we need to accept that Alex is coming and figure out what we want to do."

With one last look of contempt at the hacker, Amba turns away and addresses Esmae. "Our one advantage is that Alexi wants the crown of Kali," she says. "He wants to come home. He's not here to destroy the kingdom. We can use that against him."

Esmae turns back the holographic simulation of the kingdom. She looks at it with an expression I recognize from watching her play Warlords.

"He'll want to make this as quick as possible," she says, "so that there's as little destruction as possible to the kingdom he wants to rule when this is over. That means he'll come *here*, to the palace. The easiest way to end this would be to force us to surrender."

"You should consider it," Kirrin says quietly, materializing out of nowhere.

Max's eyes flash. "You were here right before the shield came down. You could have warned us."

"I promised Alex I wouldn't."

"Get out," Max snarls.

"Max, *listen* to me. You don't understand. This has to end quickly. If it doesn't, the devastation will be unthinkable."

"You have gone too far one too many times, little brother," Amba says, her voice icy. "Leave."

Anguished, Kirrin obeys. Amba straightens her spine with difficulty, exhaustion flitting across her face. I feel peculiarly pleased. I rather like seeing her struggle.

"Why are you smiling like that?" Max asks me, and I jump, annoyed that I forgot how he never seems to miss anything.

"Was I?" I shake my head. "I don't know. I guess I'm still getting used to how the muscles in my face work."

He narrows his eyes but turns back to the hologram. "We can position a third of the ships we have at strategic points above the palace," he says, pointing. "And use them to fire relentlessly on any ship approaching. The rest of our ships can attack directly, from these angles here. That should keep Alex's fleet away from the palace."

"Alex won't want to win this from inside a ship," says Esmae. "He'll leave some of his fleet high up, to fire from a distance and to keep our own fleets occupied, but he and a portion of his soldiers will find ground to land and they'll attack the palace on foot. Alex will want to take the crown from Elvar with his own hands." She points to two of the palace exits. "Those are his best entry points. We should evacuate the palace and barricade those doors." Her eyes flash. "We don't know how many other people are working with him. We can't have anyone letting him in."

"Agreed," says Max. "And those of us who aren't going to fly the ships will wait here, outside the palace." He glances over his shoulder at Juniper. "Get everyone armed and ready."

She nods and bolts.

"The university will be safe," Max goes on, with another glance out at the window at the approaching fleet, "and it's close enough for Mother, the servants, the children, and anyone else who can't fight to get to before Alex gets here."

"The children?" I repeat, my hackles rising. "You'd better not be including me in that category."

"You're a child, Titania, whether you like it or not," Max says.

"I can be useful!" I protest. "The people in this room are all I have! How can you ask me to go and hide somewhere safe while you're all out here dying? Let me help!"

"That's not—"

"No!" the word explodes out of me, making everyone stare. "Don't treat me like I'm nothing!"

There is stunned silence in the room. No one seems to know what to say or do, apart from Esmae, who is unimpressed with my tantrum.

"We care about you, you outrageous brat," she says, with an icy wrath that makes me feel like I'm about three inches tall. "We're not asking you to hide because we think you're nothing. We're asking you to hide because it would be devastating to lose you."

"Oh."

"Titania, we all wish you still had some of the incredible abilities you possessed as a ship. I expect you wish that, too. But nobody here blames you for the choice you made. We're not angry with you for not being what you once were." A little softer, she adds: "But you do need to accept that your choice has been made. After I lost the blueflower, I remember you telling me that I had to stop acting like I was indestructible. Well, now I'm going to say the same thing to you."

My cheeks flushed with shame, I bite my lip and say quietly, "I'm sorry. I—I just—I just want to help. In any way I can. *Please.*"

Esmae considers me for a moment. "You could stay right here," she says. "We'll evacuate the palace, apart from you. This is the war room, after all. It has direct video and audio feeds from every piece of tech in the palace and every camera in the city. Having you here, keeping an eye on everything, warning us about what we don't see coming, would be extraordinarily useful. Are you up for that?"

"Yes!" I say, almost giddy at the prospect of being able to actually do something useful again. "Yes, I am." Out of the corner of my eye, I catch sight of the boy huddled in the corner of the room, his tearstained face watching us all worriedly. Something makes me say: "Sebastian should stay with me. Two pairs of eyes will be better than one."

Sebastian straightens. "I'll do it," he says at once, giving me a grateful look. "I want to help. It's what Grandfather would have wanted me to do."

No one reminds him that's not true. We all know Rickard would have sent him as far away from here as he possibly could.

"We're almost out of time," says Max. "Sybilla, get word to Mother to gather the servants and get to the university. Amba, can you lay all this out for Father and General Khay?"

"Yes," says Amba crisply. "I'll go find them at once."

Sybilla hesitates, her eyes fixed on Radha's face. "Radha, you should go with the queen and the servants," she says.

"What?" Radha says, aghast. "No! I know I can't fight, but I can still do *something*."

Sybilla casts a panicked look out the window. "We don't have time to fight about this," she pleads, the prickles around her crumbling away. "Please. If you don't go, I won't be able to do anything except worry that you're not okay."

Radha hesitates, her expression somewhere between angry and afraid. Swallowing, she says, "Okay."

"Thank you," Sybilla says, her shoulders crumpling in relief. She holds Radha's face with both hands and kisses her on the mouth. "Let's go find the queen."

The war room empties, leaving just Esmae, Max, Sebastian, and me. I move away from the hologram, letting Sebastian pull up the camera feeds on as many screens as are available in the room, and wring my hands as I try to put what I'm feeling into words. All that comes out is: "Please don't die."

Esmae gives me a hug, and Max kisses me on the fore-head. My throat feels like it's full of tears. Why does this feel like goodbye?

Before they leave, Max takes a step in Esmae's direction, the two of them silhouetted against the swarm of ships on the horizon. For just one moment, the sight of them like that, with his hands on her shoulders and her face tilted up to his, triggers a terrible, almost forgotten memory in my human brain.

The vision comes back to me, the one Kirrin showed me. Pieces of Kali strewn across a fiery, ashy hellscape. The snow. The broken throne. The red ponytail buried under the rubble. Max and Esmae, silent and gray, streaked with ash and blood.

But before that, they were standing together, just like this, Esmae's eyes shining with tears as she tried to smile.

Close your eyes, he said.

And she did.

I jerk my head, trying to blink the vision away. Why did it come back to me now? It means nothing. That future vanished when Sorsha died.

Didn't it?

When I dare to look at them again, it's the here and now again. Max's voice is hoarse as he speaks, so low I almost can't hear him. "Just in case this goes badly—"

"Don't," Esmae says, a hitch in her breath. "We're going to be fine."

They look at each other for a long moment, and then Max kisses her, an almost desperate kiss that makes me look away again.

"Remember," he says, the last words I hear. "Light the stars up."

CHAPTER THIRTY

Esmae

It's quiet outside the palace. The solar lamps in the sky are half-way to sunset, just a few hours from shifting into moonlight, and the rooftops of the city below, the cobbled paths, and the thorn forests all look like they've been painted with gold.

The silence would be peaceful, if it wasn't so chilling. There's no birdsong, no chatter drifting up from the city streets, no footsteps. There's just the hum of the base ship's engines far below us, and the hum of our warships' engines high above us.

We wait. The palace is empty, apart from Titania and Sebastian. Rickard is still there, too, but I suppose he doesn't count, does he? The thought makes my chest hurt.

A third of our forces are in the sky, in almost a hundred ships, including all of the Wych soldiers and most of the Hundred and One. The rest of us are here, on foot and in chariots at the palace gates, looking down the tiers of the city, watching the wooded paths and roads that could spit out an army at any moment. Around me, I see Max, Sybilla, Elvar, General Khay, Laika, and so many other faces I've come to know over this past year. How many of us will still be here at the end?

We wait.

Radha, the servants, the palace children, and anyone else who wanted shelter should all be safe behind the university's ancient, solid doors by now. Guinne refused to go with them in the end, choosing instead to stay with a handful of doctors and servants who also refused to go. Instead, they've set up a makeshift medical clinic behind a wall of soldiers in the palace courtyard.

Beside me, Elvar is very pale. He's been displaying nothing but confidence, insisting on presenting himself as a strong and calm king, but I know him well enough to see the beads of sweat dampening his blindfold, the way his hands tremble ever so slightly, and his too-tight grip on his sword.

"You don't have to do this, Uncle," I say quietly.

"Yes," he says, without hesitation, "I do. This is my kingdom to protect, even from my own nephew. I cannot let you, Max, and the rest of my people die in my stead."

"How about none of us does any dying?"

Elvar's throat moves as he says, "Bear is dead."

"Yes."

"Cassel's beloved boy, gone. Because of my ambition, because of my desperate need to prove myself to the ghost of a mother who hasn't been here for a very long time."

"Because of many things," I insist, thinking of my great-grandmother, alone in the Night Temple, convinced that *she* was the cause of our family's destruction.

"If I could take it back, I would."

"I know," I say gently.

There's a crackle in my ear, the sound of my earpiece activating, and Titania's voice comes through: "They're coming."

Above us, our ships begin to fire. The sky explodes in bursts of light.

And all hell breaks loose.

CHAPTER THIRTY-ONE

Radha

The idea that I would hide somewhere safe, while my friends and the girl I happen to be madly in love with fight a battle that could kill them, is almost laughably absurd.

As a stream of people make their way quickly into the university, I slip away, my heart pounding so hard it hurts. I'm not a fool. I know I can't fight. I may be able to stab a grown man with a knitting needle but put any other weapon in my hands and I'm a disaster. I have no intention of making my way into the battle.

But there's something else I *can* do.

I take the smaller, winding paths back to the rear of the palace, where I'm unlikely to bump into anyone, friend or enemy. I'm sure Titania and Sebastian can see me, if they're looking at the right tech feeds, but if they have, they haven't told the others that I'm not where I said I'd be.

It's not that I *want* to keep this a secret. It's just that I know that if Sybilla finds out I'm not safe inside the university, she'll be distracted worrying about me and it might get her killed. And I don't want to tell Esmae or Max what I'm about to do either, not when there's a chance, a very, very good chance, that it might not work. I can't let them go into this battle relying on a scheme that might fail.

I make my way into the palace kitchens through the servants' quarters then look for the dock. The yawning, tunneled exit has been sealed, so that no ships can go in or out, but the door leading from inside the palace to the shipyard is still usable.

Outside, there's a boom that makes me jump. Oh, god. It's started.

I run the rest of the way to the dock. Apart from a handful of supply ships, which are entirely useless in battle, there's only one ship left in the dock: the one belonging to the royal house of Wychstar.

After Father killed Rickard, and the klaxon went off, there was no time to decide what to do with Father. The only thing to do was have Rodi barricade Father and himself in the royal ship until there *was* time.

Which is very convenient for me right now.

Punching in the familiar code to make the ship doors hiss open, I march inside. I find Father and Rodi in the galley, Rodi trying to press a mug of hot tea into Father's hands.

"Radha, what are you doing here?" Rodi demands, looking appalled to see me. "You're supposed to be somewhere safe, not wandering around in the middle of a battle!"

I ignore him, addressing my father. "You weren't King Darshan today," I say. "You weren't the king of Wychstar, a widower, a father of four. You were Ek Lavya."

His eyes meet mine at the sound of the name, full of anguish and weariness, but he doesn't speak.

"Now I need you to be Lavya again," I say.

"Radha," Rodi protests.

I hold up a hand to stop him. "You will do this for me, Father. Because you have used me, tricked me, and lied to me. Because you love me. And because I know your heart is good when it's not choked by hate. So you will do this for me. You will become Ek Lavya one last time."

There's a moment of fraught silence, and then Father says quietly, "What would you have me do?"

The corners of my mouth lift in a smile. "We're going back to where this started, Father," I tell him. "And you're going to skewer the eye of a fish."

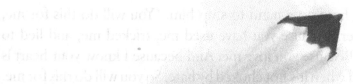

CHAPTER THIRTY-TWO

Titania

All I can see is thunder, fire, and the shine of steel. Alexi and two or three thousand of his soldiers found somewhere in the city to land and have stormed the palace on foot, just like Esmae predicted, while the rest of his fleet has stayed high in the sky to distract *our* fleet and fire down on us from above. If I could get the inner shield back up and working, I could cut them off from us and maybe give us a chance, but manipulating technology is beyond me now.

Everything's happening so fast that there is barely a moment to breathe. My head snaps this way and that, from one screen to another, as Sebastian and I try frantically to keep track of everyone we love as they are scattered into the ugly, bloody chaos of battle.

Meanwhile, I'm also keeping an eye on the forces coming from Elba, Shloka, and Skylark, all still hours away. I want to scream in frustration. Without them, we are at the mercy of Alexi's ships in the sky. Without them, we're hopelessly outnumbered.

And with Leila Saka in charge of Alexi's army, the battle on the ground is nothing short of a massacre.

Alexi's fleet fires relentlessly, while our ships fire back. With each boom of gunfire, with each flash of light, the palace trembles, like it knows what's coming and it's afraid.

Amba, in her celestial battle gear, is a creature of glory in the middle of ugliness. Though mortal and weakened, she has experience, brilliance, and skill on her side, and her sword sparkles like starlight, moving so fast that it seems like enemies are scarcely able to touch her before they drop.

A howl in the distance, and then three enormous wolves leap into the fray, their chests heaving with growls, sending Alexi's soldiers scattering in terror. Elsewhere, on another screen, Sybilla darts in and out of the battle like a devil, small, wickedly sharp twin knives in her hands, leaving blood behind.

"King Elvar!"

I turn quickly at the sound of Sebastian's yelp, and I see that Elvar is on the ground, his armor shredded, his shirt soaked with blood, while a pair of soldiers in Alexi's colors tower over him.

I start to shout a warning into Esmae's earpiece, but she's already there. A blink of an eye, and the soldiers crumple like puppets whose strings have been cut, and Esmae is kneeling beside Elvar.

"Cassel's nose," Elvar rasps hoarsely, his hand stroking Esmae's face. "I will tell him you send your love."

"You're not going to see him just yet, Uncle." Putting her fingers between her teeth, she lets out a piercing whistle that summons two of the Hundred and One to her side almost immediately. "Take the king to the clinic. He needs medical attention at once."

As they haul Elvar off to get him the help he needs, I look for Max, scanning the screens until I find him, running to help Juniper. Soldiers come at him as he runs, but he miraculously dodges all of them, never faltering in his breakneck race to keep Juniper from getting killed. I think it's just wildly good luck, at first, but then I see a small bird following Max, trilling in his ear. Tyre, I assume.

Sybilla darts across another screen, one of her knives missing. She passes General Khay, who is in a throng of enemies. Ilara crushes a soldier's windpipe with her mechanical arm, but they just keep coming and coming. There are so many of them.

Two of our ships go down in flames. In the sky, the fleet comes closer.

Elsewhere, the rumbling roar of a beast draws my attention to Laika, the raksha demon, who is in her powerful lion form as she springs at Leila Saka's throat. General Saka dodges, fast and lithe as a snake, and her face is unafraid, even giddy, as she drives her sword down at Laika's head.

Laika growls and knocks General Saka's arm aside with one massive paw, but then there's another dagger, a yowl, and Laika crumples.

Esmae runs to her, bending over the enormous, silent lion. "Laika," I hear her cry, "Laika, can you hear me?"

But Laika is gone. Even on a screen, I can see that she's completely still. Esmae stands and turns to face General Saka, trembling with fury. A smile twitches across the older woman's face, as if she's been waiting for this battle for a very long time.

"She'd still be alive if I'd killed you in the snow," Leila taunts, gesturing at the lion.

Snarling, Esmae leaps at her.

With a prosthetic thumb on her right hand and a less trained left hand, Esmae is not quite able to fight the way she used to, and so she and Leila Saka are more or less evenly matched. They dance and dodge around each other, both favoring quick, darting blows over brute strength, and their swords clash over and over.

Then, out of the corner of my eye, I see something on another screen that makes my heart sink like a stone.

Sybilla is cornered. And not just by anyone.

By Alexi.

She doesn't stand a chance.

"Sybilla's in trouble!" I shout into Esmae's earpiece, making her startle. "Alexi has her! You have to help her!"

Max steps up to Esmae's side, his dark eyes fixed on Leila Saka. As she strikes, he blocks her blow. "Go," he says to Esmae.

"Is Juniper okay?"

"She's fine. Just a scratch." Max angles his sword again. "Go save Sybilla. I can handle Leila."

"Can you?" General Saka asks, pausing to cock her head to one side curiously. "Then it is time, young prince, to see if you are better than your teacher."

With only the briefest hesitation, Esmae turns and runs.

And all I can do is watch, completely useless once again, as Max faces a bloody, smiling Leila Saka on one screen, and, on another, Esmae confronts her twin brother for the last time.

CHAPTER THIRTY-THREE

Radha

There is no fish, of course, and no eye to skewer. Just a grid, a switch, and a gap big enough for an arrow.

My father, brother, and I stand at the top of the north tower. Below us, out of sight somewhere on the other side of the palace, is the battle. High above us are hundreds of small, deadly corpse ships, from both sides, zipping around each other, unleashing thunder and fire as they battle their way past the onslaught of gunfire from our ships. Our far fewer ships.

"It's not safe up here," Rodi says, the wind this high whipping his hair back from his forehead. "If any of the people in Alexi's ships see us up there, we're done for."

"Then we'd better be quick," I reply. My teeth are chattering from the cold, but I squint past the sun lamps, at the faint glitter of the glitch in the outer shield, and feel just the smallest spark of hope. "Can you do this, Father?"

Father's head is tilted up and his eyes are on the glitch. He's holding one of the last bows left in the palace armory and an arrow. His stance is lithe, graceful, and completely different from the hunched, weary posture that's become so familiar. It's like he can't hear me, like he can only hear the rustle of the wind, the vibrations of the gunfire, the beat of his own heart. I asked him to be Lavya one last time, and that is what he has done.

He places the arrow against the nocking point and pulls the bowstring taut. I hold my breath.

He fires.

The arrow slices through the air, fast and lethal, and the force of the bowstring snapping back into place makes the wind whip against my cheek. The arrow soars into the sky, so far that we lose sight of it. All we can do is watch the glitch instead, that tiny anomaly on the faintly shimmering outer shield where the failsafe is, and as seconds pass, one after another, I wonder if we failed, if we need to try again, if this is even *possible*.

Then there's a crackle, so faint I wonder if I'm imagining it, the sound of something made out of energy coming back to life. I clutch Rodi's arm, fingernails digging into his skin, as something starts to spread across the sky, a thin veil of shimmering light, just like the outer shield beyond it.

The inner shield flickers into place, stranding Alexi's fleet on the other side.

CHAPTER THIRTY-FOUR

Esmae

"Alex!" I shout.

He freezes, the blade of his sword just inches from Sybilla's throat. She's on the ground, clutching a wound in her side, her face ferocious and defiant as she prepares to die. At the sound of my voice, she turns her head, her eyes going wide. Hope and horror battle each other in her expression.

Alex's grey eyes meet mine, hard and glittering. His chest heaves with the adrenaline of battle. I step closer, cautiously now, agonizingly aware of that blade's proximity to Sybilla. "Let her go," I say. "We can end this ourselves, you and me. Let her walk away."

"Esmae," Sybilla starts, furious, but I silence her with a look.

"Alex, let her go."

He clenches his jaw, but he gives a curt nod. "Go," he says.

"Max needs you," I say to Sybilla, who stands up, wincing in pain, but makes no move to back away. It's the only thing I can say that will make her leave me. "Go, Sybilla."

Trembling with rage, her white skin covered in a sheen of sweat, she backs away until she's side by side with me.

"I love you, Esmae Rey," she says softly, and leaves.

I don't watch her go. I keep my eyes on my brother, who doesn't take his off me, either. The Golden Bow shines on his back, the bright mirror to the Black Bow on mine. Around us, the noise of the battle seems muted, far away. Bursts of light from the gunfire high above us seem like dust motes in sunlight, not quite real, not quite here. The thorn trees rustle and gusts of wind blow past, chilling the sweat and blood on my skin. But all I see are a pair of gray eyes exactly like mine.

The end is here, and there's just us. There are no giants to hide behind, no apocalyptic weapons to balance each other out. Sorsha and *Titania*, the starsword and the astra, all cleared off the board. Right now, in this moment, it's just him and me, the twin in the sun and the one in the dark, just as it should have been from the very start.

Neither of us makes any move to strike. We assess each other, each a mirror of the other as he holds his sword in his right hand and I hold mine in my left. His eyes blaze with something dark and ferocious: hate, perhaps, or wrath, or just determination. I watch every tiny twitch of his muscles, every small rise of his chest as he breathes.

So, when his sword comes down, mine is already in place to meet it. Steel hisses, a screech that overpowers all other sound, making all the fine hairs on the back of my neck stand. At once, Alex pulls back, striking hard again, and this time I duck the blow, darting around him, driving my sword backward as I go. He dodges and we face each other again.

Alex and I have never fought like this before, with swords, with *intent*, but I know how he fights. I studied it for years as a child, back when I admired him and wanted to be like him, and I've seen him fight countless times since we met at the competition. He's an elegant, deliberate warrior, fond of formations and gestures, devoted to sportsmanship. Where I am fast and savage, he is strong and graceful, never flustered, perfectly balanced.

There is nothing graceful or balanced about the boy in front of me. His strikes are too intense for such an early point in the battle, sweeping wildly, wasting energy. He'll tire out in minutes. I wonder if that's because he thinks I'll be easy to beat quickly, but I dismiss that possibility as soon as I look in his eyes. That madness is there again, the same madness I saw at the Night Temple. There is nothing deliberate or cautious about any of his choices. He's throwing himself into this, recklessly and furiously, and I don't know if that's a good thing for me or not.

I allow myself to blink, to get sweat out of my eyes, and when I open them, Alexi isn't front of me anymore.

Instead, there's only a child, maybe four or five years old, his sword far too big for him, his gray eyes wide, innocent and eager to please.

"Let me try again, Father," he says, in a high, merry voice. "I can beat you this time!"

Alex.

My sword wavers mid-strike, my arm falling to my side. It's the opening Alex needs to strike me down, but he doesn't. I think that's because he falters, too, jerking back in shock, as if he, too, has seen something that shouldn't be there.

When I blink again, the child is gone, and Alex is fully grown once more. Bloody instead of fresh, furious instead of enthusiastic. Childlike joy put right out, like a blanket thrown over the last embers of a fire.

"Did you see—" I can't help asking the question.

His jaw tightens. "I saw you, but you were a child. You asked me to tell you a story, except you called me Amba."

"I assume this is Kirrin's work?" I raise my eyebrows. "Maybe he thinks showing us visions of our childhoods will make us less likely to kill each other?"

Alex opens his mouth to give what I can only assume will be a scathing reply, but then something flashes high above us and he jerks his head up. I look, too, and see that, somehow, the inner shield is back in place, shimmering gloriously across every horizon.

Alex's fleet is on the other side, cut off from him. All he has left are Leila Saka and the soldiers he landed with. We're not outnumbered anymore.

And in the distance, far, far away, I see the specks of more ships. Shloka, Elba, and Skylark. They can't reach *us* with the shield in place, but they can reach Alexi's stranded ships.

My heart thumps. We can win.

"This doesn't change anything between us," Alex says, his eyes flashing. "Nothing that happens up there will make any difference to this battle between you and me."

He comes at me harder than ever, but with hope pounding in every one of my heartbeats, I fight back. I may not be as good as he is anymore, but I fight harder and better because I have a family here, and I'm fighting not for a crown, but for them. I'm fighting so that they'll live, so that I'll get back to them when this is over, because they need me and I need them.

SANGU MANDANNA

Another swing of the sword, another blink, and the small child is back. Only this time *I'm* a child, too, and our swords are grotesque in our small hands.

Again, I falter, and this time it costs me. Pain lances through my right shoulder, the blade of the sword slicing right into the muscle. I stagger back, blinking again, and the bloody, wild, real version of Alex is back, advancing on me and knocking my sword out of my hands.

I trip over the root of a thorn tree, landing hard on my knees. Alex's eyes burn, watching me, and he sheathes his sword. At first, I wonder if it's because he thinks he's won and this is over, but then I see him reach for the Golden Bow on his back.

There's a dull roar in my ears as his lips move, uttering the incantation that activates the celestial power of the Golden Bow, making it glow.

Once activated, it can kill one enemy. There's no stopping it.

Except—

Except with a bow of equal power. A bow that can *also* be activated, a bow that can destroy the Golden Bow if its wielder is fast enough.

My shoulder throbs as I yank the Black Bow off my own back. If I unleash my bow before Alex unleashes his, mine will destroy his and he won't be able to kill me outright. I open my mouth to speak the ancient, powerful incantation—

—and nothing comes out.

I don't know what to say.

I—

How is this possible? I *know* the incantation. I was taught it, made to repeat it until it was carved into my brain. I know it.

236

Why can't I remember it?

Oh.

Reeling, the words of a curse come back to me.

You stole knowledge you weren't entitled to, so when you need it most, that knowledge will fail you.

How could I have ever forgotten that Rickard's curse was in the dark, waiting for its moment?

I can't activate my bow.

I can't stop his.

It's over.

CHAPTER THIRTY-FIVE

Titania

As I watch Alexi's Golden Bow glow with the power that will surely kill Esmae, I let out a piercing, anguished cry. And something inside me just

snaps.

I turn away from the screens. I am done watching. I am done standing by helplessly. One way or another, I will be *Titania* again, powerful and unbeatable. I will put an end to the madness of this war.

At last, says the voice inside my head, satisfied.

CHAPTER THIRTY-SIX

Esmae

I let the Black Bow slip out of my grasp and I sit back, exhausted, on my heels. In a way, I'm glad that Rickard died before he could see his curse come to pass. He regretted it, in the end, and it would have broken his heart to watch me fall like this.

Alex's brows knit together, confusion and suspicion crossing his face. "Why aren't you doing anything?"

"Because I can't."

"You don't need your thumb to activate the Black Bow," he says, like he can't understand when I became such a fool. "You just need the incantation."

Leila Saka would not have bothered to say any of this. Nor would my mother, or Lord Selwyn. None of them would have cared one bit about whether I could defend myself before they unleashed the power of the Golden Bow on me.

But Alex is not any of them. No matter how he may feel about me, the boy who was raised to value honor and chivalry above all else must hate the idea of using his powerful, celestial bow against an opponent who hasn't even the slightest protection from it.

"I can't use the incantation," I say, my teeth gritted as my cold, inglorious defeat stares me in the face. "I've forgotten it."

"*Forgotten* it?"

"Because of a curse."

Anger darkens his face. "You're lying. You think you'll be too late by the time you activate the Black Bow, so you think you can stop me from using the Golden Bow by pretending you're helpless."

I'm not surprised he thinks that. *I* was not raised to value honor and chivalry, and he knows it. We both know full well that I am not above such trickery.

"Think what you like," I snap, outrageously bitter that, after everything, *this* is how I'm going to lose. On my knees in the dirt, with the thorns of the forest beneath me, hunted by a curse that has finally caught up to me.

I was born in the shadow of one curse, and I will die in the shadow of another. It's almost poetic.

"I suppose you think I should spare you now," he says furiously.

"I think you're going to do whatever you want," I bite back. "Just like you have all your life."

"All my life?" He lets out a mirthless laugh. "You obviously know nothing about my life if you think I've had everything I ever wanted."

"You were the darling of the star system."

"And how much do you think that meant to me when my father was dead?"

I have no answer to that.

"You took everything from me," he says, his voice cracking with the weight of his devastation. "Without the crown, I have nothing. *I'm* nothing. I've lost everything because of you!"

I start to object, but then I stop. Is he wrong? Haven't I taken from him all our lives? Oh, other people did the killing and exiling and lying, but wasn't it all because of me? He lost his father. He lost his home. He lost his brother. And his mother, well, she drove him away herself, but I can see how he might trace that back to me, too.

Our tragedy started a long time ago, and now, at long last, he's going to end it.

As I look up at him, I feel suddenly overwhelmed by pity. Because the truth is, I have been very lucky. All those years I kept looking to the horizon, wanting more, I *had* more. I had the dearest, most loyal of friends, who made me laugh, who sat beside me in the royal schoolroom and scribbled notes to distract me, who loved me so wholly that he died so that I would not. I had a teacher, who made long journeys every week just to help me grow, who let me see his warmth and tenderness and flaws, who loved me until the moment he died. I had a war goddess, who I mistook for stern and uncaring, but who also loved me, and guarded me, and told me stories, and tried in vain to keep me away from the path that would lead to calamity.

And even after I lost Rama, even after it seemed that I had been betrayed and abandoned by everything I believed in, I was still so very lucky. I had an uncle, who, for all his failings and mistakes, put his trust in me. I had a prickly, devoted friend, who, even bleeding and stumbling, did not want to leave me to fight this last battle alone. I had a ship, who tried to chart me the safest and brightest path across the skies. And I had love, dazzlingly real, dizzying love, with all the laughter, passion, joy, and heartbreak that comes with it.

I had so very much. I *have* so very much.

Can't I let him have this?

My throat is tight as, piece by piece, I dismantle my pride and my pain and, quietly, say the words that will end this.

"The crown is yours."

He blinks, going very still, the Golden Bow still glowing in his hand. "What did you say?"

"You can have it. The crown, the throne. Your home."

"Why?" He's suspicious again. "You can't expect me to believe you'd rather surrender than die."

"Dying in battle isn't everything the stories tell us it is, Alex," I reply. "I'd quite like to live."

"I could choose not to accept your surrender. I could still kill you."

"Yes, you could."

"This isn't how this is supposed to go!" he says, as anguished as if I had wounded him, as if I've taken something else from him. "You're supposed to fight me until the bitter end. Even if you can't use the Black Bow, you're supposed to find another way. You're supposed to get right up and wrestle me to the ground if you have to. I know you, Esmae. You don't give up."

It's all true. I *don't* give up. All I have done since the moment he met me is fight. It's not at all like me to stop fighting now.

Especially since we both know that with his fleet on the other side of the inner shield, and with Amba and Max and *our* ships still in play, he could still lose this war. And even if I fail at a last, desperate bid to overpower him and can't save myself from the Golden Bow, and I don't survive, we both know I would die with the knowledge that I fought to the end and that those I love will probably win after I am gone.

But I shake my head. "Every minute this goes on, more of us die," I tell him. "There's a moment, in a game of Warlords, when the right thing to do is resign. I could fight you, and keep fighting you, but I don't *want* to do that anymore, Alex. I want to live. I want everyone else to live. I want *you* to live."

The Golden Bow, still aglow, wavers in his hand. His eyes are wet. "Maybe," he says, the words coming out so low I almost miss them, "Maybe *I* don't want that."

My heart gives a sharp, painful thump as understanding settles over me.

"Oh," I say.

And suddenly, that strange, skewed vision sweeps over me again, over *us*, turning him into a small, earnest boy and me into a small, lonely girl. My heart feels like it's splintering all over again as I, the Esmae before the blood and the grief, reach for him, the Alexi before the loss and the dark. The Golden Bow, oversized in his child's hands, tumbles to the ground, the glow dying to nothing, as I grip his hands in mine.

"I don't know who I am without them," he says, his voice young and afraid. "I don't want to be here if they aren't."

"You have time," I tell him. "You have your whole life to figure out who you are. You may think you have nothing left, but that isn't true. You have a cousin who has been fighting to keep you safe for years. You have an uncle who has hurt you, but who wishes he hadn't. And you have me, whether you want that or not." Tears track down my face, but I don't let him go. "We can start again."

Gray eyes lift to meet mine. "We've hurt each other."

Yes, we have. And I don't know if it's possible to find a path forward without more hurt or hate, but we'll never know if we don't try.

"We have to stay," I say, thinking of Amba, who stayed for me, yes, but also because she couldn't leave without righting her mistakes. "It may be easier to go, but we have to stay to remake everything we've broken."

He doesn't say anything. Doubt and fear are written all over those heartbreakingly young eyes.

"Alex," I say. "Please. Let's end this here. Let's not swallow any more stars."

I close my eyes, because Alex has always done what our mother has told him to, what Kirrin has told him to. He's afraid to choose on his own, but I can't choose for him. I've done my choosing. This last part, this is up to him. And if he chooses to reject this, to reject *me*, and wrench his hands out of mine, and pick up his bow once more, I don't want to watch.

But when there's only quiet, I open my eyes.

He's eighteen years old again, the Golden Bow is still dark on the ground, and my brother hasn't let my hands go.

CHAPTER THIRTY-SEVEN

Titania

The problem is this kingdom, the voice in my head says, kind and understanding. *You do see that, don't you? All the hurt around you is because of this realm. If there was no Kali, there would be no war.*

A pause, in which I bite my lip, unsure.

Then the voice adds, gently, *Perhaps you could even save Esmae if you act fast enough.*

Hope clutches me, pushing the doubts away. Alexi is about to use the Golden Bow on her. If there's a way to save her, if there's a way to end this war before anyone else dies, I have to act.

I have been the arrow for too long. It's time to be the archer.

You know what must be done, the voice says. *Use the boy.*

I take my earpiece out and deactivate it. Keeping secrets has never led me anywhere good before, but I can't let anyone hear me.

They won't understand, the voice agrees. *They love this kingdom too much. It holds them hostage.*

"Sebastian," I say, and he tears his eyes away from the screens for the first time since the battle started, looking surprised. "I know how to end this. And you and I are going to be the ones to do it."

"Really?" His young, tearstained face lights up. He longs to be a hero, for his grandfather. "How?"

"Esmae told me that she accidentally unlocked Rickard's secret drawer one time. And you were with her. Do you think you could unlock it again?"

"Yes," he says doubtfully. "I don't see why we need to open it now, though. All we found inside was a love letter."

"And the code to trigger Kali's emergency shutdown," I remind him.

Sebastian's eyes widen. "How will *that* make anything better?"

"Because it's time for Kali to end," I say. "It's destroying us all, Sebastian. You know that. All this death and bloodshed is because of this kingdom."

"My grandfather loved Kali!"

"And look what it did to him," I point out. Esmae's time is running out. "A lifetime of service and devotion, and it got him killed. Now Alexi is about to kill Esmae. This kingdom is going to get her killed, too."

"But what will happen when the base ship shuts down?" Sebastian asks anxiously. "Won't people get hurt?"

"Of course not," I say, echoing the words I can hear inside my head. "As soon as the base ship begins to shut down, the kingdom will evacuate. Everyone will go to Wychstar, or Winter, or anywhere else they please. And we'll start new, better lives free of the shadow of this cold, warmongering realm."

"Shouldn't we ask someone—"

I want to shake him. There's no time for this!

"No one will help us," I cut him off, my tone much sharper than I intended it to be. "Because no one sees how poisonous Kali is. We're the only ones who know better."

Tell him Rickard told you he dreamed of a new beginning before he died, says the voice in my head.

I don't remember Rickard ever saying such a thing to me or to anyone else, but I suppose it could have happened when I was still a ship and it's one of the pieces of data I've lost since I became human. After all, I can't be lying to *myself*, can I?

Invoking Rickard's dreams is the right thing to do. Sebastian takes me back to Rickard's suite without any more protests. Keeping his eyes averted from his cold, still grandfather lying on the floor under a blanket draped over him out of respect, he opens the secret drawer and hands me the code.

"Now go back to the war room and check on the others," I say, giving him a huge, beaming smile. "You've done so well. I'll do the rest."

Quick, says the voice in my head. *You may still be able to save Esmae.*

I run to the closest elevator, jabbing the button that will take me all the way to the base ship below. The elevator gives a gentle jolt as it starts to move.

As I wait impatiently, I notice something out of the corner of my eye. Someone else, standing in the elevator with me. I jerk my head around, my heart jumping in a way that's both unfamiliar and alarming, but the other person is only my reflection. The back wall of the elevator has a mirror on it.

But as I look at my reflection, it skews and warps, and suddenly there's a man staring back at me. A tall, handsome man with leonine blond hair and cold eyes.

I've seen him before. But where?

You're seeing things, the voice in my head says, not as kind as before.

I blink, and the man is gone. The reflection in the mirror is just me.

The elevator comes to a halt and the doors open, casting all thoughts of familiar men in mirrors out of my head. I run down the bright, metallic hallways of the base ship, peering through the glass doors of different rooms until I find exactly what I need.

The tablet is propped on a table, in a small, white empty room, and its screen blinks with a string of empty boxes. Waiting for me, for the string of numbers clutched in my clammy hand.

I enter the room, letting the doors slide shut behind me. I lock them, just to be safe.

And not a moment too soon: something slams against the glass doors. I turn back and see Kirrin outside, his expression frantic, his fists pounding on the glass.

"Titania, don't do this! Don't listen to him!"

Him? Who is he talking about?

He's the god of tricks, says the voice, cold and angry. *He lies.*

I tilt my head, intrigued by the fact that Kirrin hasn't just materialized *inside* the room. This room must be shielded, the same way King Cassel's cottage and Esmae's broom cupboard were shielded, to prevent any interference from powerful celestial creatures.

"Remember what we saw?" Kirrin is shouting. "The ruins and the ash? Everyone dead? This is how it happens, Titania! That future is what *will* happen if you put that code in!"

The ashy red ponytail under the rubble. The shattered mullioned window. Max telling Esmae to close her eyes.

I pull my hand away from the tablet. What if Kirrin's right?

He wants Alexi to win, the voice in my head hisses. *He wants Esmae to die. If you trust him now, you might as well kill her yourself.*

There's too much truth there to deny. Kirrin has constructed so many tricks to get Alexi a victory, including my own creation, and Esmae has almost died half a dozen times because of those tricks. Even Amba and Max don't trust him anymore. How can I?

So I turn away, ignoring his pleas, and, with the greatest care, I put the code in.

CHAPTER THIRTY-EIGHT

Radha

I have no idea what happened, but the battle is over. I must have missed some sign that someone has called an end to it, but I don't care as long as it *is* over. I don't even know who won, if you can call the bloodshed in front of me any sort of victory, but I'm not sure I care about who won or lost either, as long as I find the people I love alive and safe.

As I run across the courtyard to the palace gates, passing the noisy, busy medical clinic, I can see the battlefield down the hill. There are soldiers backing away from each other, generals calling orders, ships retracting their weapons and lowering their engines to a hum. People are rushing to put out the fires of wreckages.

At the gates, I walk past Kirrin, who stands out not just because of his blue skin, but because of how *clean* he is. No blood, no ash, no sweat. He is ancient, untouched, eternal. He's not looking at the battlefield, but at something over my shoulder instead.

"The palace is still standing," he says quietly, more to himself than to anyone else.

I have no idea why *that*, of all things, is what he's decided to observe right now, but I have never pretended to understand the way the gods think.

I keep going, making my way down the hill to where the smell of blood and burned flesh is almost unbearable. I make myself look at each corpse I pass, to make sure it's not someone I love and also to make sure I remember each wound, each face. How monstrous we are, to be able to do this to each other.

Then, just when I think I might have to resort to screaming out the names of everyone I need to find, I catch a glimpse of something near the thorn forest. A gloriously red ponytail.

I run, almost tripping over my own feet, blundering down the grassy knoll to the opening of the forest, where the ground is stained an ugly, sticky red and soldiers tend to the wounded. There's Max, staggering to his feet, carefully pulling his sword out of the heart of Leila Saka, who is bloody and filthy and angry even in death. I allow myself a moment to be glad that he's okay and then I stumble past him.

Sybilla turns right before I reach her, and her face lights up with dazzling, perfect joy. She takes a step and then I'm there, tangled in her arms, and we hold each other so tightly that I'm no longer sure where I end and she begins.

CHAPTER THIRTY-NINE

Esmae

Alex comes up beside me, torn fabric from his sleeve clutched in his hands. "Let me see your shoulder," he says.

"No," I protest, trying and failing to step past him. "I have to find the others."

"You won't find anyone if you bleed to death."

I grimace, but stay put, mostly because I don't think I can get past him. I grumble a little as he puts a painful amount of pressure on my shoulder, right over the wound his sword left there, so that he can bind it tightly and stop the bleeding until I can get hold of a laser.

"Bear should be here with us," he says quietly, tying a knot.

The way he says *us* sends a needle right through my heart. "I know."

"All he wanted was for us to be on the same side."

"Well," I say, "We can do that for him."

He finishes binding my wound and takes a step back. "I have to check on my people," he tells me, a little awkwardly. He isn't quite sure how to tread through this new, uncertain future of ours, but neither am I. "I'll find you after."

I nod, and we part ways. I turn back up the hill, quickening my steps as I make my way back to the other edge of the thorn forest, where I left Max with Leila Saka. I see him almost at once, watching me get closer, a crooked smile on his face.

"There you are," he says.

I'm less than two paces from him when he crumples. Just like that, like his legs forgot how to hold up him.

"Max!" I drop to my knees beside him, more confused than worried, and help him sit up a little against the fallen trunk of a tree. "Hey. What's the matter?"

He looks at me for a long moment and then, reluctantly, moves the hand that had been pressed to his thigh. Horror floods my body, turning it icy cold, as I see the wound. The artery that must be cut. The blood.

"No," I whisper, clamping my hands down over his thigh, pressing firmly down on the pulse beating wildly there. "No, no, no, no. Max, please. You can't. It's okay. I can fix this."

"What happened?" Sybilla's spiky, urgent voice is the most welcome sound in the world.

"Get the queen," I tell her. "She can save him. *Now*, Sybilla! Get Guinne!"

I take deep breaths, in and out, in and out, refusing to let myself slip into a panic. Max's eyes flutter, but they stay open. He's going to be fine. Because if there ever, *ever*, was a time for Guinne to use her boon, this is it. This is what she saved it for. She will come and she will reverse what happened to him and he'll be fine.

Everything's going to be fine.

And then she's here, the bottom half of her face pale as death beneath her blindfold, clutching Sybilla's arm tightly as Sybilla guides her to us. They stumble over the uneven ground in their haste. Amba is right behind them, limping, her face pale and set.

"You can save him, can't you?" The words tumble out of me as the panic I tried to quash rises up anyway. "You can reverse this?"

"Yes," Guinne says at once, so confidently that I feel instantly better. "Yes, it hasn't been more than a few minutes since it happened. I can do it. I just have to take my blindfold off."

But before she can, before she can even touch it, an unexpected sound makes us all go quiet.

It's a klaxon, but not like the one that triggered when the inner shield came down. This isn't loud and shrill. This is muted and whiny, just one long beep after another.

Like something is counting down.

Amba's face loses what little color it had.

"That *sound*," Guinne says, her lips almost bloodless. "We are never supposed to hear that sound."

Then silence. Absolute, total silence. I look around, bewildered. Did the klaxon stop?

No, *everything* has stopped.

As I stare, stunned right out of my panic, I see that everything around me is frozen into utter stillness. There is no sound and no movement. Even the wind has died. Max's hand is halfway to my cheek, Sybilla's ponytail is mid-swing, and everyone else around us, all the way up and down the hill, they're all frozen, too. Like a tableau of sculptures, painstakingly placed in a grotesque, macabre theatre.

Then someone crouches down beside Max, and I look up into the grim, austere face of a god.

"Ah, nephew," Ash says quietly, one hand on Max's shoulder. "How many times must I watch you die?"

"He's not going to die!"

He looks at me then, with those impossibly dark, bleak eyes. "You do not understand, do you?"

"I understand that, somehow, you've stopped time."

"Suspended it," he corrects, "and only for a moment, so that I might speak with you. That klaxon is the sound of the base ship shutting down."

"What?" I just stare at him, incredulous. "That's not possible. No one would do that!"

With something like pity on his face, Ash waves a hand. Beside us, translucent, moving holographic images appear, much like the recording Titania made me when I was trying to find out how my father died.

I watch as Titania, in human form, approaches a sleeping man shrouded in a strange, otherworldly glow. Curious, she reaches for him. A holographic version of Ash interrupts her, but not before her fingers make contact with that peculiar glowing energy.

"That's Ness," I say. "Isn't it? Amba's father? Max told me he's been sleeping in the Temple of Ashma for centuries."

"When Titania touched the energy around him, she woke him," says Ash. "Not completely, not his body, but *just* enough for his mind to form a connection with her. It was useless to him when she went back to being a ship, but when she became human, that connection reactivated. She did not understand what was happening to her, and I did not see it until it was too late."

"Wait," I say, shaking my head, my stomach clenching around itself. "You're not saying Titania triggered the shutdown?"

"I am saying that Ness did," says Ash, "through Titania. He manipulated her, preyed on her fears that she is no longer useful, used her love for you. He convinced her that she would be helping you by destroying Kali. He let her believe that there would be time to evacuate the kingdom."

"But there isn't, is there?" I ask in growing horror. "Because the emergency shutdown isn't supposed to be triggered until *after* the kingdom has already been evacuated. That's why the klaxon sounds like it's counting down. It's supposed to be just enough time for one person to put the code into the system, get in a ship, and fly to safety."

Ash nods. "Kirrin had a vision of Kali's destruction. He thought Sorsha might have torn the kingdom apart in battle, but he did not take into account the snow. There was snow in his vision."

"It doesn't snow on Kali," I say quietly. "But it does on Winter."

"What he saw was all that was left of Kali after the kingdom, having lost its atmosphere and gravity, crashed into Winter."

"Why?" I ask, my voice somewhere between grief and fury. "Why would Ness want to kill half a million people?"

"He does not care one way or another about killing half a million people," says Ash. He turns his head, looking at Amba, standing frozen just a few feet away. "He did this to kill *her*."

I shouldn't be surprised. Stories have an unsettling way of coming full circle, and with lives and stories as tangled as ours are, why does it surprise me that the god who swallowed his children, and who was slain by his daughter, has found a way to punish her one last time?

"I imagine he could have manipulated Titania into killing Amba herself," Ash says quietly. "But he saw too much in Titania's memories. He saw that Amba sacrificed her godhood for you. And he knew that there could be no better way to destroy her than to have her die powerless, knowing as she did that the person she loved most was going to die, too."

I want to scream in fury. By shutting down the base ship, Ness will kill not just Amba and me, but also Max, who is his son reborn, and Alex, who one of his other sons loves. In one cruel blow, Ness is going to strike down two of his children and devastate the others. Kirrin, for one, will never recover from losing Amba, Max, *and* Alex.

And for the sake of his vendetta, Ness will wipe out hundreds of thousands of innocent people, too. It's monstrous.

"Is there any way to stop it?" I ask. "You must have come to speak to me for a reason."

"You already know the answer to that," Ash says. "You just don't want to know. The shutdown cannot be stopped, but, with a powerful boon, it *can* be reversed."

Reversed.

My heart breaks apart. "No!"

But he's gone, time is no longer suspended, and I am in pieces.

As the chaos around me continues as if there were no pause, I can't bring myself to speak. I just look at Max, memorizing every detail of his face.

"You must use your boon to reverse the shutdown," I hear Amba say to a horrified Guinne. Ash must have spoken to

SANGU MANDANNA

her, too. "That is the only way to thwart my father and save hundreds of thousands of lives."

"No." I say the word again because I feel like I have to, like saying it enough times might actually make a difference. A sob slips out of my throat. "No."

"It's okay," Max says quietly, his breathing ragged and shallow. "I've died before. I'll find a way back to you."

"There has to be another way!"

"Esmae," Amba says, only the slightest tremor in her voice. "You know there is nothing else we can do. Even if Max is saved, he will die when Kali falls. You know that's not what he wants. You cannot dishonor him by allowing thousands to die just to give him a few more minutes."

"I won't *let* thousands die!" I say fiercely. "I'll find another way! I won't let Kali fall. I won't let a bitter, cruel god take everything from us. I'll find a way."

"There is no time," she replies.

Max's tired, half-glazed eyes move to his mother. "Mother, reverse what Ness did."

And I know this is what has to happen, I *know* that, and yet every part of me wants to scream childishly that this isn't fair, that we shouldn't have to lose him to save everybody else.

"Mother," Max says again, his breathing shallower than ever.

Guinne's mouth trembles, but she nods. "Of course." She runs a shaky hand over his hair. "Goodbye, my boy."

Then she stands, the picture of quiet dignity, and turns her back to us. Her hands reach up behind her head as she unties and peels the blindfold from her eyes. Her shoulders shake.

258

A tear slides down Amba's cheek as she places a hand over Max's heart. "The stars will be lucky to have you, brother," she says softly. "Go in peace."

Don't go in peace, I want to shout. *Don't you dare. Stay. Stay. Stay.*

Instead, I just hold Max tighter. My tears drip all over his bloody shirt, but he doesn't seem to care. "I found you once," I whisper in his ear. "I got my fingerprints all over you. I'll find you again."

He smiles, that special small, crooked smile that he only ever lets me see, and his eyes crinkle at the corners. "I know," he whispers back.

Behind us, there's a clap of thunder. It rattles my teeth, sends electricity skittering across my skin.

Then, quiet.

The whine of the klaxon is gone. The sun lamps blaze back to life, like dawn after a dark night. The kingdom is saved.

And Max stops breathing.

CHAPTER FORTY

Esmae

At some point, when the wounded have been tended and the dead returned to their families, when the city is quiet with grief and relief, someone thinks to ask how the battle ended. And who won.

I open my mouth to tell them about my surrender, but Alex gets there first. "No one," he says, his eyes meeting mine. "No one won."

But what of the crown, someone asks.

My uncle, brother, and I all have a claim to it, but none of us wants it anymore. It is, after all, a crown soaked in blood. It cost us Rama and Sorsha and Bear, Laika and Leila and far, *far* too many others.

It cost us Max.

And even if all of that weren't true, well, I know that I, at least, am nowhere near ready to rule a kingdom. I may *never* be ready. I don't know how to be fair and wise with that kind of power.

It's not a big leap from there to question whether *any* one person should have that kind of power.

I'm the one who suggests that it may be time for the House of Rey to come to an end. It'll take *years* to make such a transition, to lay out all the ways in which the kingdom must grow and become better. But I'm not the only one who likes the idea of a future in which Kali is ruled by a government of its people and not by a king, queen, or war council.

Elvar, tired and grieving, is not opposed to it, but he's afraid. "What will we be," he asks, "without our House?"

"We'll be a family," I tell him.

CHAPTER FORTY-ONE

Titania

For the first time since I became human, I am whole.

Ash severed the connection between Ness and me, so I can see now how he slipped into the cracks between my memories, how insidiously he distorted me. The peculiar, ugly outbursts of anger and resentment are gone. The cruel thoughts are gone. I am myself again.

It is agony. I will not see anyone, will not speak to anyone. I cannot bear to see what I might find in their eyes. Instead, I take to haunting the south tower like a ghost, hiding among the turrets where no one will think to find me, the closest place I can get to the stars.

There is no happiness in food or in touch anymore. I don't *deserve* happiness. I wish I had never become human.

All it has done is cause intolerable grief. If I had remained *Titania*, the indestructible, unbeatable ship, the arrow in the hands of better archers, there would have been no invasion. Ness would have had no hold over me.

And Max would still be here.

One night, I find Esmae waiting for me on the south tower. There's a white plate balanced on one knee.

"Come here," she says, patting the ledge beside me.

I want to tell her to go away, but she's the one person I will never say that to, so I obey. I see that there are two generous slices of moist, freshly baked lemon cake on the plate.

Esmae holds the plate out to me, but I don't take it. "I don't want it," I say, even as the scent of lemon makes me almost dizzy.

Shrugging, she takes an enormous bite out of one of the slices. "You're punishing yourself," she says, mouth full.

I glare at her, eating with such enthusiasm. "And so what if I am?" I ask petulantly. "I deserve it. In fact," I go on before she can tell me it wasn't my fault and Ness was to blame, "I've *earned* the right to sulk. I hate being human. Everything about it is rotten and wrong and ruinous. You should never have let me make such a stupid choice."

She nods gravely, like she's seriously considering the absurdity of my words. "You're right," she says, swallowing her mouthful of cake and putting the plate to one side, out of my reach. I hate that I even notice that it's out of my reach. "Except," Esmae goes on, "for one thing."

There's a click as she taps her watch and a holographic recording flickers to life in front of us.

"Max showed me this," she says.

It's me, on Ashma. My face flushed and aglow with excitement, my feet stumbling with fawn-like uncertainty, the sound of my giddy laughter. And off-screen, the sound of someone else's laughter. His.

"You know what this is?" Esmae asks.

I don't answer, because my throat is clogged with what I now know are tears and my eyes burn and we both know the answer anyway.

But she says: "This is joy, Titania. You had a dream, and it came true. This is what being human *really* means to you. I think you know that, but you think it would be selfish to accept it. We've all done things we wish we hadn't. That doesn't mean we don't get to live, *really* live."

All I can do is shake my head, a quick, sharp jerk. "How can I?"

"This is what he wanted for you," Esmae says, gesturing to the glowing face and the sounds of laughter in the recording. "Let him have it."

I watch the recording until it finishes, until it loops back to the beginning and starts to play again, until I've watched it so many times that the sound of Max's laughter, and my own, is imprinted on my memory.

As Esmae clicks her watch off, I swallow the lump in my throat and say, in a shaky voice:

"I'll take that cake now, please."

CHAPTER FORTY-TWO

Esmae

The remaking of shattered things doesn't happen overnight. Twins torn apart by ill luck and a long series of choices don't mend their friendship in a single instant. Families and kingdoms riven by war don't heal straight away. These things will take time, and heart, but fortunately I have both of those things.

We all do.

Apart from the starting the long, slow, painstaking transition into a new form of government for Kali, there's a lot for all of us to do. Alex and Elvar have grieving families to visit, soldiers to thank, and apologies to make to our people, to the allies they used badly, and to the friends whose loyalty they repaid with none of their own.

I have to do some of the same, but mostly, I have smaller, softer things to patch up: Guinne's grief, Amba's trauma, Titania's broken heart, and Kirrin's guilt. He hardly ever leaves Alex's side, but when he does, it's because I make him go see Amba, so that they can find some way to heal together. Their father took one brother away from them. They don't have to forgive or forget all that has happened, but they needn't let Ness take away anything else.

As for King Darshan, it is his idea, in the end, to retire to the Night Temple for the rest of his days.

"Rodi will be a better king than I was," he says. "And it feels like the right place for me to go. It's where I went to pray for my revenge. Now it's where I must go to pray for my redemption."

Unlike Grandmother, he accepts visits from his children, his grandchildren, and even from me. After some time, he's able to convince Grandmother to as well. Neither of them will admit it, but I think they're becoming friends.

Mother does not come back to Kali. We don't know where she is. Alex says that's because she doesn't want us to know. But Grandmother tells us that sometimes, when she's out walking in the courtyards of the Night Temple, she catches a glimpse of a woman in a window, her face obscured by thick, frosted glass. The temple acolytes say the woman has a metal hand.

I suppose some people would say that all three of them deserve greater consequences for all that they've done, but I don't have the heart. I'm tired of looking back.

The past belongs to them. The future is ours.

And speaking of the future, Sebastian and Titania are both given places in the Hundred and One. I'm quite sure there are more than a hundred and one of them now, but the old name sticks. They're not a small army anymore. Max never wanted them to be. They still train, under the exacting eye of General Khay, but only because they like it. The rest of the time, they help rebuild the things that were destroyed in the battle, and they find work in the city, and they go back to school. Titania, in particular, is *most* excited by her apprenticeship at a bakery.

No, they're not an army. Just brothers and sisters bound by something stronger than blood.

Alex and I spend quite a lot of time together. It's awkward, and odd, and sometimes we still get angry and remind each other of all the terrible things we've done to the other, but for the most part, it's nice. Most nights, we play Warlords in a quiet, cozy parlor, him against me, Amba against Kirrin, and there's a lot of laughter, swearing, and, in Kirrin's case, many, *many* accusations of cheating.

In the quiet moments, between the work and the new relationships and the slow process of remaking, I let myself feel how much it still hurts. How much I miss Max. When either Sybilla or I needs to cry, we find the other and we cry together, because we both loved him in our different ways and we will never be the same now that he's gone. Sybilla and Radha have each other, for which I'm genuinely, truly glad, but I'd be lying if I said I didn't envy them. They have a long, dazzling life together ahead.

Meanwhile, three wolves insist on crowding me out of my own bed.

Then, on a blustery autumn day, months after the battle, a visitor summons me to the top of Max's tower, above the room no one has touched since he died.

"We're still here," I say to Ash, the destroyer. "Why haven't you used the astra?"

"You could have won," he says. "You knew that, and yet you gave your brother the one thing he wanted."

"I didn't want the crown. He did."

"That's not what he wanted and not what you gave him," says Ash. "What he wanted was a reason to live."

I blink in sudden understanding. "It wasn't Kirrin who kept showing us those visions of us as our younger selves, was it?" I say. "It was you."

"I only gave you a nudge. You did the rest. You offered your brother the crown and gave him something far more important than that. And you did not do it because you thought it would change my mind about the astra, or because you thought you could trick him into letting down his guard, but because you chose to be kind instead of cruel. You chose peace over your pride. And that," he adds, "was all *I* wanted."

I smile a little. "So this world gets another chance, then?"

"Yes. And I will say this, too: you have lived well, these past few months. After the battle, it would have been easy to retreat into fury once more, to choose the dark instead of the light, but you did not do that. You have been kind and brave, in spite of your pain. It has been well done."

Gods should not be able to make me blush after everything I've seen and done, but it would seem it's still possible. "Is that why you called me up here? To tell me that?"

"You really must learn to be more exact in your questions," he says. "I called you up *here* because I deeply dislike the confines of human homes."

"You don't like being indoors?" For some reason, this makes me laugh.

He chooses to ignore this stunning lack of respect, and says, "As for why I wanted to speak with you, which is the question I presume you were actually asking, it is because I wanted to offer you my apologies."

That takes me aback. "Why?"

"I did not intend to make you wait as long as this, but I needed time." Something curious happens to his face. His cheekbones redden, like he's feeling awkward.

Ash, the oldest and most powerful god in the universe.

Feeling awkward.

"Time for what?" I ask, struggling not to laugh again.

"To say goodbye," he says. "I let Ness go."

"Oh," I say softly.

A small smile lifts one corner of his mouth. "There is power in the true death of a god. Long ago, a king of Kali lived because Valin died. You are alive here, today, because that king survived to have children, who had their own children, and so on. When I let Ness go, I was able to harness the power of his death. I have brought you a gift."

He waves a hand. Beside him, stardust materializes out of nothing, sparkling and glowing, coalescing into a shape that becomes more and more solid.

Until it becomes human.

Until it becomes *him*.

I can't breathe. I mustn't. Breathing might fracture this moment, might break this spell, might take away this beautiful, impossible thing.

Max smiles crookedly. "I hear you've been busy."

Abandoning all grace, I burst into a display of the loudest, snottiest tears known to humankind. Then his arms are around me and one of his hands is in my hair and his heart is beating, beating, *beating* under my wet, snotty face.

"Rama says he's proud of you," he says in my ear.

There will always be pain, and there will always be more to remake. There will always be something else that needs to be done, some crisis, some storm, but there will always be a new day after. Rage and sorrow will always be a part of my life, but so will joy. There will always be new ways to grow, and new ways for a heart to break, and new ways for it to mend again.

That's what it means to live. To have a future. And there are no shadows over mine anymore. There are no more curses and no more prophecies. No more devoured stars.

Just bright ones, twinkling forever in the sky.

THE END

ACKNOWLEDGMENTS

I started writing this trilogy in October of 2014, so I've now lived with these characters and their stories for almost seven years (seventeen if you count the decade that was 2020!). And while I'm ready to say goodbye to Esmae, Max, and the others, with the certainty of knowing that I've told their stories completely and as well as I'm able, it's still such a weird thing to pack away something that's been a part of my life for so long.

And, as something that has been a part of my life for so long, it stands to reason that an awful lot of other people have been involved, too. I wish I could name every single one of you, but that might make this section longer than the actual story, so I'll try to limit myself to just a few people without whom I wouldn't have been able to write this third and final book in the series.

To Mum and Dad, for a childhood filled with the luxury of unlimited books and stories.

To Steve, the most patient, loving, and supportive husband, who makes sure I remember to eat even when I'm in a drafting frenzy.

To Jem, Henry, and Juno, for all the joy and inspiration you give me every single day.

To Penny Moore, for steering me the right way every time.

To Eric Smith and Alison Weiss, for your friendship, your support, and for being the very first people in publishing to believe in Esmae's story.

To Nicole Frail, for your patience, enthusiasm, and keen editorial eye over the course of three often messy books.

To Kate Gartner, Joshua Barnaby, and the rest of the team at Sky Pony Press, for years of incredible covers, beautiful page interiors, publicity plans, and all the other pieces that make up the vast jigsaw puzzle that is publishing a book.

To the booksellers, librarians, reviewers, and bloggers who work so hard to make sure these books find homes.

To my author peers, inside and outside of the YA community, who are all so funny, talented, passionate, and endlessly supportive.

To the seventy-seven-year-old reviewer who wrote, back in 2019, that you loved *A Spark of White Fire* and weren't sure you'd live to see the rest of the series. I so, so hope you're still around. I hope *A War of Swallowed Stars* was everything you wanted it to be.

And last of all, to you. For giving this book a chance, for sticking with Esmae to the very end, and for coming on this adventure with me. Thank you.